Linda Pr...
675 26 1/...
Grand Junc...

P9-BBP-521

RAVES FOR *SAND SHARKS* AND MARGARET MARON

"Every Margaret Maron is a celebration of something remarkable."
—*New York Times Book Review*

"Deborah remains a rewarding companion whose affectionate take on the North Carolina rural landscape and its peculiar inhabitants add greatly to the enjoyment."
—*San Diego Union-Tribune*

"Entertaining...Maron's fine evocation of [the beach] area adds to the pleasure."
—*Booklist*

"This series is like sweet iced tea on an August day in North Carolina—near impossible to resist."
—*Atlanta Journal-Constitution*

"Top pick!...a well-written plot...It has the strength and weight of all her books, as well as the humor and excellent writing."
—*RT Book Reviews*

"There's nobody better."
—*Chicago Tribune*

"Maron writes with wit and sophistication."
—*USA Today*

"Maron's homespun evocation of people and place is typically pitch-perfect, her use of the judicial milieu skillful—and her engaging heroine as welcome a companion as you could wish for under a beach umbrella."
　　　　—Publishers Weekly

"Opening a new Margaret Maron is like unwrapping a Christmas gift."
　　　　—Cleveland Plain Dealer

"Maron has a pleasant, easygoing style that's smooth, generous, and perceptive...a delightful, thoughtful, good-natured series."
　　　　—Providence Journal

"Always a writer gifted with the ability to convey an enthralling sense of time and place...Reading Maron is like sipping a Carolina cooler—solid comfort together with fascinating sensations."
　　　　—Greensboro News & Record (NC)

"Intriguing and enjoyable...Maron is an accomplished author and her previous books have all been bestsellers. SAND SHARKS is just as good and highly recommended for those who crave a superior mystery."
　　　　—Shelf Life

"The mystery is a good one, but the real pleasure in SAND SHARKS comes from the humor and social observations...will delight fans."
　　　　—Connecticut Post

"Maron is a master...[The characters] are compelling and unique and the fast-paced plot is entertaining."
—**MyShelf.com**

"Clever and entertaining."
—*Fayetteville Observer* (NC)

"Maron skillfully paints subtle clues for her sharp-witted judge...Readers who haven't been to Wilmington will be tempted to visit after reading Maron's descriptions of lulling waves and drifting pelicans."
—*Our State* (NC)

"Entertaining and thought-provoking...something to celebrate."
—*Contra Costa Times*

Deborah Knott novels:

SAND SHARKS
DEATH'S HALF ACRE
HARD ROW
WINTER'S CHILD
RITUALS OF THE SEASON
HIGH COUNTRY FALL
SLOW DOLLAR
UNCOMMON CLAY
STORM TRACK
HOME FIRES
KILLER MARKET
UP JUMPS THE DEVIL
SHOOTING AT LOONS
SOUTHERN DISCOMFORT
BOOTLEGGER'S DAUGHTER

Sigrid Harald novels:

FUGITIVE COLORS
PAST IMPERFECT
CORPUS CHRISTMAS
BABY DOLL GAMES
THE RIGHT JACK
DEATH IN BLUE FOLDERS
DEATH OF A BUTTERFLY
ONE COFFEE WITH

Non-series:

LAST LESSONS OF SUMMER
BLOODY KIN
SUITABLE FOR HANGING
SHOVELING SMOKE

SAND SHARKS

MARGARET MARON

GRAND CENTRAL
PUBLISHING

NEW YORK   BOSTON

If you purchase this book without a cover you should be aware that this book may have been stolen property and reported as "unsold and destroyed" to the publisher. In such case neither the author nor the publisher has received any payment for this "stripped book."

This book is a work of fiction. Names, characters, places, and incidents are the product of the author's imagination or are used fictitiously. Any resemblance to actual events, locales, or persons, living or dead, is coincidental.

Copyright © 2009 by Margaret Maron
Excerpt from *Christmas Mourning* copyright © 2010 by Margaret Maron
All rights reserved. Except as permitted under the U.S. Copyright Act of 1976, no part of this publication may be reproduced, distributed, or transmitted in any form or by any means, or stored in a database or retrieval system, without the prior written permission of the publisher.

Blackstone's Commentaries on the Laws of England: Volumes I–IV by Sir William Blackstone, originally published 1765–1769 (The Avalon Project, Yale Law School)

Roman Civilization: Volume II by Naphtali Lewis & Meyer Reinhold © 1955 Columbia University Press

"The Lake Isle of Innisfree" by William Butler Yeats, 1893

Grand Central Publishing
Hachette Book Group
237 Park Avenue
New York, NY 10017
Visit our website at www.HachetteBookGroup.com.

Grand Central Publishing is a division of Hachette Book Group, Inc. The Grand Central Publishing name and logo is a trademark of Hachette Book Group, Inc.

Printed in the United States of America

Originally published in hardcover by Hachette Book Group
First mass market edition, November 2010

10 9 8 7 6 5 4 3 2 1

ATTENTION CORPORATIONS AND ORGANIZATIONS:
Most HACHETTE BOOK GROUP books are available at quantity discounts with bulk purchase for educational, business, or sales promotional use. For information, please call or write:

Special Markets Department, Hachette Book Group
237 Park Avenue, New York, NY 10017
Telephone: 1-800-222-6747 Fax: 1-800-477-5925

To North Carolina,
which has given me more than I can ever
repay.

Here's to the land of the long leaf pine,
The summer land where the sun doth
shine,
Where the weak grow strong and the
strong grow great,
Here's to "down home," the Old North
State!

—Official North Carolina Toast

Acknowledgment

My thanks to all the members of the North Carolina Association of District Court Judges, who over the years have let me sit in on their conferences, shared their stories of humor and heartbreak, and answered my endless questions. I could not have written these books without their generous help.

SAND
SHARKS

CHAPTER
1

By marriage, the husband and wife are one person in law.... If the wife be injured in her person or her property, she can bring no action for redress without her husband's concurrence.

— *Sir William Blackstone (1723–1780)*

I should never have suggested perfume. If I'd stuck to something plain vanilla like a lacy bed jacket or some pretty note cards or even a box of assorted chocolates, it would have been fine. But no. I had to stop at a cosmetics counter in Crabtree Mall for a tube of my favorite moisturizer and say to Cal, "What about that?"

"That" was a small white porcelain bottle shaped like a single perfect gardenia.

My stepson shrugged and said, "Okay," plainly bored with this shopping trip. He and Dwight were going to drive up to Virginia the next morning. Dwight hoped to finish cleaning out the house Cal had inherited from his mother and to put it on the market, before driving on up to Charlottesville to teach a couple of sessions at a law-enforcement training seminar. Although Cal would be staying with a friend while Dwight was gone, he would certainly be seeing his grandmother during the visit. Yet he was no more enthusiastic about buying her a gift than he had been for the new jeans and shirts and sneakers he so desperately needed.

Cal turned nine last month and he's going to be as tall as his dad. A recent growth spurt now puts him almost shoulder-high to me, which means that he's outgrown almost every article of clothing he owns except for socks and the oversized Carolina Hurricanes T-shirt he was wearing—a shirt I have to wash by hand so as not to fade the team signatures on the right shoulder.

"Is that a gardenia scent?" I asked the clerk behind the counter.

"Sure is!" she chirped, and spritzed the back of my hand with a sample bottle.

"What do you think?" I asked Cal, holding my hand under his nose.

He took one sniff and went pale beneath his freckles. His brown eyes filled with sudden tears and he slapped my hand away, then bolted from the store and out into the mall.

Belatedly I remembered that smells can be even more evocative than music and I realized that I had thoughtlessly brought back all the grief and terror he had felt when Jonna died. He hadn't reacted at all to the first few blooms of the season that I had cut for our dining table last week, had even given them a cursory sniff, their sweet aroma diffused by cooking odors. But here on my hand? In concentrated strength just when the return to Virginia had to be on his mind?

Six months of healing ripped away in a moment by the

exaggerated smell of gardenias that must surely evoke the circumstances surrounding his mother's death.

I took some of the clerk's wipes and scrubbed the back of my hand till it was almost raw and every trace of the gardenia perfume was gone, then I grabbed our shopping bags and hurried out into the mall to find Cal.

I was halfway down the long space and beginning to panic before I finally spotted his red Hurricanes shirt. He was scrunched down beneath an overgrown ficus plant outside a video store. His back was against the wall, his shoulders slumped, and his face was buried in his arms, atop his drawn-up knees.

I so wanted to go put my arms around him and say how sorry I was, but he usually reacts awkwardly to my hugs and kisses or else shies away completely, and this wasn't the time to try again. Not when I was the reason he had fallen apart. There was a bench several feet away, so I parked the shopping bags and sat down to wait for the worst of his misery to pass.

A mall guard paused to look inquiringly at him and I caught her eye.

"It's okay," I murmured softly.

She grinned. "Can't have the video game he wants, huh?"

I smiled back as normally as I could and she moved on. If only Cal's hurt could be eased by something as simple as an electronic game.

Eventually, he raised his head and looked around. He did not immediately see me among all the people passing back and forth and his eyes darted apprehensively from one face to another until they met mine. Was that resentment or resignation on his face?

Whichever, there was nothing I could do about it, no matter how much my heart ached for him, no matter how much he missed his mother. He was stuck with me—had been stuck with me ever since Jonna was murdered back in January and he came to live with Dwight and me, less than a month after our Christmas wedding.

I held out the bag with his new sneakers and he dutifully got up and walked over to help.

"That's enough shopping for one day," I said briskly. "Let's go home."

As soon as we were in the car, he stuck the buds of his iPod in his ears and stared out the window without speaking.

Normal behavior.

What wasn't normal was the way he unplugged one ear after we had been driving a few minutes and looked over at me.

"Do I have to go to Shaysville? Can't I stay with Aunt Kate while y'all are gone?"

Kate is married to Dwight's brother Rob, and she keeps Cal during the week while Dwight and I are working. Unfortunately, Kate and Rob and their three children were flying up to New York the next day to spend some time in the city. Kate still owns the Manhattan apartment she shared with her late first husband and the tenant was happy to have her and her crew to come dog-sit while he went off to Paris for a week.

When I reminded Cal of this, he went to Plan B. "Then can I go with you?"

Another time and I might have been thrilled that he would choose me instead of Dwight, but this?

"What's going on, honey?" I asked gently. "Don't you want to see your grandmother and your old friends?"

He sank lower in his seat and didn't answer.

"Your dad's going to need your help with the house, Cal."

"No, he won't. He's got Uncle Will, so why does he need me? I won't be in the way at your meeting, Deborah. Honest. I can stay in the pool or watch television or something."

"Is this because of your Aunt Pam?" I asked.

He turned back to the window and stared out at the setting sun without answering.

Jonna's sister is bipolar and his last experience with her had been a terrifying ordeal. No wonder he was apprehensive about the possibility of a repeat.

With my left hand on the steering wheel, I reached over and touched his shoulder. "You absolutely do *not* have to worry about her, honey. She's still in the hospital and won't be coming out anytime soon. I promise."

I gave him a couple of miles to process my assurance, then added, "Jimmy Radcliff's going to be really disappointed if you stay home."

Jimmy's dad, Paul, is the chief of police up in Shaysville. He and Dwight are old Army buddies and Paul had promised to take Cal and Jimmy camping on the New River while Dwight attended his conference.

Some of the tension went out of Cal's small frame. "Okay," he said with a nod.

"Pam's a big part of it," I told Dwight when we lay in bed that night, "but I think he may be dreading the house itself. It's going to make him remember Jonna and what his life was like before she died, so cut him a little slack if he gives you a hard time, okay?"

He stopped nuzzling my ear long enough to murmur, "Okay," then turned his attention back to where his hands were and what they were doing and after that, I have to admit that I did, too.

"I'm gonna miss you," he said later when we lay face-to-face in the darkness with our legs entwined.

"Me, too, you," I said, kissing his chest.

"This is your first judges' conference since we got together."

Uh-oh.

Dwight and my brothers were inseparable as kids and I've known him since I was a baby. After he and Jonna split and he came back to Colleton County to become Sheriff Bo Poole's second in command, we would hang out together whenever we were at loose ends and not seeing anyone. I used to cry on his shoulder about relationships that went nowhere and he would unburden his guilt about missing Cal's childhood and whether or not he should take Jonna back to court to amend the custody arrangements. He was smart enough not to give details about his romantic entanglements but I always talked way too much about mine, some of which did indeed begin with the summer conferences at the beach or end with the fall conferences up in the mountains.

"Remember that you're a married lady now," he growled. "Or should I ask Judge Parker to keep an eye on you for me?"

Luther Parker was the first black judge elected in our district and he takes a semi-paternal interest in me.

"You can ask," I said, "but he's in bed every night by nine o'clock."

"Just see that you are, too," he said. "Alone."

I laughed. His tone was light, but I heard the tiniest touch of apprehension in his voice.

Nice to know your husband doesn't take you for granted, right?

Will called the next morning to confirm the time and place to meet with Dwight. He's three brothers up from me and makes his living as an estate appraiser and an auctioneer. Even though he's never had any formal training for either, he's pretty savvy and seems to know instinctively the value of a piece of furniture or a porcelain figurine. Occasionally he messes up on the worth of a chest or a family portrait, "But hell," he says, "that's what keeps the fancy-pants dealers coming to my auctions. They think I'm so ignorant that they're going to get something good for pennies on the dollar. Once in a while they might do, but most times they wind up buying what I'm selling for more than they meant to spend. It all evens out."

After Jonna's death up there in Virginia, he offered to go through the house with Dwight and to help move everything of sentimental or monetary value back down here so that we could get a better sense of what might be important to Cal someday and what could be disposed of now. This was the first chance they'd had to go up and even now it was only because of that training seminar up in Charlottesville.

Dwight planned to help Will load the truck, list the house with a real estate agent, go to the seminar on Monday and Tuesday, then pick Cal up on his way home on Wednesday, the day before I was due to get back.

Cal understood that the house and most of the furniture had to go, and he was enough a child of the age to be interested in how much money might wind up in his college fund when everything was sold. At least that's what we hoped.

"Peanut butter or chicken salad?" I asked him now as I opened a loaf of whole-wheat bread to pack a lunch for them.

He frowned at the carrots and apples I'd pulled from the refrigerator. "Dad and I always stop at McDonald's," he said, referring to the times he and Dwight had driven back and forth to Shaysville whenever it was Dwight's weekend to have him.

"This is better for you guys," I said lightly, mindful of my new nutritional responsibilities to a growing boy.

Dwight entered the kitchen, freshly shaved, and carrying his duffel bag. "Ready to hit the road, buddy?"

He set the bag by the back door and went over to pour himself a final cup of coffee.

Cal immediately took advantage of his turned back and said, "Can we stop for lunch in Greensboro, Dad? Like we always do?"

"Sure thing," Dwight said, completely oblivious to what was going on here. "Uncle Will's never said no to a cheeseburger."

"Fine," I said and shoved the stuff back into the refrigerator. I did not slam the refrigerator door and I did not stomp out of the room.

"Something wrong?" asked Dwight, who had followed me into our bedroom.

"Not a thing," I snapped. "I love being overruled in front of Cal."

"Huh?"

"I told Cal I was packing y'all a healthy lunch and then

you came in and said you'd stop for greasy cheeseburgers and french fries."

"I did? Sorry, shug. You should have said something."

"Right. And make myself the evil no-fun stepmother again? Thanks but no thanks." I headed for our bathroom to take a shower.

"Oh, come on, Deb'rah. What's the big deal? An occasional cheeseburger's not going to kill him."

I paused in the doorway and made a show of looking at the clock. "You'd better go if you're going to meet Will."

"Deb'rah?"

I ignored his outstretched hand and slammed the door between us, half-hoping he'd follow, but before I had fully shucked off my robe and gown, his truck roared past the window.

And no, dammit, I was *not* crying.

CHAPTER
2

But man was formed for society; and, as is demonstrated by writers on this subject, is neither capable of living alone, nor indeed has the courage to do it.

—*Sir William Blackstone (1723–1780)*

I stood in the shower, water sluicing down my body, and lathered shampoo into my hair. I was so furious with Dwight, it's a wonder the water didn't sizzle as soon as it touched my skin.

Hadn't we agreed to present a united front? For six months I had bent over backwards, trying to make up to his son for the mother he'd lost, trying to be consistent and fair and walk the line between understanding his loss and giving order and security to his life, and this was the thanks I got? Why did Dwight automatically assume I was in the wrong when I knew damn well I wasn't? Everybody says that junk food and poor eating habits make for obese kids. Did he want Cal to grow up fat and unhealthy? And just as importantly, was Dwight going to let Cal do an end run around me every time I made a ruling that he didn't like?

I sighed, finished rinsing the shampoo from my hair, and turned off the water to towel myself dry. I had one stepson.

One.

My mother had acquired eight when she married Daddy. How on earth did she wind up winning their love while asserting her authority?

"*She didn't,*" the preacher who lives in the back of my head reminded me. *"Not right away anyhow."*

I sighed again. It had taken her years with some of the older boys, but they had all come around in the end. I just wasn't sure I had her stamina and patience.

Well, the hell with it. If Dwight wanted to go storming off like that, I wasn't going to sit around here feeling sorry for myself.

Today was only Saturday, but there was nothing to keep me home. Although the summer conference of district court judges would not officially start until Monday, I was on the Education Committee and we planned to get together Sunday evening to begin brainstorming for the fall conference program. But hey! It was June, the hotel was right on Wrightsville Beach, and I had a new red maillot that didn't look too shabby on me. I called the hotel, and when they told me I could check in that afternoon, that's all I needed to hear.

I printed out the files I would need, then quickly packed and whistled for Bandit.

Daddy had volunteered to keep Cal's dog while we were away, so I drove through the back lanes of the farm to the homeplace with Bandit on the seat beside me. Paws on the dashboard, he peered through the windshield as if he knew he was in for a great weekend.

Daddy was sitting on the top step of the wide and shady front porch when I got there. The porch catches every bit of breeze but the air was dead still today and felt as if it'd already reached the predicted high of ninety when I opened the door of my air-conditioned car. Daddy scorns air-conditioning and our muggy heat seldom bothers him.

As always, his keen blue eyes were shaded by the straw panama that he wears from the first warm days of spring till the first cool days of autumn. His blue shirt was faded and his chinos were frayed at the ankle, part of the I-ain't-nothin'-but-a-pore-ol'-dirt-farmer look that he adopted during his bootlegging days and has never seen the need to change, no matter how many nice shirts and pants his daughters-in-law and I give him. (Maidie, his longtime housekeeper, just rolls her eyes and puts everything through the washer a time or two with bleach before he'll wear something new without nagging.) His long legs stretched down till his worn brogans rested on the lowest step.

Ladybelle, a dignified seven-year-old redbone coon-hound, lay on the dirt near his feet, and Bandit was all over her in bouncy excitement the minute I let him out of the car.

Daddy stood up and shook his head at so much canine energy on such a hot day. "He don't seem to've calmed down much since he come, has he?"

"That's the terrier in him," I said. "He's getting better at home. You sure he's not going to be too much trouble? Andrew said he'd pen him in with his beagles if you don't want to be bothered with another house dog."

"Naw, he won't be no bother. He *is* housebroke, ain't he?"

"He wouldn't be a house dog if he wasn't."

"Well, then, he'll be just fine. Ladybelle'll let him know if he gets out of line with her."

"Thanks, Daddy," I said, standing on tiptoe to kiss his wrinkled cheek. "Dwight and Cal should be back Wednesday and they'll be over to pick him up then. I'll get home on Thursday. Maidie has our phone numbers if anything comes up."

Daddy's aversion to telephones was formed back when long-distance phone calls cost real money, and no matter how cheap they are these days, he's never going to change.

"Ain't nothing gonna come up worth a phone call," he told me firmly.

Minutes later I was meandering through a maze of back-country roads that would take me over to I-40. Despite all the new developments that had obliterated so many of the county's small farms, there were still fields of tobacco along the way. Here in the middle of June, few of the tops were showing any pink tuberoses yet. I passed a four- or five-acre stand of corn where a red tractor was giving the plants a side-dressing of soda. And there were still parcels of unsold fallow land where tall oaks and maples were in full leaf, where honeysuckle competed with deep green curtains of kudzu that fell in graceful loops from power wires to drape all the weaker trees. Goldenrod, daisies, and bright orange daylilies brightened the ditch banks.

Once I hit I-40, heading southeast, the wide green dividers bloomed with beds of delicate pink poppies and eye-popping red cannas. Grass and trees and bushes were so lush and green that the line about being "knee-deep in June" kept looping through my head. Robert Frost? Eugene Field? I often wish I had paid more attention to poetry in my college lit courses. Someone once described poetry committed to memory as "a jewel in the pocket."

My pockets have holes in them and most of the jewels have fallen out.

I-40 came to an end about ninety miles later where the highway splits. To the right is the town of Wilmington proper with its meandering boardwalk along the Cape Fear River, its many seafood restaurants, the courthouse, and street after street lined with live oaks and antebellum mansions with black-and-gold historical plaques affixed to the front.

The left fork of the highway leads over to Wrightsville Beach, past a dozen or more strip malls, shopping centers, and upscale gated communities until you reach the high-rise hotels and densely packed beach houses that line the wide beaches of sugar-soft sand.

I turned in at the conference hotel and maneuvered past the cars loading and unloading to park near the entrance.

As I pulled my roller bag across the polished marble floor to the reception desk, I heard someone call, "Well, hey there, girl!"

I turned to see Chelsea Ann Pierce, a colleague based in Raleigh, and her sister, Rosemary Emerson, who's married to a Durham judge. Chelsea Ann's a generously built easygoing blonde with an infectious laugh. Rosemary's the older prototype, with darker hair and a cynical sense of humor that cracks us all up.

I get my share of gooey, inspirational God-loves-you-

and-so-do-all-the-women-you-know emails from various friends and relatives and those I usually delete without reading, but I never automatically delete the jokes and funny pictures or off-the-wall news items that Rosemary sends. She's never yet duplicated anything that's been circling through the ether for years, and it's always something that makes me laugh out loud and then forward to a PI friend in California with a similarly warped outlook on life.

"Three minds with the same thought?" I asked, even though they were in clam diggers and bright cotton shirts. "Ya'll figure to get a little beach time in first, too?"

Chelsea Ann shook her head. "Nope, we're off to check out the consignment shops." She recently sold the big suburban house that was part of her divorce settlement and bought a condo in Raleigh's Cameron Village. "I need a narrow table for my new entry hall and the Ivy Cottage is supposed to have the best selection of used furniture around. Want to come? We'll wait for you to check in."

I shook my head and gestured toward the nearly deserted beach that lay beyond the clear glass walls. "Y'all go ahead. I haven't been in salt water all season and I'm dying to get out there. I'm free for supper though. Want to meet at Jonah's? Six-thirty?"

My hotel room on the fifth floor came with the standard king-sized bed, a decent-sized desk for my laptop, and a mirrored alcove that surrounded a Jacuzzi big enough for two. French doors opened onto a minuscule balcony that held two of those ubiquitous white plastic club chairs that seem to have taken over the world. It overlooked the beach and pool area, and my view of turquoise water was spectacular.

I immediately opened the glass doors and stepped outside. The ocean's warm briny fragrance carried with it a faint whiff of chlorine from the pool and three hot tubs directly in front of the terrace that lay below my balcony. Too hot to sit out today though. Not when I could be down there. I didn't bother to unpack anything except my bathing suit, beach jacket, floppy hat, and flip-flops. After slathering myself with sunscreen till I felt like a turkey getting ready for the roasting pan, I took the elevator down to the pool level. There were piles of thick white towels by the door and I grabbed a couple as I went past. The heat hit me in the face again as soon as I opened the outer door but a light breeze was blowing off the water and gulls were kiting on the currents overhead. A line of pelicans swooped past so low that they almost skimmed the tops of the waves. Although the pool was drawing a fair crowd, the beach was practically empty, and the lifeguard appeared to be playing a game on his cell phone. I saw no one I knew on my stretch of creamy beige sand as I spread out the towels, took off my jacket, and lay down on my back with my hat over my face to let the sun bake my body.

"*Summertime and the livin' is easy,*" my inner pragmatist sang as he spread his own towel.

Until I felt the tension draining out of my joints and muscles, I didn't realize how much stress I'd been under these last five months, adjusting both to marriage and to having Cal with us full-time. This would be the longest I'd been away from both of them since January, but there on the hot sand, I finally admitted to myself just how much I had been looking forward to this week.

No personal demands, no stepmother tightropes to walk. Only the give and take of professional life, and I wasn't going to feel guilty about enjoying it or let my anger with Dwight ruin it for me.

Or so I told myself, because lying on my towel, I was beginning to feel thoroughly miserable.

"Just as you should," scolded the preacher from the shade of his beach umbrella. *"You know good and well that Dwight was clueless. If anyone needed to be jumped on, it was Cal."*

The pragmatist, who only wanted to soak up sun, gave an impatient scowl. *"He's a child. Dwight's son. She comes down hard on him, who's Dwight gonna side with?"*

The preacher shrugged. *"So? Any other child—one of her nieces or nephews—and she'd either laugh it off or tell him, 'Good try, kid, but it's peanut butter and apples driving up. Y'all can stop for hamburgers on the way home.' She wouldn't take it out on Dwight. He was right. What's the big deal?"*

"Cal doesn't respect her decisions."

"He's nine, for Pete's sake! If she's going to drop down to the nine-year-old level every time they butt heads, why should he respect them? Stomping off sure doesn't help."

"I didn't stomp," I said.

"You stomped," they chorused.

"Very mature," the preacher sniffed. *"That only tells Cal that he won the round. Some role model you are."*

"Go to hell," I said and blanked my ears to everything except the cry of seagulls and the rhythmic swoosh of waves breaking on the beach.

* * *

I was almost asleep when someone lifted my hat and said, "Cynthia?"

I blinked up at a vaguely familiar face.

"Oops, sorry!" said the man. "I thought you were someone else."

"Jeffreys?" I asked. "Peter Jeffreys?"

He nodded and gave me a closer look as I retrieved my hat and sat up cross-legged on the towel.

"Deborah Knott," I told him. "District 11-C."

"Well, damn!" He gave a self-deprecating laugh. "I should have remembered. You taught a class for new judges over at the School of Government last year, right?"

I nodded. "Who's Cynthia? Your wife?"

"Oh, hell, no! We split up three years ago. Cynthia Blankenthorpe's a new judge from out in Mecklenburg County. Got appointed in January. This is her first conference and I promised to show her the ropes, introduce her to people."

I'll just bet he had, I thought, giving him a complete examination from behind the safety of my dark glasses. Pete Jeffreys is from Greensboro, District 18. He came on during the last election, one of those princes of the bench, ambitious for higher glory. There was already talk of his running for superior court in the next election cycle. Even on tiptoes, he wouldn't stretch to six feet, but he carried himself like a taller man and was easy to look at. Hazel eyes, a thick head of straight brown hair, cleft chin, and—now that I was seeing him stripped down to swim trunks with a towel draped over one shoulder—a slender build that was nicely muscled. Not even the slightest hint of love handles. How had I overlooked him when I was still free and single?

"*He was married,*" my inner preacher reminded me sternly. "*And so are you now.*"

"*Yeah, yeah,*" said the pragmatist, taking off his sunglasses for a better look. "*But there was something else…*"

Then Pete Jeffreys said, "Any chance you could rub some of your sunscreen on my shoulders?" and what had been a normal friendly smile morphed into a conceited smirk.

Men who think they are irresistible have always been a big turn-off for me and smirks make me want to slap the entitlement right off their faces.

"Sorry," I said with my sweetest smile. "I'm afraid my bottle's almost empty and I'll burn if I don't keep it on, but I'm sure you can find some at the gift shop."

"No problem," he said easily. "There's Cynthia now. She probably has enough to share. See ya 'round."

"*Not if she sees you first,*" said the pragmatist as Pete moved on down the beach to where a woman was spreading a colorful striped beach towel.

Even from this distance, it was clear that Cynthia Blankenthorpe was at least five years older and several pounds heavier than me. Had Pete really mistaken those muscular thighs for mine?

So not good.

On the other hand, with that name, she was probably part of the Blankenthorpes who were connected to big-time banking in Charlotte. If he was already building a wider network for future campaigns, maybe it was wishful thinking on his part.

I tucked my key card inside my hatband and headed for the water. The tide was low and still receding. A group of teenage boys and girls were further out with bright green, red, and turquoise boards but the waves were way too gentle for any real surfing, which is okay with me. I'm not a strong swimmer and big waves intimidate the hell out of me, but I do love to bobble on the swells and paddle around in the shallows.

Which I did until I was pleasantly tired. It felt downright hedonistic to go back to my room, shower, and even lie down for a nap that might have stretched right through the night if Chelsea Ann hadn't called me to ask if I could bring along an extra sweater.

"We want to eat outside, right? If the wind's off the river, it could get a little chilly."

I had planned to wear my white cotton sweater tonight, but I put it aside for her and opted for a red one over a red-and-white print sundress. Dangly hoop earrings, red straw sandals, and I was ready to roll.

CHAPTER
3

For all these crimes it has been decreed that capital punishment shall be meted out.

—*Paulus (early AD 3rd century)*

When the down elevator stopped at my floor, the car was crowded. "Make room for the lady in red," called a voice from the back.

"Thanks, Chuck," I said as I squeezed on.

Judge Charles Teach from further up the coast is well named although he's better looking than Edward Teach, aka Blackbeard. Still there's something piratical about those flashing dark eyes and the black-as-tar beard that he keeps trimmed to a neat Vandyke instead of the greasy curls his namesake favored. Early forties and still a bachelor, his reputation as a brilliant, hard-working jurist is tempered by his reputation as a womanizer who plays as hard as he works. And yes, there might have been some heavy breathing on both our parts one year at fall conference, but lust turned to liking before things got out of hand or into bed.

He usually shares a suite that automatically turns into party central. Indeed, when our elevator reached the lobby, two of his suitemates were there to get on. Steve Shaber and Julian Cannell, colleagues from the Fort Bragg/Fayetteville area, had commandeered a valet's luggage cart and, judging by that large cooler and some lumpy brown paper bags, they had brought enough supplies to stock a small saloon.

I got warm hugs from both of them and even warmer injunctions to come up to Room 628 after dinner.

A couple of judges from out near Asheville were waiting for Chuck and, as we headed for our cars, they invited me to join them.

"Thanks, but I'm meeting Chelsea Ann Pierce and Rosemary Emerson over on the river," I told them.

"Jonah's? That's where we're going," Chuck said. "You can ride with us."

Fifteen minutes later we had crossed the causeway, and were soon driving down one of the port city's main thoroughfares. That part of Market Street nearest I-40 begins with block after block of small businesses, fast-food joints, and cheap motels, but it winds up in the old part of town to become a beautiful divided street with stately homes on either side, historical markers, and live oaks whose limbs drip with Spanish moss and almost touch overhead to form a dark green tunnel.

The street ends at the Cape Fear River where Chuck turned left and drove along Water Street till he reached a graveled parking lot. This early in the evening there were still a few places left beneath the huge old mulberry trees along the riverbank, and he wedged his car in next to a black SUV with an NCDCJ license plate that belonged to

Chelsea Ann. Across the water from us, the superstructure of the USS *North Carolina* was silhouetted against a cloudless blue sky. The body of the ship itself was nearly obscured by a thicket of trees.

Instead of walking along uneven cobblestones to the front entrance of Jonah's, we took some nearby wooden steps up to the Riverwalk, a wide promenade of treated lumber that stretches about a mile, connecting Chandler's Wharf with its shops and restaurants at the south end to the Chamber of Commerce at the north end. In contrast to the old battleship permanently moored as a museum, a modern supertanker had just cleared the raised bridge downriver.

We watched for a minute and were moving on when, from behind us, we heard a dog's bark, then a sharp yelp and men's voices hot with anger.

"He didn't touch you!" cried a young man, who tugged on a retractable leash to restrain a lunging brown boxer. "Dammit all, you didn't have to kick him."

"Just get him the hell away from me or I'll have you arrested," the older man snarled.

It was Pete Jeffreys. "Frickin' dog tried to bite me," he told us as he mounted the steps, trailed by Cynthia Blankenthorpe.

"Like hell!" shouted the dog's owner. "You're the one needs arresting, kicking him like that."

Jeffreys started to turn back and answer him, but Judge Blankenthorpe caught him by the arm. "Let it go, Pete. Don't push it."

Still muttering angrily, Jeffreys allowed her to lead him away. I looked back and saw the ruggedly handsome man kneel beside his dog and run his hands over its head as if to make certain nothing was damaged. There was something about the man's face that made me look again although I was sure that he was no one I knew.

At the restaurant, the host who greeted us was a fresh-faced collegiate-looking kid who led us over to outdoor tables overlooking the river where Rosemary and Chelsea Ann were at work on frozen margaritas.

"Dave not coming?" I asked Rosemary when I realized that her husband wasn't there.

"He's skipping summer conference this year," Chelsea Ann said. "It's just Thelma and Louise this time."

"Actually, he's here," said Rosemary.

"What?" Chelsea Ann stared at her in open-mouthed surprise and Rosemary flushed brick-red. Both sisters had fair skin and green eyes but Rosemary's hair was more strawberry than golden and she reddened more easily when flustered.

"It was a last-minute change of plans," she said.

"How last-minute?" Chelsea Ann asked tightly.

"That was who called me while we were in the Cotton Exchange. He thought we'd be eating at the hotel and he was going to surprise us, but someone told him we were over here."

"So he's coming?" I asked, thinking to diffuse whatever was happening between them.

Rosemary shook her head. "He thinks he may have had one too many beers to drive, so he's going to chill out in his Jacuzzi and then grab a sandwich or something at the hotel bar."

"Let's hope that's all he grabs," Chelsea Ann muttered in my ear.

Huh? Although I knew Dave Emerson liked to flirt

and talk trash to pretty women, I'd always assumed the marriage was basically strong. Certainly I'd never heard Rosemary express regret for giving up her own law career to further his while staying home to raise two high-achieving daughters. Of course, I don't know as much about her personal life as I do her sister's. Still...

I lifted an eyebrow at Chelsea Ann, who gave a don't-ask-me-now shrug. Rosemary appeared not to have heard, so I filed it for future reference and let it go.

We weren't the only ones who had arrived in town early and who had decided to gather there for dinner. As often happens at conventions and conferences, tables meant for four soon accommodated six, and other tables were pushed together until we had taken over the whole left front corner of the open porch. Like the Emersons, some judges were there with spouses to make it a family vaca-tion. After table-hopping to speak to colleagues I hadn't seen since the last conference, I came back to my original table and took an empty chair beside white-haired Fitz Fitzhume and Martha, his tall, angular, and opinionated wife, even though that left me with my back to the water.

A reedy young waiter with a weak chin arrived with the Fitzhumes' drinks, took our orders, and agreed to bring me a margarita to replace the one I'd finished at an-other table.

"Kyle's trying to break into television," said Martha, a true people person who can't help getting the life his-tory of almost everyone she comes into contact with, from lawyers to janitors and certainly with the wait staff. "He got to be on-camera for a crowd scene in *Dawson's Creek*."

"And when I was a little kid, I was in a courtroom scene on *Matlock*," the waiter said. "In the row right behind Andy Griffith."

"Then you're from Wilmington?" I asked politely.

"Myrtle Beach actually, but my aunt lives here and she knew one of the crew members on the show, so that's how I got on."

I'm no judge—well, no judge of acting ability anyhow—but it seemed to me that his voice was too thin and just a little too arch for anything except the lightest of comedies. He was poised to tell me the rest of his brushes with the spotlight until Martha gently reminded him that his current role was waiter and that she, for one, was hungry.

"Nice kid, but too much fluff between the ears," said Martha. "He may sleep with a director, but that's about as far as he's gonna get in show business."

"Cynic," I said.

"Not cynical, sugar. Just realistic. Now Hank over there"—she pointed to the young man who had shown us to this part of the porch—"he wants to go into hotel management and I'd say he has the chops for it."

Indeed, he was in the act of seating a bearded man with two young children, a girl and a boy. He brought them crayons and a coloring sheet and was fitting one of the chairs with a booster seat for the little boy when Pete Jeffreys approached the table. The father half rose from his chair to shake hands and introduce his children, who shyly ducked their heads. The headwaiter stood by discreetly until the introductions were over, then handed the man a menu and signaled for a waitress.

"Now how you finding married life?" Judge Fitzhume asked me.

"Just fine," I lied. "And don't you and Martha have a fortieth anniversary coming up?"

"Forty-two," he beamed. "And it seems like only four since I got her to the altar."

Courtly, soft-spoken, and always polite even when disagreeing with drunken felons, Fitz had announced his retirement a few months earlier. Although he would probably continue to fill in as an emergency judge when needed, he and Martha planned to spend the next year traveling around the world to visit far-flung grandchildren. They were telling me their itinerary and had gotten themselves as far as Rome when Pete Jeffreys came up with Cynthia Blankenthorpe in tow.

I have called Pete Jeffreys one of the princes of the bench, but that impression was formed at the first fall conference he attended year before last where I watched him move confidently through the halls and meeting rooms with easy charm and instant camaraderie. He had skipped last summer's conference and I had skipped the fall, so I hadn't seen him interact with our colleagues in over a year. Now I noticed a distinct chill when he approached our table to introduce the new judge to Fitz, and I realized that Martha had drawn back stiffly in her chair and kept her strong fingers firmly around her drink, deliberately ignoring his outstretched hand.

Dear, ever-courteous Fitz assumed the hand was meant for him and, after a slight hesitation, shook it amiably enough.

"Bastard!" said Martha when Jeffreys and his protégée had moved on.

"Now, Martha," he murmured.

"Not you, honey," she assured him.

Before I could ask her to explain, the deep-fried soft-shelled crabs we'd both ordered arrived, crisp and succulent on beds of baby greens.

As far as I'm concerned, blue claws are the tastiest crustacean in the Atlantic. You can have my lobsters if you'll give me all your blue crabs, especially when they've just molted, before their shells start to harden.

Fitz gave a sigh of pure pleasure as his own plate was set before him, and was moved to tell his favorite crab joke.

"This was back when the world was young and urgent messages went by Western Union rather than cell phones or emails," he said, squeezing lemon juice over a plate of buttery linguini heaped high with lumps of back-fin meat. "A man sent his mother-in-law on a vacation at the coast to get her out of his hair. Two days later, he got a telegram from the hotel manager. 'Regret to inform you your mother-inlaw washed ashore this evening covered in crabs. What shall I do?' "

Everyone within earshot of his voice sang out, "Ship the crabs and set 'er again!"

"Oh," he said. "Y'all've heard it before?"

Martha patted his hand. "Every time you order crabs, sweetheart."

Across the table from me, Chelsea Ann's blue eyes widened. "Omigawd!" she said in an awed whisper. "It's him!"

"Who?" I asked, suddenly aware that the level of conversation out here on the deck had dropped in that electric moment of awareness that sweeps over a room when a celebrity enters. I turned in time to see a man tethering his dog to the railing by its leash. It was the same man who'd yelled at Jeffreys out in the parking lot.

By the time he had finished with the dog and joined his party at the nearest table, our group had stopped staring and the noise level had risen again.

"Who's that?" I asked Chelsea Ann, who kept glancing over surreptitiously.

"Stone Hamilton."

The name meant nothing to me.

Chelsea Ann couldn't believe my ignorance. "Stone Hamilton. He plays the lead on *Port City Blues*. Don't you watch it?"

I've never seen the program itself, but its advertising trailers are shown so often on one of the networks that I now realized why he had looked somewhat familiar. I saw that our waiter had quickly appeared at his elbow with order pad in hand even though that was probably not his table. Indeed, a waitress with jet-black hair streaked with fuchsia immediately went over and sent him packing.

Wilmington likes to bill itself as "Hollywood East," but this was the first time I'd ever seen an actor from one of the several shows that had been filmed around town. The closest I'd come was when trying a custody case between two prominent attorneys down here last fall. Every courtroom was tied up because, in addition to the usual calendar, a show was being filmed in the courtroom next to mine. The halls were full of extra people, power cords snaked along the floor, and a couple of wardrobe racks and some odd pieces of equipment had wound up in the back of my courtroom.

The custody case was complicated by lengthy narratives to explain and rationalize lapses of judgment on both sides. After we were interrupted for a second time, I told the young man who seemed to be the crew's gofer that he was not to come back in until I had recessed for lunch.

Minutes later, a scowling man with a ponytail of long gray hair and the attitude of a horse's ass erupted though the side door, trailed by the younger one.

"What do you mean he can't come back in here till lunchtime?" he snarled.

"Sir," I said, "we're trying a case here."

He glared at me. "And I'm trying to shoot some very important scenes. I need access to these clothes. Do you know who I am?"

"No, sir," I said with more courtesy than I was feeling, "but if it's clothes you're interested in, I'll be glad to have you fitted with an orange jumpsuit and paper slippers if you or any of your people come back in here again before I adjourn."

As my words sank in, the young man behind him grinned and gave me a thumbs-up.

"Bailiff," I said, "would you escort this gentleman out?"

Angrily ordering his flunky to wheel out the clothes racks, the director stomped away and peace reigned in my courtroom for the rest of the day. I still don't know what show it was.

Although Chelsea Ann continued to glance over my shoulder to the Hamilton party, I found my own eyes straying back to Pete Jeffreys, who now seemed to be introducing Blankenthorpe to that bearded man with the two kids. Why did he look so familiar? Maybe the children and husband of a judge I didn't know well?

Before I could ask someone, I noticed a familiar face at the restaurant next door.

Like Jonah's, it, too, has open-air dining out on its
porch deck and it was doing a brisk business as well,
including one diner well known to me—my handsome
cousin and former law partner Reid Stephenson. I had
known that the Trial Lawyers Association was supposed
to meet this weekend, but that was at Sunset Beach, a
good forty minutes down the coast and only minutes
from the South Carolina border. What was he doing up
here?

His eyes eventually met mine and he lifted his glass in
greeting. I gestured for him to come join us, but he shook
his head and remained where he was. There were no women at his table, only men, and he knows several of the
judges, so I didn't understand his reluctance.

"Order me another margarita and don't let them take
my plate," I told Martha. "I'll be right back."

I walked over to the gate onto the Riverwalk and gave
Stone Hamilton's boxer a pat on the head when he greeted
me with a wiggle of his stubby tail.

Reid and his friends politely came to their feet as I
joined them, even though I told them not to bother. Like
the male judges in my party, they were casually dressed
in chinos or khaki shorts and colorful knit golf shirts instead of their accustomed suits and ties. They pulled up
a chair for me and an attorney from Fuquay-Varina said,
"What are you drinking, Your Honor?"

"Margaritas," Reid said. "Right, Deborah?"

What the hell? No one was waiting for me in my hotel
room. The night was young, I wasn't driving, and I could
sleep late tomorrow.

"Sure," I said. "Thanks."

"You know everyone here, right?" my cousin asked.

I did. If not by specific names, certainly by their familiar faces. All except one, a pleasantly homely man with a long thin face made even longer by a hairline that had receded to the top of his head. Late thirties, early forties, keen blue eyes and a mouth so wide that it literally did seem to go from ear to ear when he smiled at me and extended his hand. "Bill Hasselberger, Your Honor. I've heard a lot about you from Reid here."

"I hope you don't believe everything he's told you," I said, smiling back. He had long thin fingers and a firm handshake that hinted at a wiry strength.

"Bill and I were in law school together," said Reid, "and I was an usher in his wedding."

My drink came and when the others went back to the discussion I'd interrupted—something about the association's proposed name change—I turned to Reid and said, "So why you didn't come over and speak to Fitz and Martha? He's retiring this fall."

Reid's dad, Brix Junior, was a close friend of the Fitzhumes and they had known Reid since he was a little boy.

"I'll catch 'em later." He downed the rest of his drink in one long swallow. "No way I'm going over while that asshole's there."

"And which asshole would that be?" I asked.

"Jeffreys." He spat out the name like an expletive.

Surprised, I asked, "What'd he ever do to you?"

"Drop it, okay?"

That's when I realized that this was not his first drink. Probably not his second, either, but the hostility in his voice made me shrug and back off.

A few minutes later, I finished my own drink, said all

the polite and proper things to the others, and headed back to my own group. As I passed Pete Jeffreys, he gave me a sour look and deliberately turned his back on me.

First Dwight, then Reid, and now Jeffreys?

When did I turn into Typhoid Mary?

By eleven o'clock the tables out on the porch were deserted except for a young couple on the far side, holding hands by candlelight and lost in each other's eyes. My own eyes filled with sudden tears and I wondered if Dwight and I would ever sit like that again.

The rest of our crowd had already called it a night and Chelsea Ann and Rosemary had been urging me to leave for the last twenty minutes, but I insisted on finishing my final drink even though I hadn't touched it lately. For some reason, those crabs and hushpuppies weren't sitting too easy, although the four—or was it five?—margaritas might have had something to do with it. In any event, I was reluctant to move till everything settled down.

"C'mon, Deborah," Chelsea Ann said at last. "This isn't like you. What's wrong? You and Dwight having troubles?"

Eventually I let them help me to my feet. I wasn't really tipsy, but I did seem to have trouble walking. While Rosemary settled our bill, Chelsea Ann helped me down the steps to the Riverwalk. I almost made it back to the parking lot when my stomach finally rebelled.

"Oh God!" I moaned and hurried on past the steps to get as far ahead of them as I could. Even in my misery, I had the sense not to hurl into the wind. Instead I hung over the railing on the backwash side and lost both my dinner and all that tequila.

Chelsea Ann and Rosemary waited a discreet distance away till I had finished retching.

When I could finally lift my head, I noticed something odd. On the muddy riverbank only six or eight feet away from me, something bobbled on the outgoing tide, half hidden by overhanging shrubbery. In such dim light, it was almost unnoticeable amid the trash and driftwood that had collected in the branches.

It took me a minute to process what I was seeing and to realize that those two dark wet logs floating side by side were a man's sodden pant legs. Pete Jeffreys hung face up from a low-lying tree branch, his body almost completely submerged in the water.

One crab clung to his fingers, a second scuttled up his bare arm, and as I backed away from the railing in horror, Rosemary called, "What's wrong?"

Like another wave of nausea, Fitz's ancient joke rose in my throat and I couldn't stop it. "Ship the crabs and set 'im again!" I croaked.

CHAPTER
4

*The credibility of witnesses should be carefully
weighed.*

—*Justinian (AD 483–565)*

12:33. Sunday morning.

The nausea was pretty much gone, but my head was
pounding like a military parade gone wrong—everybody
marching to a different drummer and nobody on the beat,
despite the three aspirin tablets I'd swallowed.

Chelsea Ann and her sister shared a bench behind a
closed candle shop across from the parking lot, while
I leaned on a nearby railing that overlooked the river.
Chelsea Ann's SUV was still parked beside Judge Jeffreys's BMW, and both vehicles were nosed up to the
riverbank where I'd found him. The police had set up
a perimeter of yellow tape around the whole lot so that
every inch could be processed for clues as to how he had
wound up dangling in the water. The SUV blocked our
view of whatever they were finding on the ground next to
Jeffreys's car. Until they finished, we were stuck here to
twiddle our metaphorical thumbs.

My friends leaned their heads against the wall behind them and closed their eyes to block out the glare of the floodlights. High in the sky, the nearly full moon added even more light. During that interminable wait, I tried to keep my head as motionless as possible and fixed my eyes on the huge bridge at the mouth of the river as it slowly raised its middle span like an elevator to let a tanker pass beneath. Smaller leisure boats cruised past us, their lights reflected on the water. A cool breeze kept the mosquitoes at bay and made me glad I'd worn a light sweater.

Any man's murder is regrettable, but none of us knew Jeffreys well enough to feel any grief. Although I had privately decided to make discreet inquiries tomorrow, that didn't stop me from speculating with Rosemary and Chelsea Ann as we waited. Like me, they had also noticed a coolness from some of our colleagues as he moved from table to table.

"I've been thinking," Chelsea Ann said. "Remember the guy that carjacked and killed a girl last fall? How he wasn't even supposed to be on the streets because he'd violated probation. Didn't Jeffreys handle that case?"

It's always a judgment call between time in our over-crowded prisons or supervised probation. I couldn't remember the details, only that it's a judge's worst nightmare: that we'll set a bail too low or give probation to someone who then goes out and kills.

"Wasn't there something about a custody case when he first came to the bench?" asked Rosemary.

"I thought it was about the way he ran his campaign," said Chelsea Ann. "Some mud he slung at Hasselberger?"

"Hasselberger?" I asked. "Bill Hasselberger? Is that who he ran against?"

"Yeah, you know him?"

"Not really. He was here with Reid tonight at the restaurant next door and Reid introduced him. I thought he was a local, though."

"He is now," said Chelsea Ann. "I heard he was so pissed when he got beat that he moved his practice down here so he wouldn't have to plead a case in Jeffreys's court."

"I'll bet Roberta Ouellette would know," I mused. "Isn't she in his district?"

After a half hour of going round and round, we lapsed into weary silence and I turned back to the distant bridge, which had now lowered itself back into place. Despite the late hour, headlights flashed back and forth from an intermittent stream of cars and trucks.

The local newspaper and television reporters had left shortly after the body was loaded onto a gurney, but a boyish young blonde in baggy blue cotton trousers and a white tank top had figured out that we weren't part of the crowd that had gathered to gawk and she casually made her way down the Riverwalk to where we were. She looked like a teenager out too late until she flashed press credentials that ID'd her as Megan Somebody-or-other from WHQR, the local NPR station. She just happened to have a tiny voice recorder in the pocket of those baggy slacks and she was polite about pointing the mic at Chelsea Ann and Rosemary on the bench. "I hate to bother you, but would you mind talking about what happened here tonight?"

My friends shook their heads and she gave me an inquiring look.

"Sorry," I said, "but we really can't discuss it."

I should have kept my mouth shut because she immediately homed in on me. "Could you at least confirm that you were the one who found the body?"

Almost against my will, I nodded and that cute little camel nose edged itself further under the tent flap. "That must have been such a shock."

She reminded me of my niece Emma. I didn't say anything, but just like Emma, this budding Anne Garrels was not easily deterred. "You're all judges, right? Down here for the conference at Wrightsville Beach? I'm supposed to interview Justice Parker out there on Tuesday."

Our identities would soon be common knowledge, so again I nodded, ignoring the fact that Rosemary was the wife and sister of judges, not a judge herself.

"Did you know him? Was he a friend? A close colleague?"

"I'm sorry," I said again. "Look, I know you're just doing your job, but I really don't think I should say anything else. I'm sure your police department will give you a statement when it's appropriate."

"Okay," she said cheerfully. The recorder and mic disappeared back into her pocket. "But maybe you could give me a little background on Justice Parker? I mean, I know she's only the third woman to be chief justice of the state's supreme court, but what's she like as a person?"

That seemed harmless enough, so I cautiously told her about Sarah Parker's professionalism, the esteem with which her peers held her, that she had a quietly impish sense of humor and that she seldom spoke on or off the record without weighing her words.

"Never married?"

I shrugged. "I know absolutely nothing about her personal life."

"Then what about her public life? What could I ask her that a million other reporters haven't already?"

"You could ask about her journals."

"She keeps a journal? Where all the bodies are buried?"

I laughed. "I don't have the foggiest idea. But if she says she does, let me know, okay?"

"Sure. You have a card?"

I actually had my purse open before I realized what she was really after. "Good try, kid."

She laughed, too, then turned serious. "If he was a friend, I really am sorry you had to be the one to find him." She paused and considered. "Or even if he wasn't your friend, it still sucks, doesn't it?"

A moment later, she was down the wooden steps and eeling her way onto Front Street, past the dozen or so curious people who stared over at the police activity as if waiting for something more exciting to happen.

"Hey, guys," one of them finally called. "Where's Jill Mercer?"

I hadn't known who Stone Hamilton was, but Jill Mercer got her break as the good girl gone bad in an action video Dwight had rented back when we were just friends in a strictly platonic relationship. According to Chelsea Ann, who says she only watches *Port City Blues* because it's set in Wilmington and not because Stone Hamilton is hot, Mercer plays a sexy, trash-talking judge.

"Just your run-of-the-mill district court judge who moonlights in an after-hours blues club," Chelsea Ann had said.

"Oh great," Rosemary said now. "They think we're shooting scenes for that show."

Chelsea Ann squinted at her watch. "Five more minutes," she muttered, "and then we're out of here even if I have to commandeer a squad car. I have a breakfast meeting first thing in the morning and y'all know what I'm like if I don't get at least six hours of sleep."

Almost as if he'd heard her, the lead detective came over to us.

"Sorry to keep you waiting, ladies...uh, ma'ams? Or is it Your Honors?" Amused by his own confusion, Detective Gary Edwards shook his head and smiled at us. "I've never addressed more than one judge at a time. Do y'all have a collective title?"

Cute.

Chelsea Ann, who's currently between guys, sat up to give him a second and third look.

Early forties. Blond. Starting to beef up just a little through the waist.

And yeah, even though there's now a wedding band on my own third finger, I found myself automatically checking out his.

No ring. No sign that he'd ever worn one.

Hmmmm.

(*"That's quite enough of* that, *missy,"* the preacher said starchily.)

(The pragmatist shrugged. *"She's allowed to look, long as she doesn't touch."*)

Rosemary yawned and said, "Can we go now, Detective Edwards?"

"Sorry," he said again. "I know you gave statements to

the responding officer, but I need to hear it from Judge Knott myself if you don't mind, ma'am."

I did mind. I minded very much, but he pointed his own voice recorder at me and once again I had to tell the humiliating story of losing my dinner, which was how I had come to see Judge Jeffreys dead in the water.

"What about earlier?" Edwards asked. "Who was he seated with? Who didn't like him?"

"Sorry," I said. "I didn't know him that well and I didn't pay much attention to him." No way was I going to have him focus on Martha Fitzhume or Reid before I had a chance to find out why they thought Jeffreys was a prick. "He came by our table with one of the new judges, Judge Blankenthorpe from Charlotte. I think he was with her most of the evening."

"She staying out at the conference hotel?" he asked.

"Probably. She was on the beach there this afternoon."

Chelsea Ann and Rosemary offered up two or three more names of judges they'd seen with Jeffreys and I described his run-in with Stone Hamilton over Hamilton's dog.

"Dog?" Edwards asked sharply. "Hamilton's dog bit him?"

"Tried to. Or so Judge Jeffreys said. Hamilton didn't think so. Anyhow, the dog was on a leash," I said.

"You didn't happen to notice what kind of a leash, did you?"

I shook my head and then winced as those marching drummers in my head banged their sticks against my temples.

"Blue," Chelsea Ann said from her bench. "One of

those retractable nylon bands. He used it to tie the dog to the railing while he ate. Why?"

Edwards walked back to her and said, "That's what he was choked with."

"Stone Hamilton's leash?" Chelsea Ann fluffed her blonde hair back into its usual curls and shook her head. "Never. He and his group *and* his dog left while Pete Jeffreys was still here."

"You a fan of his, Your Honor?"

"Absolutely, Detective Edwards." She pulled out her keys and jingled them purposefully. "Now, if you'd just ask one of your men to move the tape so I can get my car out, I'd really appreciate it."

He stepped back with a mock salute—"Yes, ma'am!"—and called over to tell one of the uniforms to let us leave.

Once we were in the car, I could see Chelsea Ann's face in the rearview mirror. "Did you just twinkle at that Edwards guy?" I asked. "You did! You twinkled at him."

As the uniformed officer lowered the tape at the exit of the parking lot and signaled for us to drive through, Chelsea Ann grinned and said, "So?"

Rosemary sighed and laid her head against the seat. "I thought you said that a chest for your new entry hall was the only thing you intended to bring back from the beach this year."

Chelsea Ann gave her sister a reassuring pat on the arm. "I haven't loaded him in my trunk," she said. "Yet."

CHAPTER
5

The principles of law are these: to live uprightly, not to injure another man, to give every man his due.

—*Ulpian (ca. AD 170–228)*

Except for a lone desk clerk, the lobby was deserted when we got back to the hotel.

"Me for bed," Chelsea Ann said as she and Rosemary exited the elevator for the room they were sharing.

I meant to follow their good example, but the car stopped at the next floor and there was my own chief judge, F. Roger Longmire, who was on his way back up to Room 628 with a couple of clean glasses in his hands.

"Deborah!" he exclaimed. "What the hell's this about you finding Pete Jeffreys dead in the river?"

I gave him an abbreviated version, omitting my reason for hanging over the Riverwalk railing, but when I tried to get off at my floor, he insisted that I come on up with him and brief the others.

* * *

Room 628 was actually a suite—two bedrooms, four beds, and two baths with a Jacuzzi in one. The large living room had couches and chairs and a wet bar that was now fully stocked with the usual hard and soft drinks and the most popular mixers. A nearby table held olives, an assortment of cheeses, and several bags of crackers and chips.

I stepped into one of the bathrooms to freshen my lipstick and realized that somewhere along the way I'd lost an earring, a trio of red-and-white enameled hoops that matched my dress. I put the remaining one in my purse and hoped that its mate had fallen off in Chelsea Ann's car and not into the Cape Fear River.

When I emerged from the bathroom, the aspirin had finally done their job and I let Chuck Teach pour me a glass of ginger ale as I was deluged with questions.

I told them everything I knew, again leaving out the reason I'd been hanging over the railing. After the usual exclamations and head shaking, someone immediately wondered who would be appointed to fill his seat.

"Too bad Bill Hasselberger's not still living in that district," said Steve Shaber, one of our hosts.

Julian Cannell, who was sharing the suite, shrugged. "Maybe he'll move back now."

"I doubt it," said Jay Corpening, the local chief judge, as he offered me an open bag of pretzels. "I think he's happy where he is right now. He argued a civil case in front of me last week. Took it on contingency and convinced the jury to give his client everything she was asking for. Which is not to say he won't run for the bench down here."

"Jeffreys's death is sure gonna make life easier for Tom Henshaw," Chuck Teach said.

I shot him a raised eyebrow.

"He's filling out Judge Dunlap's term," he explained, referring to an elderly colleague who had abruptly decided to retire to an ashram out in the mountains. "You'll probably meet him at the reception tomorrow night."

I sipped my ginger ale and told him that I didn't understand. "I thought Dunlap's term expired this fall. What's that got to do with Jeffreys? He's not due to run for another two years."

"Ah, but you're forgetting that Jeffreys wanted to run for superior court in two years," Steve said. "Dunlap's seat would give him a safe position for that race."

Enlightenment dawned. In North Carolina, you can't run for two offices in the same election, but if you hold a seat that's not up for election, you can go ahead and run for a different judicial position, yet still keep your own seat on the bench if you lose.

Devious.

"Would he have won?"

Chuck shrugged and Steve said, "Tom's doing a good job, but Pete had better name recognition in that district and he's raised a hell of a lot more money. Your average voter doesn't keep up with local judicial races. You know that. They might not've voted for him if they'd known he had ulterior motives, but Tom Henshaw wouldn't have had the money to get that word out."

"Was Henshaw at Jonah's tonight?" I asked.

Steve frowned. "I didn't see him there. You thinking he took out Jeffreys?"

"Somebody did," I said. "I doubt if it was a stranger killing."

That sobered the mood for a few minutes, and I could

almost see them running a mental eye across the twenty or more familiar faces at the restaurant tonight, trying to think which one might have had a grudge against Pete Jeffreys serious enough to risk killing him. Human nature being what it is, though, the discussion soon turned to speculation about Jeffreys's possible successors and from there, conversation among those still in the suite returned to the normal mix of politics, recent rulings from the appellate court, and new acts of the state legislature that would affect our own rulings.

Chuck and Julian backed a couple of state representatives who were up for election into a corner of the room. Tweedledee and Tweedledum wore pastel seersucker suits, one pale green, the other a light, almost white, pink. I don't care how hot and muggy our summers can be, it takes a lot of confidence in your own manhood to wear a pink seersucker suit. That's probably why he was drinking his beer from the bottle.

District court judges are warned not to lobby members of the general assembly, but we're allowed to "educate and inform" and I had no doubt that those two representatives were getting a raft of informed statistics about how badly we need more judges to help with our caseloads. I'm pretty sure they were also being educated about the widening gap between superior court salaries and ours. That's the price you pay if you want to press the judicial flesh.

And don't think they don't. Every election, judges get asked, "Hey, who should I vote for in this race?" Even though we can't officially endorse anyone, candidates know that our words can influence a bunch of voters.

Beth Keever, chief judge in Cumberland County, was

deep in a discussion with some others about how best to shelter the children of high-conflict divorces and how to protect domestic violence victims from their batterers when exchanging children. Beth waved her diet soda to make a point as she gave facts and figures about the feasibility and logistics of visitation centers. It's an ongoing discussion—a good idea that probably won't get funded.

When the pretzel bag came around again, I snagged a couple to ease the hollow in my stomach and joined a group that included Roger Longmire and Cynthia Blankenthorpe, who had not looked particularly shocked when I described finding Jeffreys's body.

She had changed into a pair of white duck walking shorts that emphasized her muscular thighs and calves and reminded me of Tour de France cyclists. Those could have been Lance Armstrong's legs. If they'd been mine, I'd have tried to disguise them in a long skirt or looser pants, but she sat like a man, with her left ankle resting on her bare right knee. Her unpolished nails were cut short and there were raw-looking red scratches on her right hand. Her bangs and the ends of her shoulder-length hair looked sun-bleached, as if the rest of her light brown hair had been protected from the sun by a helmet or cap. Maybe she really was a cyclist. Face, arms, and legs were certainly well tanned. No worries about skin cancer here.

"I'm sorry about your friend," I said.

"Did they say if it was quick?" she asked as Roger shifted over to make room for me on the couch. She had an easy air of confidence that probably came from growing up a Blankenthorpe in Mecklenburg County.

"I would imagine it was," I said, with more assurance

than I felt. "I've been told it only takes a few seconds for the brain to shut down."

I tried not to think of those few seconds. It's all relative, isn't it? As Einstein pointed out, an hour passes in an instant when you're sitting with a lover. When you're sitting on a hot stove, a few seconds stretch into eternity.

"His car's still there," I said. "Didn't you ride over with him?"

"I did," she said, reaching for the bowl of cashews on the coffee table. "But when I was ready to leave, I couldn't find him, so I hitched a ride back with the Fitzhumes."

"What time was that?"

She shrugged. "Around ten or so. Why?"

"The police are asking who saw him last."

"I doubt that was me."

"Did you know him long?"

"Not really." She took a hefty swig of whatever was in her glass. "I have to run this fall and to give him his due, he was willing to introduce me to his donors and to the other judges here."

"Sounds like you didn't care for him all that much," I said.

She shrugged. "He came on a little strong. For some reason, he decided he was going to be my mentor...give me advice on how to run my campaign, show me the ropes, he said."

The short man perched on the arm of her chair rolled his eyes and said, "Yeah, I just bet he did."

He was built like a bowling ball—round and solid, with the same amount of hair. I felt as if I should know him, but I couldn't put a name to his pudgy little face.

"Bernie Rawlings," he said, intuiting my lapse. "From the mountains of Lafayette County. You covered court for my brother last fall. Almost got yourself killed, I hear." He described the outcome of a murder investigation from my time up there in Cedar Gap. As I expected, a lack of evidence had kept one of the culprits from being charged even though everyone was pretty sure he was the killer.

As we talked, others had come and gone, mostly gone until there were only a half dozen of us left. Steve and Julian began to gather up the empty cans and bottles and to store the cheese and olives in the small fridge. It wasn't exactly here's-your-hat-what's-your-hurry, but yeah, it was pushing two a.m. and well past time for re-spectable judges to call it a night.

I always ask for a room near the elevator, which means that I'm also near the ice machine and vending area. When I said good night to the others and exited at my floor, I heard someone filling an ice bucket. Martha Fitzhume emerged from the alcove with an ice bucket and a can of Coke and seemed surprised to see me.

"I didn't realize we were neighbors," I said.

Her white hair was rumpled as if she'd slept on it wrong. In lieu of pajamas, she wore gray knit pants and an oversized purple T-shirt from Fitz's last election. A sheen of moisturizer glistened on the bony angles of her patrician face.

She was equally observant. "You look like hell, sugar. I heard about Jeffreys. You all right?"

"Just tired," I said, key card in hand. "Couldn't you sleep?"

"Not me, Fitz." She shook her head ruefully. "Those

damn crabs. He ate all of his and half of mine, too, and now he has indigestion. I thought maybe a Coke would settle his stomach. You reckon there was something wrong with them? I heard you got sick, too, or was that because of finding Pete Jeffreys?"

"Probably the margaritas," I admitted.

"I suppose the police questioned you about this evening?"

I nodded.

"You didn't find it necessary to repeat what I said about him, did you?"

"No."

"Good. Fitz is always telling me I run my mouth too freely at times."

"But why *did* you dislike him, Martha?"

"Just stuff," she said with a vague wave of the Coke can. "You know how word goes around."

"What stuff?" I persisted.

"Don't get me started." She moved past me toward a door down the hall that had been left on the latch. "It'd probably take an hour and I need to get back to Fitz. Don't you worry though. I didn't kill the bastard. Fitz wouldn't't've let me."

I couldn't help smiling as I swiped my key card in the lock. No way could Martha have strangled Pete Jeffreys and dumped him into the river, but there was also no way Fitz could've stopped her from trying if she'd set her mind to it.

Moonlight spilled through the windows of my dark room, and without switching on the lamps I crossed over to the balcony doors and stepped out into the humid night air. Beyond the multilevel pool decks, the gazebos, and the deserted pool lay the ocean. No whitecaps and almost as calm as a millpond. The tide was dead low and what waves there were rolled gently onto the sand and quietly dissolved in white foam. The moon was three or four nights from being full and it sparkled on the slowly undulating water like a handful of golden sequins tossed by a careless mermaid.

The moon, the stars, the thick brine-ladened air—I had stood gazing out to sea like this on dozens of other summer nights and memory held me in its grip, sending kaleidoscopic images coursing through my head of weekends with Mother and Daddy and my brothers back when I was a child: musty summer cottages borrowed from a more affluent aunt or uncle, pallets of quilts on the floor, sand underfoot no matter how often the floors were swept.

A week at the beach for high school graduation, chaperoned by my brother Seth and his new bride: beach music and shagging the night away on the boardwalk at Atlantic Beach and sneaking sips of beer when Seth's back was turned, trying to forget for a few hours at a time that Mother would be dead by the end of that summer.

Then, after I was grown, that heady mixture of freedom and abandon, and yes, the mild flirtations with a colleague or two here in this very hotel during summer conferences.

But I had never been to the beach with Dwight. No memories of kissing him with salty lips, of making love to him in the moonlight on a deserted stretch of sand.

I sighed and stepped back into the air-conditioned room, switched on the lights, and drew the curtains. My cell phone lay amid a clutter of tissues and lipsticks

where I had unthinkingly left it when I changed purses
earlier in the evening. I'm not quite as bad as Daddy
about talking on phones, but the fact is that I don't like
being tethered to one and the older I get, the more often
I seem to forget to carry mine or to switch it on. It exas-
perates the hell out of Dwight, who never turns his off.
I flipped it open and saw that I had missed several calls.
Chelsea Ann's number was there, along with my friend
Portland's, and several I didn't recognize, but Dwight's?

   Nada.

CHAPTER
6

*Augustus took care that no persons should hold office
who were unfit or elected as the result of factious com-
binations or bribery.*

—Dio Cassius (ca. AD 230)

Despite my late night, I was wide awake by 8:30. Reid
had left his riverfront table long before I did, so if I
was up, he might be, too.

He answered on the fourth ring and did not sound all
that happy to hear my voice. "Do you know what the hell
time it is?" he asked.

"Sorry," I said unrepentantly, "but I wanted to catch
you before you left for your first session."

"First session?"

"Isn't today the opening session of your conference?"

"Yeah, but we don't plan to get down there till this
afternoon."

"You mean you're still in Wilmington?"

"Yeah, why?"

I heard him yawn, which made me yawn, too, of
course.

"Deborah? You still there?"

"I'm here." Another yawn overtook me. "How about we have breakfast together? Where are you?"

"At my friend Bill's house. Bill Hasselberger. You met him last night, remember? He said I could stay with him this week. Save on hotel bills."

"Ask him where's a good place to get breakfast."

"It's too early for breakfast," he grumbled, but after a muffled conversation on his end, he said, "Bill says for you to come on over here. He claims he makes an awesome frittata."

I got directions and we agreed I'd be there within the hour after I'd showered and dressed. From his lack of questions, I gathered that neither of them knew about Pete Jeffreys's death. Good. Maybe I'd get to see their faces when they heard. Not that I suspected either of them. All the same...

Forty minutes later I turned off Market Street, counted three blocks, turned left, and pulled up in front of a modest white clapboard bungalow with dark red shutters and a porch that was shaded by a large mimosa tree covered in thousands of puffy pink flowers. Only a few miles from the ocean and not quite 9:30 in the morning, but the white-hot sun shone fiercely in a sullen blue sky and the air was already muggy when I opened the car door. My antiperspirant gave up the fight before I could make it up the front walk to the shady porch.

Hasselberger's rolled-up Sunday paper lay by the steps where his delivery person had thrown it.

Reid met me at the door, along with the odor of bacon, basil, and sauteed onions. A night's growth of stubble darkened his jawline and he was still in a faded T-shirt and loose knit pants. Like all my male Stephenson relatives, he's tall and good-looking and he loves women. With his broad shoulders, curly brown hair, and clear hazel eyes, they love him right back, which is the main reason his marriage fell apart. He still acts like a kid in a candy shop with an unlimited allowance, but it cost him the love of his life and the mother of his son.

He didn't notice the newspaper and I didn't call his attention to it. Instead, I followed him into the air-conditioned coolness, past a pullout couch in the living room where he had slept last night and into the kitchen, the source of those entrancing aromas. Except for the unmade sofa bed, the house was tidy enough, but it had the temporary air of a bachelor's place—mismatched furniture, odd lamps, clashing colors.

Reid may have been a member of Hasselberger's wedding party, but evidently that marriage had gone the way of Reid's. Clearly no woman lived here. Had ever lived here. Not with these furnishings anyhow. The severely tailored couch was cranberry verging toward plum, the overstuffed recliner next to it was a gold-and-brown plaid, while the three floor lamps were modern chrome-and-steel rods and were more suited to an architect's office. It looked to me like the leavings of a bad divorce settlement.

Not that I was there to criticize any man who would immediately hand me a mug of strong fragrant coffee. Not when I could see the frittata that had my name on a wedge of it almost ready to emerge from the broiler of his electric oven.

"Glad you could come," he said, wiping his bony

hands on a pink dishtowel before shaking mine. Once again, his smile split his face from ear to ear. The warmth of that smile lit up his long thin face and brown puppy-dog eyes.

"Thanks for asking me," I said. "Y'all got away last night before I could tell Reid to meet me at a pancake house this morning somewhere between here and Sunset Beach. This is much nicer."

"Is something up?" my cousin asked. "We see each other almost every day back home. Why down here?"

"Does there have to be a reason? We haven't really talked in ages. And then you left early without coming over last night. One minute you were there, the next minute you were gone."

He shook his head at me. "I'm surprised you noticed. You looked well on your way to getting smashed."

"I was just tired," I said defensively.

His lifted eyebrow showed me just how much he believed *that*, but he didn't push it. Instead, while Hasselberger poured us glasses of juice, we talked generalities and about the agenda before the Trial Lawyers this weekend. One of the main pieces of business was to vote on changing the association's name to Advocates for Justice.

"Everybody pretends that the new name better describes what we do," Bill said, "but we all know that it's because 'trial lawyers' has become a dirty word."

True. They're constantly being slimed by certain pro-business elements who oppose big judgments against corporations and their insurance companies, never mind whether said corporations are grossly negligent or merely indifferent to the possible harm their protocols might cause.

I waited until the frittata was out of the oven and we were seated at the table with heaped plates to say, "So, Bill, how come we never met when you were on the bench?"

Reid kicked me under the table, but Bill flashed another one of those warm smiles, this time with a hint of mischief. "Actually, we did meet. Fall conference one year and here last summer a couple of years ago."

"Really?"

"Reid had told me all about you, so I knew who you were, but I guess I was just part of the crowd. Hard to get your attention with Chuck Teach there, and then the next summer—"

Reid's fork, laden with cheese and tomatoes, paused in midair. "You and Judge Teach hooked up?"

"It was nothing more than a few drinks and dinner," I said.

"Yeah? Does Dwight know?"

"Who's Dwight?" Bill asked, proffering the coffeepot.

Reid held out his cup for a refill. "Dwight Bryant. Her husband."

"You're married now?"

I wiggled my left hand to show him my rings. "Going on seven months."

"Well, damn!" he said with a laugh. "I finally get a chance to register on your radar and it's half a year too late. Is he with you this week?"

I shook my head. "No, he had a seminar up in Virginia." I took another bite of that delicious mixture of eggs and herbs and cheese. "I don't mean to be tactless, but was it hard leaving the bench?"

Reid rolled his eyes. "C'mon, Deborah."

"It's okay, pal," Bill said. "I'm pretty much over it. Yeah, I liked being a judge, so I was sorry to leave, but it wasn't leaving the bench itself that I minded so much as the way I was pushed off."

"Pete Jeffreys?"

"You got it. It was a bad time all around and he played into it. My wife and I were going through an ugly divorce, so he started a rumor that she kicked me out because I was gay and that I made a couple of DWIs go away for some gay friends. You know how hard those things are to stop once enough people believe it. You don't need any fire if there's enough smoke. And I did dismiss a DWI for a friend who happens to be gay, but it was for cause and thoroughly justified. My dismissal rate for DWIs was a lot lower than his is."

"He doesn't just dismiss the cases in open court either," said Reid. "It's an open secret that one of his big-donor attorney friends has a drawerful of blank dismissal forms that Jeffreys signed for him."

I wasn't as shocked as I should have been.

Like it or not, I doubt if there's a courthouse in the state where that hasn't happened.

"The worst of it is that he's lazy," Bill said. "Sitting on a bench is a damn sight easier than maintaining an office, chasing down cases, and working actively for a client who may or may not pay you for your services. I'm absolutely convinced that the main reason he ran for judge wasn't the prestige and certainly not because he could make a difference, but because of the salary and the pension plan and it's a first step toward higher office. He shoots from the hip with his rulings and half the time he doesn't bother to read the whole case file. Just last fall, he put a guy on probation who was already on probation and hadn't once reported to his probation officer. If he'd read the file, he would have seen an escalating pattern of criminal behavior—robbery, car theft, and a felony breaking and entering that was really a burglary because he broke into an occupied home at night."

"Why didn't Jeffreys keep him in jail for that?" I asked, since even first-time burglaries carry hefty jail time.

Bill shrugged. "He pleaded to the lesser charge and Jeffreys hadn't read the file."

"Is this the case where the guy left court and then murdered a girl?"

Grim-faced, Bill nodded. "Two days later he carjacked a waitress who was working her way through college. Raped and killed her and put her body in the trunk, then drove around for three days, using her credit cards and checkbook before he was picked up and they opened the trunk. He'll probably get the death penalty when it comes to trial, but Jeffreys ought to be charged, too. Of course, he blames the DA and the probation officer for not alerting him to the guy's record, but it was all there in front of him if he'd bothered to read it."

"And now he wants to run for superior court," Reid said, hotly indignant on his friend's behalf.

"I guess everyone knows there's no love lost between the two of you," I said.

"After the way he helped screw up my life? Not that my ex didn't do her share, too. She never exactly said I was gay, but she never came to my defense either. She just gave a little martyred smile and let the allegations stand so that our so-called friends wouldn't blame her for catting around the courthouse on me."

"She's an attorney, too?"

He nodded. "That's why I moved down here. I had to go back into practice, and I wasn't going to stand up in a courtroom and call him 'Your Honor' after what he'd done. Besides, I didn't want to keep running into my ex or one of her lovers every time I crossed the street. They'll both get theirs one of these days but I wasn't going to stay there and wait for it."

"As far as Jeffreys is concerned, your wait's over," I said, speaking more flippantly than I felt. "He got his last night."

"Huh?" said Reid.

"Someone strangled him last night in the parking lot near Jonah's and threw him in the river."

I kept my eyes on Bill's face as I described the scene. The news seemed to surprise him, but then most lawyers have trained themselves to contain their emotions and to cultivate a poker face.

Both asked a dozen or more questions. In the end Reid leaned back in his chair and lifted his coffee cup as if toasting his friend. "They say you can't go home again, but maybe now you can."

"Not while Lisa's still there," Bill said grimly.

"One down, one to go."

"Don't joke," I told Reid. "Once the police come up with a list of his enemies and learn that Bill was in the vicinity, they'll want to know what time y'all left the restaurant last night."

"Us? Oh hell, Deborah, you know we didn't have anything to do with his death."

"Well, as long as you can alibi each other," I said. "You did drive back here together, right?" I said.

There was a split-second silence as the two men locked eyes.

"Actually," said Bill, "we were in separate cars. Reid said he'd get the check and I needed to pick up some half-and-half for breakfast, so I left first and got here about thirty minutes before he did."

"Where were you parked?"

"Up Ann Street, across from Jonah's."

"Did you see Pete Jeffreys in the parking lot?"

"No. When was he killed?"

I had to admit that I didn't know. The last time I'd noticed him was right after I came back from talking with Reid. My cousin's hostility to Jeffreys had been enough to make me look around for him to see if he'd suddenly sprouted horns and a tail. I now realized that the sour look he'd given me was probably because he'd seen me at Bill Hasselberger's table.

As we ate, our talk turned from murder to gossip about mutual friends.

"So ol' Fitz is finally retiring?" Reid said.

"And he's being honored at a reception tomorrow night," I told him. "Why don't you come?"

"Maybe I will," he said and entered the information as to where and when on his BlackBerry.

We'd finished eating and Reid began to make noises about getting down to Sunset Beach before lunch, so I thanked Bill for his hospitality and drove back to Wrightsville Beach.

I was halfway there before it hit me. Why had it taken Reid so long to pay the check that he'd gotten back to Bill's house a half hour after Bill?

CHAPTER
7

The municipal laws of all well-regulated states have taken care to enforce this duty: though providence has done it more effectually than any laws, by implanting in the breast of every parent that insuperable degree of affection, which not even the deformity of person or mind, not even the wickedness, ingratitude, and rebellion of children, can totally suppress or extinguish.

—*Sir William Blackstone (1723–1780)*

The SandCastle Hotel is as friendly to children as it is to judges. The decor in the spacious lobby is vivid turquoise and coral with terra-cotta tiles and couches upholstered in soft sand-colored leather. Bowls of taffy wrapped in wax paper twists sit on the registration counter. A floor-to-ceiling saltwater aquarium filled with exotic and colorful sea creatures lines the wall of a hallway that leads to the restaurant. In the middle of the lobby itself, beneath the large circular skylight, is a round shallow tank that holds an inch or two of white sand and six or seven inches of water. It's chest-high to a four-year-old and kids are encouraged to touch the living sand dollars, sea urchins, snails, and skates or watch a school of tiny minnows dart through the water.

Adults can play there, too.

When I returned to the hotel that morning, the first person I recognized was pudgy-faced Bernie Rawlings from Lafayette County, who stood by the tank running his fingertips through the wet sand with a dreamy expression on his face. He wore sandals and a white tennis shirt and his bald head was covered by a blue cotton hat that matched his blue shorts. He smiled when he saw me. "This reminds me of when I was a boy and we'd come down from the hills in the summer to rent a place on the beach. My dad would set up a small tank so we could catch fiddler crabs and snails and minnows. He had a shore guide to marine life and we'd spend the week trying to identify everything. It was always sad when we had to leave and put them back in the ocean."

"We must have had that same book," I said. "My mother was always trying to get us interested in nature. Only instead of a tank, we used a plastic shower curtain."

"Shower curtain?"

I nodded. "My brothers would scoop out a hole in the sand and we'd line it with an old shower curtain. That's where we'd put the things we found. Like you did. Only we had to empty it out every evening so the tide wouldn't take it away."

We were joined by a pudgy-faced child in shorts and tank top who looked exactly like Bernie except that he was only half as tall and he had a headful of hair that was cut in a modified mullet. He also had a clump of taffy in each hand and was busily stuffing his cheeks full.

I was about to tell Bernie how much he and his son looked alike when he said, "Emily, this is Judge Knott."

The girl stared at me unblinkingly as Bernie finished the introduction, her mouth too full to speak.

Bernie tried to interest her in the hermit crab that was moving its heavy whelk shell ponderously over the sandy floor of the tank, but she handed him a wad of wax paper wrappers to dispose of and said, "Can we go back upstairs now? I wanna watch *SpongeBob*."

"Honey, you watched that thing three times on the drive down. Look! These are live ocean animals. Starfish! Horseshoe crabs!"

She scowled. "You promised! Momma said."

Bernie sighed. "Okay, okay. Go ring for the elevator." He gave me a sheepish smile. "What can you do with 'em at this age? And I did promise my wife that I'd amuse Emily so that she could have the day to herself to shop and go out with some of the other wives."

"You're a good husband," I said, feeling charitable.

He beamed and hurried after his bratty daughter while the pragmatist whispered in my ear, "*Good husband, stupid dad.*"

Some of my brothers claim that I was spoiled, being the only girl and the youngest after a string of eleven boys, but no way would my parents have let me program their free hours like that.

I lifted a scallop from the shallow tank and waited till it slowly, cautiously opened a narrow crack to reveal a ring of shiny blue metallic eyes.

My earliest memory of the beach was of sitting in the gentle waves at Harkers Island. I was probably three or four at the time, so the older boys were either married or working summer jobs. The younger ones were there, though—Zach and his twin Adam, and Will, the oldest of my mother's four children. If Jack was there that week, I can't remember, but Seth, who's five up from me, was my protector when the others wanted to dunk me or hog the inner tubes we used as floats. Ben was there, too, but he was always pestering Daddy for the car keys so he and Seth could go juking at Atlantic Beach.

If Mother had hoped to turn any of us into marine biologists with her shower curtain aquarium and the *Golden Guide to Seashores*, it didn't work. I doubt if any of my brothers could tell a lettered olive from a tulip shell anymore, but when it was time for the hermit crab races, Will had an unerring knack for finding the fastest.

Check out all the whorled shells in a tidal pool till you find one inhabited by a hermit crab. Draw a big circle in the sand, put your crab in the center, ante in a dime. If your crab makes it out of the circle first, you take the pot. Losers go back in the water, winners are kept until deposed.

At five or six, I looked for crabs with the biggest, prettiest shells and usually came in last, but Will always put his money on one that had taken over the shell of a lightweight moon snail. One summer he found a crab that won so consistently that we stopped racing with him. Next day, he made a big show of throwing his champion back into the water and hunting for another. We lost two rounds to his new contender before it dawned on us that it was a ringer he'd thrown back, not the champ. Daddy made him give our money back, but I overheard him tell Mother, "Takes after his daddy, don't he?"

"I don't know that the world's ready for another Kezzie Knott," Mother had laughed.

Will still plays the angles whenever he can get away with it. I wondered how things were going up in Virginia and if he was on his way back yet. I also wondered if Dwight had made an inventory of whatever Will had loaded onto his truck. Not my worry though. Dwight's known my brother longer than I have and he's well aware that Will's moral compass is a few degrees off true north.

But thinking of them only reminded me that Dwight still hadn't called.

I put the scallop back in the tank and watched it jet away, then stepped into a waiting elevator and mashed the button for my floor. As the doors were closing, I saw a cute little girl dart across the terra-cotta tiles to the touching tank. She was trailed by a smaller boy and the bearded man I'd seen Jeffreys talking to at the restaurant last night. There was something teasingly familiar about the man, but I couldn't think where, if ever, we'd met before.

Up in the room, the telephone on the desk was flashing its message light. The first message was from Chelsea Ann at 9:45. Her breakfast meeting had ended early and if I hadn't had breakfast yet, come on down. The second, at 10:12, was from a local newspaper reporter who hoped to catch me around the hotel before he left. The third was Detective Gary Edwards only fifteen minutes earlier, asking me to return his call.

Too late for breakfast and no, I didn't want to talk to a reporter. Nor did I particularly want to talk to Detective Edwards. How about I went to the beach instead and pretended I didn't get his message?

"You're an officer of the court," scolded the preacher, *"and it behooves you to cooperate."*

"*Besides,*" said the pragmatist, guiding my fingers to the dial pad, "*you know you want to hear what's happening with his investigation.*"

So I called his number and learned that he was in the hotel, too, in one of the small conference rooms off the main ballroom, and would I join him for a cup of coffee?

Thinking I might still get in some pool time before lunch, I changed into my red swimsuit, topped it with a jungle print skirt and matching shirt, and made sure I had sunscreen in my raffia tote bag before heading out.

Down in the lobby, I ran into Chelsea Ann, who was drifting back from breakfast with the Sunday paper under her arm. She wore a peach-colored knit shirt that flattered her golden hair, gold hoop earrings, and a short white skirt that showed off her long tanned legs.

"You were up and out early," she said. "Or were you in the shower when I called?"

"I had breakfast with Reid and his friend over in Wilmington," I said. When I told her that I was on my way to meet with Detective Edwards, she immediately invited herself to come with me.

"Only let's duck into the ladies' room first and let me put on fresh lipstick."

Why was I not surprised?

Edwards on the other hand *was* surprised. Pleasantly, if I could judge by his big smile when he saw my friend as we came down the hall to where he stood in the doorway. "I see you got my message after all."

"Message?" Chelsea Ann said.

"That I wanted to see you again."

She wasn't quite twinkling at him, but a mischievous

smile curved her lips as her big green eyes met his. "In your official capacity, Detective Edwards?"

"Of course, Your Honor." He tried for deadpan and missed by a nautical mile.

"Should I come back later?" I asked with mock irritation.

He laughed and ushered us into the conference room. It was small and windowless but vivid seascapes brightened the sand-colored walls, the chairs were upholstered in a flame pattern of aquamarine, yellow, and coral, and the long rectangular table was bleached oak.

There was a coffee station just outside the door and Edwards made sure we were both well supplied before we sat down across from him. Instead of asking us to repeat last night's account of finding the body, he gave us each a sheet of paper printed with blank round circles meant to represent the porch tables at Jonah's.

"We're trying to get a snapshot of the evening," he said, "so if you would, try to remember as many people as you can and write down where they were seated. Also the approximate time as closely as you can where Jeffreys was the last time you saw him."

"Does this mean you don't think it was a random act of violence?" I asked.

"Well, robbery doesn't seem to be a motive," said Edwards. "His wallet was in his pocket with over two hundred dollars in cash and a credit card in every slot. His car keys were on the ground next to the driver's side."

"Like someone came up from behind him with that dog leash as he was about to unlock his car?"

"That's what it looks like. The parking lot isn't brightly lit. Lots of deep shadows under those trees, but still enough to recognize faces, so we don't think this was a stranger killing. Whoever did it had to know it was Jeffreys."

I soon saw that the diagram did not include the restaurant next door. I briefly considered not mentioning it. What the hell though? Reid couldn't have had anything to do with the murder and Bill Hasselberger might not have been the only one at their table with a reason to hate Jeffreys. So I drew a right angle to indicate the adjoining porch and wrote in the names of the four lawyers I had recognized.

"I saw Jeffreys twice with a man at this table," I said, touching a circle that was somewhat removed from the area we had occupied. "Did you know him, Chelsea Ann?"

She looked up from her own diagram and frowned. "Describe him."

"Late forties, early fifties. Dark hair, a little longer than most. Short beard, bushy mustache. Had a little girl and a smaller boy with him."

"Oh, yeah. I saw them when they came in. Don't know him though."

"You say Jeffreys went up to him twice?" asked Edwards.

I nodded. "The first time he was by himself. A little later, I saw him introducing Judge Blankenthorpe."

"Really?" Edwards leafed through several sheets of paper that were already covered with scribbled names. "That's odd. You're sure that's the table?"

"Pretty sure," I said and Chelsea Ann agreed.

He pulled one from the sheaf and laid it on the table between us. It carried Judge Cynthia Blankenthorpe's name and today's date. The circle in question was blank.

"Wonder why she didn't list him?"

CHAPTER
8

Not cohabitation but consent makes a marriage.

—Ulpian (ca. AD 170–228)

By the time Chelsea Ann and I finished comparing diagrams and prodding each other's memory, we had managed to name nineteen judges and their spouses plus several attorneys that we'd seen the night before. "What about Judge Henshaw?" Edwards asked.

Chelsea Ann wrinkled her nicely arched brows. "Who?"

"I don't know him and you probably don't either," I said. "He's finishing out Judge Dunlap's term."

"Never met him," she agreed.

"Steve Shaber said he didn't see him either."

We also agreed that Pete Jeffreys had been seated two tables away from ours, yet neither of us had noticed when he left.

"Judge Blankenthorpe drove over with him," I said. "What does she say?"

"That he called for the check and before it came, he

got up and left the table. She says she thought he was going to the restroom, but he never came back. She wound up paying his share of the tab and hitched a ride back here with—" He paused to decipher his notes. "With Judge Fitzhume and his wife. Do you know if they're staying here at the SandCastle?"

"They are," I said. "And for what it's worth, that bearded man may be, too. I saw him and the two children out in the lobby about a half-hour ago."

We finished up and signed our sheets, during which time Chelsea Ann and Edwards seemed to find it necessary to exchange phone numbers.

"Just in case you remember something," he said, "or I think of something else I need to ask you."

Like whether or not she was in a relationship? Or whether she would go out with him after this investigation was over? I was the one who had found Jeffreys's body and he didn't bother to ask for *my* number. On the other hand, he *was* a detective and had probably detected that Chelsea Ann's left hand was free of rings.

As we walked back down the hall, I reached over and brushed her cheek.

"What?" she said, pausing to look into a nearby mirror. "Something on my face?"

"Just getting rid of the little yellow feathers," I told her.

She grinned. "Am I looking like the cat that ate the canary?"

"And washed it down with cream," I said.

"So? I'm forty-one years old. Don't I have a right?"

"Absolutely. And speaking for every woman who's going to turn thirty-nine this summer, we do appreciate what a role model you are for the rest of us."

She smoothed her blonde curls complacently. "Thank you, thank you."

"C'mon, ol' lady," I said. "Let's go find you a rocking chair."

We put on our sunglasses and went out onto the terrace where indeed there was a long row of high-backed white wooden rockers. We dragged two of them down to the far end where we would be in the shade and out of the way of casual passersby. With a nice wind coming off the ocean, the air was hot but not oppressively muggy. The terrace overlooked the pool area with its many coral-colored umbrellas and coral lounge chairs, yet it was high enough to let us see over the umbrellas to the beach where gentle waves chased and were chased by squealing toddlers. A group of small boys worked at building an ambitious sand castle almost as tall as they were.

Maybe I should have let Cal come with me instead of going to Virginia, I thought. Maybe a few days of one-on-one without Dwight to complicate things would have let us work out our relationship and reinforce the ground rules.

I sighed and leaned back in the chair.

Unfortunately, Chelsea Ann heard my sigh. "How's being a stepmother working out?"

"Great," I said, rummaging in my tote for sunscreen. "In fact I was just thinking how much Cal would love this."

"And you and Dwight are really okay?"

"Sure." I slipped off my shirt and smoothed sunscreen on my face, arms, and shoulders. "We're fine."

"So what was last night about?"

"What do you mean?"

"You don't remember getting maudlin about that couple in the corner when we left?"

I shook my head.

"You wanted to go over and give them your blessings."

I flushed. "Must have been the tequila."

"And that's another thing. I've never seen you so completely hammered."

"Dwight and I are just fine," I said again, unhappily aware that he still hadn't called. I offered my sunscreen and asked, "But what's with Rosemary and Dave?"

The diversion worked. She took the bottle with tightened lips. "I could throttle my stupid sister!"

"Why? What's happening?"

"I think he's trying to shaft her and she's just going to stand there and let it happen."

"Huh?"

"You didn't know that he had an affair with one of the paralegals in his old law office?"

"No. When?"

"January."

"January this year?"

"That's when she found out about it. God knows how long it'd been going on." She dabbed lotion on her nose and smoothed more on her arms. "Wasn't the first time he'd cheated on her either, but she wouldn't listen to me or anyone else. She was sure that his flirting was just a automatic habit and nothing to take seriously."

"She was wrong," I said.

"He's hit on you, too?"

"At your birthday party last year." Although Dave had

made light of it when he saw how outraged I was on Rosemary's behalf, I knew, as any woman knows, that he would have had his hand up my skirt with the least bit of encouragement.

"This last time, he was just a little too careless and Rosie heard about it at school."

I knew that Rosemary had named her older daughter after herself but I hadn't seen the child in two or three years. "She's what now? Thirteen? Fourteen?"

"Sixteen, and the girl who told her is the niece of one of Dave's former law partners. Rosie came straight home and threw up all afternoon. Seeing Rosie like that really shook her up. She made Rosie promise not to say anything to Dave till she could confront him herself, then she made a few phone calls and learned that it was true."

She capped the sunscreen bottle and handed it back to me. "When he wouldn't move out, she applied for a divorce from bed and board. You didn't hear about it? It was all over the courthouse in Durham."

I reminded her that Durham's almost fifty miles from Dobbs and unless the details are particularly salacious, rumors about a colleague's personal life don't always travel outside that judge's district.

All the same, a "divorce from bed and board" constitutes a public and legal separation under North Carolina law. Rosemary would have had to prove that Dave had committed adultery, but that shouldn't have been hard. If they stayed separated for a year, the divorce would be almost automatic.

"So what are they both doing here this weekend?" I asked.

"She asked if she could come down with me. Said we could have a girly weekend. Said Dave had told her he was going to skip the summer conference."

"But he's here and she still stayed?"

"I told you I want to wring her neck. You heard her last night. She lied to me. She knew he was going to be here, but he sweet-talked her into coming anyhow. He's spent the last two months courting her like they were teenagers. Flowers, funny cards, presents. He's convinced their daughters that it was a one-time aberration and they're ready to forgive him. You remember how Rosemary took on Mom's care when she broke her hip after Christmas?"

I nodded.

"He told the girls that the affair was partly Rosemary's fault for neglecting him then."

"And they bought it?"

"They're not alone," Chelsea Ann said angrily. "Rosemary's buying it, too. I'm pretty sure she slept with him last week. And it's not as if she doesn't have a law degree."

As judges, we both knew what Dave Emerson knew and what Rosemary must surely know, too. If marital relations are resumed after a divorce from bed and board has been granted, that nullifies the divorce action.

"Maybe he really does love her," I said, remembering how my cousin Reid really had loved his wife even though that didn't stop him from cheating on her time after time.

"You think?" she asked cynically. "Or do you think that it's because a fault-based action usually means that the cheating spouse gets the short end of the stick when it comes to alimony and property rights? If he can get her back to bed with him down here and enough of our colleagues realize that they're sharing a room and cohabiting..."

"Condonation," I said, a term which means that the aggrieved party condones, i.e., forgives the adultery by resuming marital relations. That effectively erases the charges of adultery and levels the field if they later decide to divorce after all.

"You got it." Chelsea Ann's tone was bitter. "And speak of the devil."

I followed her line of sight and saw Dave Emerson walk out onto the balcony of his room a few floors up. He was bare-legged, as if just out of the shower, and wore one of the hotel's terry cloth robes so loosely tied that his hairy chest was exposed. Carrying a mug in one hand and newspapers in the other, he sat down on one of the chairs, set his mug on the small table, and began to read. He did not seem to see us and Chelsea Ann certainly did not wave.

Just then Fitz and Martha spotted us and walked over to speak. Both were in flip-flops and green bathing suits and both wore white cotton sun hats. Fitz had a towel around his neck and looked trim enough for a sixty-five-year-old man, Martha wore a short white beach jacket and her legs were still good.

"A police detective's looking for y'all," I said.

"He can just keep looking," said Martha. "We plan to get a swim in before lunch and the pool gets too hot."

As they started to move away after the usual pleasantries, Martha said, "Oh, look! There's Rosemary and Dave."

Chelsea Ann groaned when she saw Rosemary join Dave on the balcony. She, too, wore a terry robe. Although her belt was tied tightly, it was clear that she had nothing on underneath.

"I'm so glad they're back together again," said Martha, effectively squelching any hope Chelsea Ann might have harbored that none of our colleagues suspected that the marriage was in trouble or that they would witness anything that looked like condonation on Rosemary's part.

She looked so troubled that I jumped to my feet and tried to pull her up, too. "We're paying beach rates for our hotel rooms here, so let's get our money's worth. I'll get us an umbrella, you go change and meet me out there, okay?"

"Okay." She said it with all the enthusiasm of someone who darkly suspected there would be jellyfish.

Ten minutes later, one of the cabana boys pitched my bright coral umbrella on a fairly empty stretch of sand. I tipped him, then spread out my towels and took off my jungle print skirt. I rolled both shirt and skirt into a rough semblance of a pillow and lay down to wait for Chelsea Ann to join me.

The sand beneath my towels was warm and relaxing, and waves and gulls created a white sound that almost drowned out the squeals of laughter from the children who played in the shade of the lifeguard's stand a few hundred feet away. I told myself that I was only going to rest my eyes till Chelsea Ann came, but last night's late hours caught up with me.

I'm not sure how long I had been sleeping when I became aware of footsteps scrunching on the sand as they approached. They stopped at the edge of my towel. Thinking it was Chelsea Ann, I turned my head and looked up into the face of the bearded man who had spoken to Jeffreys last night.

"Well, hey, darlin'," he said.

CHAPTER
9

In cases of obscurity it is customary to consider what is more likely.

—Paulus (early AD 3rd century)

I sat up so abruptly that I banged my head on one of the umbrella's wooden ribs.

"*Allen?* Is that really you under all that face fur? What the *hell* are you doing here?"

"Same as you, darlin'. Enjoying the beach. It belongs to us'ns in the Triad just as much as y'all in the Triangle."

"Don't call me darling," I snapped.

"Aw now, you ain't still mad at me, are you, Debbie?"

"And don't call me Debbie," I said, enunciating each word as forcefully as I could without actually snarling.

"Well, I'm sure as hell not gonna call you Your Honor. Not after all we've been to each other."

He squatted down on his heels next to my towel and I saw that his arms and legs were as muscular as ever despite more flecks of gray in his thick brown hair and beard than when we'd last crossed paths. His white swim trunks and dark blue golf shirt were too loose for me to tell if he was still built like a brick outhouse. Too, his shirt sleeves were too long to see the full-color American flag tattooed high on one deltoid and the pair of black-and-white checkered flags on the other, but I figured they were probably still there. Once upon a brief time I had known his body almost as well as my own.

Ten or twelve years older than me, he had spent a lot of his boyhood at his uncle's farm, a farm that touched our land on the southeast. The uncle was a roughneck shade-tree mechanic, but his wife had a kind heart for a boy who was being reared up by the scruff of the neck by a trashy woman who was more into men and booze than motherhood. When Allen got tired of being punched on by the string of "uncles" his mother kept bringing home, he would run away to his real uncle and stay as long as he could till he was hauled back to Charlotte, where he eventually grew big enough to punch back.

His talent for repairing car engines was greater than his talent for drag racing, although he scraped together a living doing both at some of the state's smaller racetracks.

We had absolutely nothing in common, except that he was around the autumn after Mother died. I was mad with God that fall, mad with Daddy, not talking to eight of my brothers and six of my sisters-in-law, even mad with Mother for not finding a way to keep living. I quit college, ready to dance with the devil, and there was Allen Stancil, tapping his toe to the devil's fiddle.

We stopped by a Martinsville magistrate's office for a two-minute ceremony before going over to the racetrack where he was crewing for one of the drivers. I knew I'd made a stupid mistake before the magistrate's signature was dry on the marriage certificate, but by then I was so high on pot and tequila, I really didn't care. About a week later, Allen called me Debbie one time too many while I had a rusty butcher knife in my hand. The racing friends we were crashing with got him to the hospital before he bled to death, at which point I took a salt-shaker and crawled into a tequila bottle, hunting for the worm.

Soon as I heard Allen was going to live, I headed north and stayed gone for two years. While I was "off," Daddy and John Claude Lee, my cousin and eventual law partner, got the marriage annulled after paying Allen five thousand not to contest the action and to keep his mouth shut that it ever happened. When Allen turned up again two years ago, I learned that Daddy could have kept that money in his pocket. I was never legally married to him because he hadn't bothered to divorce his second wife.

"I guess that little girl I've seen you with is...what was her name again? Brittany?" I said.

"Tiffany Jane," he corrected me. "She's a cutie, ain't she? Gonna break a bunch of hearts some day."

"And the little boy?"

"Tyler. And yeah, 'fore you ask, he was in the oven when me and Katie got married."

"Did she get a DNA test?" I asked sweetly, remembering that the last time I'd seen him, he had gone to extraordinary (and illegal) lengths to get out of paying child support for little Tiffany Jane.

"Didn't have to. Anybody can look at him and see he's mine."

"So you and Katie are still together?"

"Well, naw. Turns out she's better at having babies

than taking care of 'em. We split. Split legal, too. This time, I'm the one getting child support."

"*You* got custody?"

"You don't have to sound so damn surprised."

"What'd you do?" I said coldly. "Bribe a judge?"

His laugh sounded hollow to me, but his words actually rang truthful when he said, "I didn't want my kids growing up like I did. Besides, they ain't got a Uncle Jap and Aunt Elsie to run to. I may not've done right by my first two young 'uns, but these here, they're gonna have a daddy that takes care of 'em twenty-four/seven."

"Yeah? How you going to raise them when you're off racing or crewing every weekend?"

"I don't do that no more. You're looking a man on his way to being a millionaire."

"Huh?"

"It's the gospel truth, Deb. I—*Ow!*" A handful of sand hit him in the mouth and sent him sprawling. "What the hell? Why'd you do that?" he sputtered, pushing himself up to a sitting position.

"You call me Deb or Debbie one more time and you're getting it in the eye," I promised him. To show that there were no hard feelings, I handed him a bottle of water from my tote bag.

He brushed the sand from his mustache and beard and rinsed his mouth several times till he had spat out all the sand, then gave a rueful shake of his shaggy head. "You always did fight dirty."

"And you were always a slow learner. So what's this about getting rich?"

"I got me a gutter business," he said proudly.

I was bewildered. "Street gutters?"

"Naw, seamless aluminum rain gutters. On houses."

"What on earth do you know about rain gutters?"

"Right much these days. See, what happened was, remember when me and Adam drove up to Greensboro so I could marry Katie?"

I nodded. I might have been killed that night if he and my brother hadn't come back to fetch Allen's truck. They had both been too drunk to talk coherently, but their arrival had scared away my attacker.[*]

"Well, we got in a poker game the night before and I hit an inside straight flush. It was double or nothing. Adam's new car against this peckerwood's gutter machine."

"Adam's car was a rental," I said.

"Well, that peckerwood did'n know it belonged to Hertz, now did he? He just saw a brand new car against his ol' beat-up van with a gutter machine in the back. My boy Keith, he'd been working with a gutter guy and he knowed how to run it, so I took him on to help me and I went and talked to a developer I knowed, used to race at Rockingham. He was building a passel of new houses out between Greensboro and Burlington and I give him such a good price—well, the short of it is, I've got a whole fleet of vans now with a big roll of aluminum and what we call a seamless gutter extruder in every van. I'm putting gutters on houses from Hillsborough to Hickory."

"I thought the housing market was slowing down."

"Not from where I'm standing, darlin'. Money's coming in faster'n I can spend it. Bought Sally a big fancy double-wide and—"

*See *Up Jumps the Devil*

"Who's Sally?"

"That's the one I was married to when you and me run off together, Wendy Nicole's mama. She keeps Tiffany Jane and Tyler for me during the week and I got Wendy Nicole learning to be an accountant so she can do the books for me. Keep it all in the family."

"Does this mean you and Sally are back together?"

"Oh, hell, no. I learned that lesson. Three times was enough." He grinned. "Four if I count you."

"Don't," I said, even though I knew I was shoveling against the tide.

"And what about you? You still going out with that game warden?"

"No."

His grin widened beneath that bushy mustache as he glanced at his watch. "I gotta go pick up the kids at the playroom in a few minutes, but how about we get together after lunch?"

"I don't think so, Allen. Besides, there's a police detective looking for you."

The grin disappeared and his eyes narrowed. No doubt a reflex from the old days. "What for?"

"That judge you were talking to last night at Jonah's."

He made an involuntary move backward. "What about him?"

"You didn't hear? He was murdered in the parking lot."

"No shit! Pete Jeffreys?"

Enlightenment dawned like sunrise over a lighthouse. "Well, I'll be damned. You *did* bribe a judge to get custody of your kids. You bribed Pete Jeffreys, didn't you?"

He looked at me anxiously. "Now you ain't gonna go

saying stuff like that to the police, are you? Besides, it won't that big a bribe. In fact, it won't even a bribe. It was more like a campaign contribution. I knowed most judges would look at my record and just because I pulled some jail time for them piddling little things I done a time or two 'fore I was full grown, they'd say Katie's a better mama than I am a daddy even though she's into the hard stuff and all I do's drink a beer when I get off work. So if a little money makes a judge do the right thing by my young'uns, what's the harm in that, darlin'?"

"Don't call me darling," I said, and reached for a handful of sand.

CHAPTER
10

To exercise a trade in any town without having previously served as an apprentice for seven years is looked upon to be detrimental to public trade, upon the supposed want of sufficient skill.

—Sir William Blackstone (1723–1780)

By now it was clear that Chelsea Ann must have changed her mind about a swim and the midday sun was too blazingly hot to tempt me any longer. I put on my shirt, buttoned my skirt around my waist, shook out the towels, and walked back across the sand to the pool area, where I dumped the towels in a hamper and climbed the stairs to the open terrace. I didn't recognize any of the people who now occupied the rocking chairs, but when I walked on into the lobby, Detective Edwards called my name.

"Talk to you a minute, Your Honor?"

"Sure," I said, following him over to a pair of soft leather chairs on the far side of the lobby. "In fact, I was going to see if you were still here. You haven't found the bearded man Pete Jeffreys was talking to last night, have you?"

He shook his head. "Don't have a name for him yet."

"Allen Stancil," I told him. "His uncle used to be a neighbor of ours. The beard's new, though, so I didn't recognize him last night."

He made a note of it on a folded yellow legal pad. "Thanks. That'll save me having to stake out a man here and stop every guy with a beard that goes in and out. I can't believe how many I've seen since you told me about him."

"So what did you want to ask me?" I said when he had folded the pad into thirds and stuffed it back into his jacket pocket.

"Somebody said you're married to a sheriff's deputy over there in Colleton County. Dwight Bryant?"

"Do you know him?"

"We've met a couple of times. Good man. He's not with you this week?"

I explained about the seminar in Virginia. "Want me to tell him you said hey?"

"Yes, but..." He hesitated, as if unsure quite how to phrase it. "See, I was thinking it'd be handy to have somebody on the inside of this conference. Somebody who could pick up on who might've had it in for Judge Jeffreys."

"And you thought Dwight could do that?"

"Well, y'all do talk about the job, don't you? My ex and I used to."

I had to smile, thinking of how Dwight and I had agreed to a separation of powers before we married. He wouldn't talk about the charges against anybody who might appear in my court; I wouldn't ask why his department had seen fit to bring those charges, and I would keep my nose out of his business. It's worked out rather well so far. Most of his cases wind up in superior court, and he's seldom involved in the misdemeanors and minor felonies that wind up in mine.

As if encouraged by my smile, Edwards said, "If you're married to a homicide detective, you have to know that small, off-the-cuff remarks can sometimes break a case, right?"

I nodded.

"I don't suppose I could get *you* to be my ears inside the conference, could I? Ask a few questions, listen to what people say?"

To be invited into a murder investigation when Dwight was always trying to keep me out of his? It was tempting.

Polishing that apple he was holding out to me, Edwards said, "Everyone I've talked to today either claims not to know Jeffreys except by sight or swears he's never done anything to make himself a murder victim. That he just happened to be in the wrong place at the wrong time."

"These are your colleagues," said the pragmatist, wistfully eyeing the ripe red fruit of temptation. *"You gonna cast doubt on their truth and honor and dirty the bench's reputation in the minds of an already cynical public?"*

"A judge who uses the office for personal gain has no business sitting in judgment of others," said the preacher. *"Pass me that apple."*

"So what do you want to know?" I asked.

"For starters, what are you hearing about him that we're not being told?"

"This is all hearsay," I warned him. "I don't have

any names or dates, but I guess they all happened in his home district." Without naming any of my sources, I then repeated Reid's allegation that Jeffreys had given signed DWI dismissals to at least one attorney in the Triad, an area centered around Greensboro, High Point, and Winston-Salem. I told him about the dirty campaign he'd run to oust Bill Hasselberger and his plans to run for the seat currently held by Tom Henshaw, someone else I didn't know.

"I've also heard he could be bribed in custody disputes, and he was the judge that gave probation to the carjacker who raped and killed his victim and then drove around with her body in the trunk for three days. I don't know if any of my colleagues were related to the victim, but I can ask."

"About Judge Pierce," he said.

"Yes?"

"Is she, um, involved with anybody right now?"

I laughed. "Sorry. That's something you'll have to ask her yourself."

"I think I'll take that as a probable no." He gave me his card and told me to call any time of the day or night.

During our talk, people from the School of Government had been setting up the conference registration table, laying out our information packets and our name tags. I paused to speak to one of the interns and to read the schedule newly posted on the message easel. As I had told Reid, our president was hosting a reception tomorrow night on the other end of the beach in honor of Judge Fitzhume on his retirement. If I knew this crowd, the tributes would turn into a roast.

The hands of the lobby clock were now straight up on noon and there was an empty hole in my stomach where Bill Hasselberger's frittata had been hours earlier.

Taking the path of least resistance, I strolled down to the hotel restaurant, pausing on the way to enjoy the beautiful, translucent jellyfish that floated dreamily through the floor-to-ceiling tank that lined the wall. Sea anemones swayed back and forth from their anchorage on a mini coral reef while small colorful fish darted in and out of the crannies. For one brief moment, I considered the possibility of an oversized fish tank at home. Not a whole wall like this, of course. Maybe more like a room divider. Then I remembered what a pain it had been to clean and care for the small tank I had briefly owned as a child, a hand-me-down from Adam and Zach, so on second thought, why didn't I just enjoy these fish while I was here?

"One?" asked the hostess when I entered the restaurant.

Before I could nod, Beth Keever waved at me from across the room to indicate an extra chair at her table. As efficient as the chief judge from Cumberland County is, I was not particularly surprised to see the rest of the education committee there. Beth smiled as I joined them and pulled out a legal pad. "We were hoping you'd turn up. We decided that if we met here and now, we could have the rest of the afternoon off."

"Fine with me," I said. I'd been wanting a chance to get down to the Cotton Exchange. "But my notes are up in my room."

"That's okay," she said. "If we miss something, you can tell me later."

They had finished eating and were ready to get down to the business of setting the agenda for the fall confer-

ence up in the mountains and for the new judges' school
at the School of Government. Suggestions flew back and
forth as to topics and speakers. I wanted a session on domestic violence and Fifth Amendment issues. Resa Harris
wanted to address the growing backlog of cases, a backlog that was aggravated by too many motions to continue.
When the subject of custody and visitation came up, I
said, "Not to get too far off the subject, but have any of
y'all heard that Pete Jeffreys took bribes in some of his
custody cases?"

There was a moment of awkward silence before one
and then another nodded.

"Me, too," said Roberta Ouellette, a fiftyish colleague
who serves in the same district as Jeffreys. "Last winter, a
year ago. I'm told that's how a man got primary custody
of his four-year-old son even though his second wife
didn't want the child in her house full-time. Nobody's
saying something bad might not have happened if he'd
stayed with the mother, but the stepmother's a smoker and
she left her lighter where the child could get it."

Judge Ouellette's green eyes darkened. "Last I heard,
the child's already had two plastic surgeries on his face
and he's lost the use of three fingers on his right hand. But
at least he's back with his own mother."

Heavy sighs ran around the table. Of all the heartbreaking issues we deal with, those involving young children are the hardest. Most judges take this part of the
job with utmost seriousness, so seriously that in districts
that have a court solely devoted to family issues, few can
stand the rotation for longer than a year or two before
begging to be assigned elsewhere. We know that our decisions can affect a child's psyche, his personality, the

kind of adult he grows up to be, and it hurts to hear that some decisions can be bought and sold like sticks of butter or a sack of potatoes.

"I was hoping he'd be caught in bed with a dead girl or a live boy," said Dale Stubbs of District 11, quoting a Louisiana governor.

That got him a wry smile. We all know that minor sexual misconduct will usually get you censured or removed from the bench quicker than major judicial malfeasance.

"What about the carjacker that he let out on probation without noticing that the guy was already in violation of an earlier probation?" I asked. "Any of y'all know the girl that got killed?"

"No, but it was really sad," Ouellette said. "She was on her way back to class after a fitting of her wedding gown when he grabbed her."

Despite Beth's attempt to get the meeting back on track, the others wanted to hear my account of last evening. None of them had been at Jonah's, but they were sure Jeffreys's death must have been a stranger killing because none of our fellow judges could possibly be a murderer.

Beth Keever and I exchanged glances that were a little more cynical.

"Okay," she said briskly, pushing back her dark brown bangs. "Back to business. Are we all agreed the new judges need the session on dress and conduct?"

Another ten minutes finished our meeting. The others called for their checks and left to enjoy the pleasures of this beach resort before the meeting of chief district court judges began the next afternoon.

I still hadn't ordered and a line had formed at the reception stand. I was about to move to a smaller table when Martha Fitzhume waved from the line and, in a voice meant as much for the six or eight people ahead of her as for me, called, "Oh Deborah! Good. You did get my message to hold us a table."

She was trailed by Fitz, Chelsea Ann, Rosemary, and Rosemary's husband, Dave Emerson. Except for dear, clueless Fitz, who kissed my cheek and murmured "Thanks, Deborah," before taking a chair beside me, the others knew good and well that Martha hadn't called and left me a message.

An attractive, college-age waitress with henna-red hair and flawless skin hurried over to hand us menus and bus the table. Like the rest of the waitstaff, she wore a coral jacket that matched the beach umbrellas beyond the outer plate-glass wall. Her smile brightened upon recognizing Martha. "Oh, hey there, ma'am! Nice to see you again."

"It's Jenna, right?" said Martha.

The waitress beamed. "Yes, ma'am, it sure is. Now what can I get y'all to drink?" she asked when she'd finished wiping down the table.

Martha ordered a glass of Chardonnay, the rest of us opted for iced tea or soft drinks.

"Be right back," the waitress promised as she left with a huge tray of dirty dishes.

"What happened to you?" I asked Chelsea Ann. "I thought you were going to come swim."

"I got sidetracked," she said. "Phone calls and then I stopped to watch the news about Pete Jeffreys's murder. My car made it on camera, but we didn't."

Dave Emerson looked up from the menu he was sharing with Rosemary. He really was a handsome man whose smile could almost fool you into thinking you were someone special when he turned it on you. Easy to understand Rosemary's kitten-in-cream glow, a glow that probably accounted for Chelsea Ann's sour expression. "Did they say if the police are close to making an arrest?" he asked.

"Nope. Just requesting anyone who saw anything to come forward."

"That police detective—Edwards? He asked us when we last saw Jeffreys," said Martha. "Any of y'all notice him much after nine-thirty?"

The others shook their heads, as did I.

"He wasn't around when Fitz and I left so we gave Cynthia Blankenthorpe a lift back here. She couldn't find him. Or said she couldn't anyhow. I don't know how hard she looked."

My head came up on that. "They have a fight or something?"

"Who knows? Why?"

"Well, she rode over with him and he was introducing her all around, but she didn't sound very upset about his death when I spoke to her in the party room last night."

Martha shrugged. "I think she was annoyed that he was treating her like a babe in the woods or somebody who wasn't smart enough to figure out the ropes herself. That's probably the real reason she hitched a ride with us."

"What time was that?" I asked.

"A little after ten."

"So nobody saw him after, say, nine-thirty?" I mused.

"He got to the restroom about the time I was leaving

it," said Fitz. "And now that I think about it, he did seem a little brusque."

"Brusque?" Martha asked.

"Well, you know how when you meet somebody face-to-face and you're trying to get out of each other's way but you don't? Most times, you just laugh and the other one'll stand still so you can get around him? Jeffreys didn't laugh. In fact, he almost knocked me down. 'Course now, he just might've been in a hurry to get to the nearest urinal."

"Was anyone else in the bathroom?" I asked. "Or coming in as you were leaving?"

"Nobody I knew, but—ah, thank you my dear, but I believe I ordered ginger ale," he said as our red-haired waitress set a glass of tea in front of him.

"Oops! Sorry," she said, and gave the tea to me.

"No, mine's the diet Coke," I said.

She did remember that Martha had ordered white wine and the rest of us eventually got our right glasses.

"Y'all ready to order?" she chirped, readying her pad.

"Jenna's studying law enforcement at the community college here," said Martha, who had naturally gotten the young woman's history at breakfast that morning. "She wants to join the SBI."

"Like ever since I was a little girl, I've been, like, just *dying* to investigate murders and stuff," the waitress agreed brightly.

"Then you need to talk to my husband," said Rosemary, patting Dave's hand with a proprietary air. "Judge Emerson's had a lot of experience with the Bureau, haven't you, darling?"

Dave shrugged. "Well, yeah. I was a DA before I ran

for judge and I worked with several agents who are still there."

"Wow! That's so cool. I wouldn't have to work undercover, would I? Like, I think I'd be too scared for that, but surveillance or profiling—that could be awesome! Is that what the guys you worked with did?"

Given the least bit of encouragement, I had the feeling that she was ready to sit at Dave's feet and soak up stories of SBI and DA derring-do, but Chelsea Ann interrupted to place her order for fried oysters. I wanted steamed shrimp and the others opted for seafood of one variety or another as well.

Keeping six orders straight seemed to try young Jenna's abilities. Either that or she was so interested in chatting with Dave about the SBI each time she arrived at our table that she couldn't match a single plate with the person who'd ordered it. Even Martha, who has nothing but empathy for a restaurant's waitstaff, sounded a little testy when she had to send her salad back because the wrong dressing had been poured on it, while Dave, who had initially been amused by her enthusiasm, was annoyed when his water arrived with a slice of lemon after he had specifically ordered it plain.

"Tell you what, Jenna," Rosemary said, stepping in to deflect the table's growing exasperation. "Instead of letting us take up your time here, why don't you give us your email address. My husband can send you the names of some Bureau people stationed in this area, right, darling? I'm sure some of them would enjoy talking to her."

I almost choked on my shrimp. I know several SBI agents myself, including more than one who would indeed be willing to "instruct" a pretty young waitress. I glanced at Chelsea Ann, who was giving her sister a glare that I interpreted as "Are you out of your fricking mind?"

"I guess I could," Dave said.

"Oh, wow!" said Jenna. "That would be awesome!"

She immediately scribbled her name and contact info on her order pad and gave it to him, then hurried off to fetch the tartar sauce she had forgotten to bring.

CHAPTER
11

The gravity of a past offense never increases ex post facto.

—*Paulus (early AD 3rd century)*

Chelsea Ann and Rosemary invited me to join them on their hunt for the perfect vestibule table for Chelsea Ann's new condo, but by the time I had changed my bathing suit for more conventional lingerie and got down to the front of the hotel where they were waiting in the car, they were snarling at each other as only siblings can.

The van's windows were down and their angry words reached me clearly.

"He's changed," said Rosemary. "If I'm going to be suspicious every time a little airhead like that wanders by—"

"Give me a break," Chelsea Ann snapped. "When are you going to realize that men like Dave don't give a damn about what's between a woman's ears? All they want is what's between her legs. Can't you see what's happening? Getting you to show yourself out on the balcony this morning? This public reconciliation in front of his peers?"

"You think it's all about legalities?" Rosemary was indignant. "Condonation? In case we can't get past this? You don't think it could be because he loves me?"

"Sorry to interrupt when y'all are having such a good time," I said, opening a back door to check the floor and under the seats, "but you didn't happen to find an earring, did you?"

"No, when did you lose it?"

"Who knows?" I ran my fingers around the seat cushions. "I didn't notice it was missing till I got back to the hotel."

Rosemary twisted around in her seat. "You were only wearing one when we were waiting for that detective to let us go. I thought maybe it was a new style. But then I'm only a naive little housewife, so what could I possibly know?"

Heavy sighs from Chelsea Ann.

Much as I love my job when I'm wearing a black robe and have a gavel in my hand, I was in no mood to spend an afternoon arbitrating between two sisters who probably had issues going back to childhood—which one was more indulged by their mother or better loved by their father, or who got spanked for something the other one did.

I closed the door and stepped back to speak through the window. "Sorry, guys, but I'm really not interested in looking at furniture. Dwight and Cal are probably going to come back from Virginia with a truckload of it, so y'all go on without me. I'll just run over to Jonah's and see if someone's turned in my earring."

Both insisted that it wouldn't be that much out of their way to swing past the restaurant, but I stood firm.

As they drove off, I heard Rosemary say, "Anyhow, just because *your* marriage went down the tubes—" and I knew I'd made the right choice.

Jonah's was having its after-lunch lull. A few people lingered with coffee or drinks under umbrellas out on the porch, but most of the indoor tables were empty. A couple of hardy souls at the bar were getting an early start on the evening.

Kyle-the-aspiring-actor clearly did not remember me from the night before, and he was only perfunctorily sorry to say he had not found an earring. "I think someone turned in a lipstick, though. You could ask Hank."

Hank-the-aspiring-hotel-manager was more accommodating if a little distracted. "Sorry," he said, as he took out a small box from under the reception stand, "but it's been crazy here today. The police only left a few minutes ago. A red-and-white earring? From last night?"

I nodded and he paused from rummaging through a box of items that ranged from earrings (none of them red and white) to sunglasses (prescription and drugstore knockoffs) and cigarette lighters (smoking is still allowed outside and in the bar). In his neat white shirt, black slacks, and preppie haircut, he reminded me of my nephew Stevie, who just graduated from Carolina: the same clean-cut wholesomeness of a kid who knows what he wants to do with his life.

"You at the university here?" I asked.

"No. UNC–Greensboro."

Before I completely morphed into Martha Fitzhume

and asked if he really did hope to manage a hotel someday, he said, "The guy who got killed? They said he was one of the judges here for dinner. You a judge, too?"

I admitted that I was.

"Was he a friend of yours?"

"Not really."

"I must have seated him, but Kyle had that table and even he can't remember which one he was. Not that y'all all look alike," he assured me with a half smile.

"You remember a bearded man last night with a little girl and boy?"

"Vaguely. Why? Was that him?"

"No, but while you were getting the children seated, he came over to speak to their father."

"Really?"

As he laid out a row of five unmatched earrings on his reservation book, I could almost see him running that part of the evening through his memory.

"Yeah, I do sort of remember him now. You think I ought to call those detectives and tell them?"

"Tell them what?" asked a familiar voice behind me.

Detective Gary Edwards.

Hank gave him a puzzled look and I quickly realized that if Edwards had been at the hotel through lunchtime, he could not have been one of the detectives here this morning. I performed the introductions and added, "Hank just realized that he did see Judge Jeffreys last night."

"He came up to the table while I was getting the customer's children seated, but I can't say that I paid him any attention after that." He turned and called to the waiter who stood staring out at the river, probably imagining himself on the prow of a ship while cameras rolled in for a close-up. "Hey, Kyle! Last night?"

"Oh, God, not more about that guy none of us can remember," the reed-thin young man grumbled as he reluctantly tore himself away from the window.

I realized he must have been looking at his own reflection in the glass.

When Hank described his encounter with Jeffreys at Allen's table—not that either of them knew Allen Stancil by name, but the children were memorable—Kyle admitted that yeah, now that Hank mentioned it, he *had* noticed the guy. "He had a dumpy little woman with him and he took her over to that man's table, too."

Dumpy little woman?

Ouch!

"That would be Judge Blankenthorpe," I reminded Edwards. "Did you get to ask her yet why she didn't label that table?"

"She thought we only wanted a seating chart for the judges. Or so she says. I saw you talking to people in the hotel dining room. Learn anything?"

"Nothing you probably don't already know," I told him. "Fitz—Judge Fitzhume? He seems to have been the last one of our group to see Jeffreys. He was coming out of the restroom as Jeffreys was going in and he said the restroom was otherwise empty and nobody he knew was anywhere around."

The phone rang and as Hank answered, I said, "Are you by any chance following me?"

Edwards smiled and shook his head. "Naw. I came down to go over the interviews my squad did here this morning. Sometimes if you go back a second time right away, somebody will have remembered something. Just like you jiggled the memory of these two. Now that they know who he was, maybe they'll remember something useful."

Kyle moved off to stare at his reflection again with a moody frown.

"Happy hunting," I told Edwards and with a nod to Hank, who was explaining to the caller that shrimp and grits would probably be back on the menu in the fall, I decided to go hunting myself for some new red earrings since mine seemed to be lost for good.

The Cotton Exchange, as its name implies, was once an export company that shipped that Southern commodity all over the world from the port of Wilmington. The buildings that grew up around it have housed a milling company, a granary, a printing company, a saloon, and heaven only knows what else over the last hundred years. Today the complex is a collection of small restaurants, boutiques, and some of my favorite specialty shops.

I headed first to Caravan Beads, a do-it-yourself shop that sells all the findings for putting together your own one-of-a-kind jewelry, and spent a relaxing half-hour creating a pair of red earrings from tiny featherweight enameled blocks.

"Balsa wood?" I asked the helpful clerk.

She shook her head. "Papier mâché."

Cool!

Down some steps and around a corner, a shop window displayed several vivid posters depicting marine life. One was a chart of colorful fishes, another showed seashells to be found in North Carolina waters. Yet another illustrated the twenty-five most common sharks off our coast, from hammerheads and bull sharks to the sand sharks we used to catch when we went pier fishing.

To my rueful amusement, the final poster was titled "Land Sharks" and cartoon drawings of various sharks had been rendered into courtroom scenes with each type of shark taking on lawyer-like aspects exaggerated for comic effect. As I bent for a closer look, Cynthia Blankenthorpe came out of the shop and paused beside me.

"Cute, huh?" She jiggled a well-filled tote bag, from which protruded a rolled-up poster. "I just bought my niece one as a gag gift for passing her bar exam. She always swore she was never going to be a land shark, yet here she is, following in her dad's and my footsteps."

Kyle the waiter had called her a dumpy little woman. She was indeed short, and yes, this was not a svelte figure. But although the tight black biking shorts she wore did nothing for her hips, she was built of solid muscle, not fat.

"You do one of those table charts for that detective this morning?" she asked, falling in beside me as I walked downstairs.

I nodded.

"Me, too, only he made me come back a second time because I left out one of the people Pete talked to. A man with two small children."

"Allen Stancil," I said without thinking.

She stopped in mid-step. "Yes! You know him?"

"We've met," I admitted.

"He contribute to your campaign?"

"No. Yours?"

"Not yet. Maybe not ever now that Pete's dead." She gestured to a nearby soda shop that was decorated like an old-fashioned ice cream parlor with little round three-legged tables and black wire chairs. The signs were all in that fat curlicue lettering that reminds me of the early 1900s. "Could I buy you a drink? Talk to you a minute?"

"Okay," I said, curious as to where this was leading.

We went inside, ordered diet colas, and took them over to a wobbly back table. She put her tote on one of the dainty chairs and sat down across from me. As she unwrapped her straw and stuck it in the icy beverage, I noticed again the wicked red scratches on her right hand that I had seen last night in the party suite, four of them, each about an inch apart.

She saw me looking and said, "I misjudged a yucca when I was out on my bike yesterday and those needles did a job on me. I'm lucky I didn't get one in the eye."

"Adam's needle and thread," I murmured, remembering Mother's colloquial name for the vicious plant.

"Haven't heard it called that since I was a kid." Cynthia smiled and for a moment her broad plain face lost the frown lines between her eyes before she turned serious again. "So what's the story on Allen Stancil?"

"Story?" I asked cautiously.

"Pete told me he was a blue-collar roughneck who's become a successful businessman. I got the impression that he donated heavily to Pete's upcoming campaign and Pete thought he might contribute to mine, too. Before I take anybody's money though, I want to know if it's clean."

"And you didn't think Pete was?"

"Oh, hell, no. I've heard how he operated when he was

in private practice. Talk about your sharks. And once he
hit the bench, there've been all kinds of rumors. One of
my friends told me he even solicited campaign contri-
butions from the lawyers in his courtroom while he was
holding court. Wanted them to pledge specific amounts
right then and there."

For some reason, that shocked me even more than realizing that he'd taken money to give Allen custody of his
children.

Most attorneys, as a matter of pragmatism, will contribute a token amount to a sitting judge's campaign, but
to to be bullied into naming a dollar amount in open
court? As if it's going to be a quid pro quo for whether
that judge will listen to your argument with an open
mind? That's like watching acid eat away at the whole
concept of judicial fairness that this country was founded
on.

"Why wasn't he reported to the ethics committee or to
Justice Parker?" I asked.

Cynthia shrugged. "Maybe he was, but I haven't heard
anything about it. You?"

I hadn't.

"If Peter Jeffreys was such bad news, though..."

"Why was I letting him lead me around?" The frown
lines between her eyes deepened. "I'm the new kid on the
block, remember? This is my first conference. For all I
knew, important people were winking at his conduct. He
came on strong. Said all the right things. I only realized
yesterday that he wasn't as smart as he thought he was."

"How was that?"

"He thought I was a Blankenthorpe heiress."

"You're not?"

She shook her head. "My dad's uncle is the one who started the bank. Not my grandfather. We're from the poor side of the family, relatively speaking."

I smiled at the pun.

"I guess that's why it ticked me off that he stuck me for his dinner. We stopped at an ATM on the way over so he had at least three hundred in his wallet, but then he went to the restroom and never came back."

"What time was that?" I asked.

"I don't know. Around nine-thirty or a quarter to ten."

That fit with what Fitz had said.

"So how come you didn't tell the police about Allen Stancil?" I asked.

"Because I'm too damn literal-minded." She set her drink cup down on the tiny metal table so hard that the ice rattled and the table almost tipped over. "He said to write down all the judges that Pete had talked to and where they were sitting and that's what I did. The *judges*. Allen Stancil isn't a judge. So is he clean or isn't he?"

"He's been known to cut a corner or two," I said, "but unless he wants a government contract to put gutters on courthouses, you'd probably be safe taking a contribution from him. He may ask for favors down the line, but you can always say no."

"Good." She finished her drink and reached for her tote bag. "Speaking of favors, can I ask you for one?"

"Sure."

"Could you take this bag back to the hotel for me? I can sling it across my handlebars, but it'll be easier if I don't have to mess with it."

"No problem," I said.

We walked out to the parking lot together and I put her

bag in the trunk of my car while she unlocked her bike chain and put on her helmet. The late afternoon heat was oppressive. Not even the hint of a breeze.

"Sure you don't want a lift back?" I said.

"Heavens, no!" she exclaimed. "Everything's so flat, I probably won't even break a sweat."

With that, she wheeled out of the lot and pedaled down Water Street.

I closed the trunk and broke a sweat just walking fifty feet to a nearby shop called Blowing in the Wind, where I bought kites for Cal and his cousins. Back in March we had spent a Saturday morning making paper kites from directions I found on the Internet, but they crashed and ripped in the spring winds. Cal's had flown the longest and he was just getting the hang of how to maneuver the string when it did a suicide dive into a maple tree.

These were made of sturdy nylon and should last longer. I even bought an extra one for Dwight and me.

Still in a shopping mode, I went on down to Two Sisters Bookery. In addition to books and book-related tchotchkes, they have the best assortment of funny, funky cards around and I always stock up when I'm in Wilmington.

I was smiling at one of them when someone bumped into me. I turned and there was a man of late middle age, about my height, wearing black jeans and black T-shirt, his graying hair tied back in a ponytail.

I recognized the director I'd threatened with an orange jumpsuit and braced myself for snarls.

Instead, he started to apologize, did a double take, and said, "I'll be damned! It's the ballsy judge. Hey, Jilly! C'mere. It's that judge I was telling you about."

A slender woman in wrinkled white clam diggers, a faded blue T-shirt, and a soiled white canvas hat strolled down from the front of the store. No makeup, no jewelry, not even a ring or watch. No sunglasses either, yet my eyes had passed right over her when I came in.

She wasn't exactly homely, but without eye makeup, her fair brows and lashes were almost invisible from five feet out; and with her signature long auburn hair bundled into the crown of that canvas hat and a nearly flat chest, she really did fade into the woodwork.

Then she flashed that thousand-watt smile, and there was no doubt that this was indeed the actress who had captivated Dwight and enough other men to lift her out of featured roles in crash-and-burn videos and into a starring role on a prime-time network show.

"Jill Mercer," she said, sticking out her hand for a no-nonsense shake.

"Deborah Knott," I told her.

"Oh, God," the man groaned. "Judge not? Lest ye be judged?"

"I do get a lot of that," I admitted.

"I still get the mercenary/mercy puns," the actress said. "And I have it in my contracts that I'll never have to work with any actor named Jack."

"School?" I asked.

"Fifth grade to eighth. The very worst time."

I nodded in sympathy. "I had to put up with the Little Debbie cupcake jokes. I still won't let anyone shorten my name."

As we exchanged childhood mortifications, the director stood beaming at us as if he were a father who had just arranged a successful playdate for his daughter.

"Come have a drink with us," he said, "and tell us all the things we get wrong in Jilly's courtroom scenes."

"Sorry," I said, newly reluctant to admit that I'd never seen their show.

Before I could dredge up an excuse, he snapped his fingers and said, "Oh wait. I forgot. We have a meeting in twenty minutes. Tell you what. Why don't you come back tonight and watch us film a car crash?"

"Do come," Jill Mercer said. "It'll be fun. You'll get to watch Stone go on his pretty little ass."

"Don't be catty, darling," said the director, whose name I still didn't know.

He told me where to be and the time and promised to buy me that drink.

"Thanks," I said, figuring that Chelsea Ann could bring me up to speed by then.

CHAPTER
12

In the case of major offenses it makes a difference whether something is committed purposely or accidentally.

—Justinian (AD 483–565)

I got back to the SandCastle a little after four and as I stepped out of my car, Chelsea Ann and Rosemary pulled in right beside me. I couldn't see anything as bulky as a chest or table in back.

"No luck?" I said, taking Cynthia Blankenthorpe's tote bag out of the trunk.

"Not for me, but Rosemary found a great patchwork quilt for Rosie's room."

"All hand-stitched cotton in a log cabin pattern," Rosemary said as she came around the end of the van with a bulky package in her arms. "In Rosie's favorite colors."

From the smiles on both faces, I gathered that they had patched up their differences as well. For the moment anyhow.

At the desk in the lobby, I called Cynthia's room. No

answer, so I left a message to say that her tote would be here at the desk, then asked the desk clerk to hold it for her.

"It's bound to be five o'clock somewhere," said Chelsea Ann, and we strolled into the bar while Rosemary went upstairs to stash the quilt in their room.

"She's still sharing with you?" I was surprised. "I thought she and Dave—?"

Chelsea Ann rolled her eyes. "Rosemary thinks it's romantic to pretend they're still legally separated, sneaking out of bed and up to his room in the middle of the night like she's still in high school and I'm the guidance counselor or something. I can't convince her that Dave's just playing the angles. She's so sure that he's finally sowed his last wild oat and that he's ready to keep that horse in the barn."

"And you're not?"

"Doesn't matter whether I believe it or not," she said wearily. "After that public display on the balcony this morning, she might as well have bought an ad in *The Star-News* that she's condoned his last affair. Just a matter of time till there's a new one."

We ordered drinks at the bar and carried them out to the terrace. Most of the rocking chairs were taken, so we sat down at one of the small tables just outside the door to the bar.

Even in the shade it was still warm, but not unpleasantly so. Sounds of children splashing in the pool drifted up to us. Out at the shoreline, eight or ten pelicans skimmed past like a string of speed skaters heading for the finish line. Further down the beach, a cloud of gulls elbowed each other out of the way to catch the chunks of bread a woman tossed into the air. I slipped off my sandals, took a swallow of my drink, and relaxed into the chair.

"So how was your afternoon?" Chelsea Ann asked.

"Interesting," I said, and told her about running into Jill Mercer and the director of *Port City Blues*.

"Jerome Stackhouse?"

"Is that his name?"

She described him right down to his graying ponytail and I nodded. "That's him."

She laughed when I told her I needed a quick cram course on the show. "He wants me to tell him what they get wrong."

"Like he really cares," Chelsea Ann scoffed. "I'm sure someone's told him that in North Carolina, the prosecution and the defense both remain seated to question a witness, but that's not as dramatic as having them stride around and get in a witness's face. Or that you don't automatically cite the grounds for your objection. Or that wearing a robe and horn-rimmed glasses completely keeps you from being recognized when you take your hair down, take off your robe, and turn into a hot blues singer at an after-hours club."

"You're kidding, right?" I said. "A female Clark Kent/ Superman thing and the Lois Lane character—"

"That would be Stone Hamilton," she interposed.

"—He never notices? Is this show played for real or is it a sort of *Get Smart* farce?"

"It's a dramedy. And in all fairness, Stone Hamilton plays the club owner, Don Harper, who's never been in Darcy Jones's courtroom. The episodes bounce back and forth between legal dramas and Darcy's after-hours life.

Something will happen in the club that makes her see a court case differently. Or a court case will open her eyes to what's happening to someone at the club. The story lines alternate, see? One week, it's mostly about Don and she's just a minor character. The next week, Darcy's the one front and center."

"Are they lovers?"

"On screen or in real life?"

"Whichever."

"I think Hamilton may be involved with someone from *Dead in the Water*, another show that's filmed here in Wilmington. I don't know about Mercer. On *Port City Blues*, there's enough sexual tension between Don and Darcy to keep viewers wondering will they or won't they, but everybody knows what happens when the guy gets the girl on these shows. Kiss of death. If they're smart, the two characters probably won't hook up till the very last episode."

While the ice melted in our glasses and the occasional judge wandered by, Chelsea Ann regaled me with incidents from the show, its legal courtroom goofs, and gossip about Jill Mercer and Stone Hamilton.

"He's real eye candy," she said. "I'm going to be so disappointed if he turns out to be gay."

"Why don't you come along with me and check him out for yourself?" I said.

Her green eyes lit up like sparklers. "Really? It would be all right?"

"I don't see why not. That Stackhouse guy said he wanted some feedback from a real judge. This way he'd be getting a twofer and you can stop me from putting my foot in my mouth."

"Like that's possible," she said with a laugh.

We agreed to meet in the lobby later that evening and maybe get supper somewhere on the drive over.

When the elevator stopped at my floor, Martha Fitzhume was waiting for the doors to open.

"Oh, good!" she said. "I was on my way up to the party suite for a drink and I hate drinking by myself."

"Where's Fitz?" I asked, allowing myself to be dragooned.

"Having a nap. Bless his heart, he wore himself out in the pool after lunch. His retirement's not coming a day too soon for either of us. He just doesn't have the stamina he used to have, Deborah, and I want him to myself while we're both still healthy enough to travel and enjoy each other."

On the sixth floor, the door to 628 was on the latch, and talk and laughter met us as we neared the suite. Martha knew everyone, of course, and I had met most of them. The one totally unfamiliar face belonged to Tom Henshaw. A barrel-shaped man in his late forties, he was completely bald in front and on top, but thick brown hair covered the sides and back of his head. I had been told that he was normally a shy, quiet man, but this afternoon he was downright gregarious.

It's not that he was celebrating the death of the man who had challenged him for his recently acquired seat on the bench, but neither was he in mourning. He greeted me so warmly that I almost expected him to hug me and thank me for finding Pete Jeffreys's body, as if I'd somehow been responsible for his suddenly safe seat. I couldn't help thinking that it was a good thing he hadn't been at Jonah's last night. Otherwise, he'd be near the top of my list of suspects.

All the same, looking around the room reminded me that I didn't actually *have* a list of suspects. Several of my colleagues had been at Jonah's, yet I couldn't visualize any of them as a killer. Yeah, yeah, given the right provocation, I'm sure a lot of people could kill in the heat of the moment, with or without true intent. Look how close I'd come to fatally stabbing Allen. A few centimeters in either direction and I could be sitting in prison right now.

But to walk the length of the parking lot? To come up behind someone and take him unawares? That's malice aforethought. Deliberate intent.

"*Surely none of these laughing, talking, pleasant faces could conceal a hatred that intense?*" said the kind-hearted preacher.

"*Oh, please,*" said the pragmatist.

Martha fixed us each a vodka collins, I snared a bowl of nuts, and we went out onto the large balcony that wrapped around the corner of the suite. Two others were there before us, Judge Lillian Jordan and a younger man who was sworn in last year. There were only three chairs at the round white plastic table and he jumped up immediately, insisting that we take his.

Lillian smiled as we watched him bolt back into the air-conditioned room. "Thanks for rescuing us," she said. "We were boring each other to death, but he was too polite to think of a good excuse to leave and—"

"—And you were too kind-hearted to tell him to push off," Martha said, handing me my drink.

Lillian is the judge I hope I grow up to be. She's maybe fifteen years older, but doesn't look a day over forty. A trim figure, light brown shoulder-length hair, a genuine interest in people, and a quick sense of humor, yet there is a gravitas about her that invokes confidence in what she says and how she rules. Some judges coast on the issues, relying on these twice-a-year conferences to keep them current on new laws and new rulings from our state supreme court. Lillian is always on top of the law and is seldom reversed. She doesn't allow any nonsense in her courtroom, but she gets her point across quietly and firmly. Most attorneys respect her even when she rules against them.

Unfortunately she's a committed Democrat in a Republican district and no longer bothers to run for election. Fortunately our Democratic governors keep appointing her to fill vacancies or act as an emergency judge. She had driven over from Randolph County this afternoon and was interested to hear about my finding Pete Jeffreys's body.

"Only if you feel like it, though," she said, taking a single cashew from the bowl I'd brought out. "It must have been horrible and you're probably tired of telling it."

"That's okay," I said and gave her the condensed version.

"As close as you are to the Triad," I said, "did you hear about any of the allegations against him?"

She nodded without elaborating and I wondered if she had spoken to the ethics committee.

Martha was more willing to talk about his flawed approach to the law and I finally learned that she had found him detestable even before he came to the bench. "It wasn't proved, but I'm pretty sure he bribed someone at a Burlington lab to give a phony result on the blood test.

My cousin's daughter went through hell before she could prove Jeffreys's client was the father of her son."

My head came up on that one. "A Burlington lab?" I couldn't quite remember the name. "Jane-something?"

"Jamerson Labs. You heard about that?"

"Heard about it? It came unraveled in my courtroom. I didn't know Pete Jeffreys was involved, though."

I remembered the lab worker's plain, chinless face. She had taken money to lie about a paternity case that I had sat on, and then I discovered that she had lied for Allen as well, in someone else's court over in Greensboro. That sweet-talking flimflammer hadn't paid her a dime, just made her feel beautiful and so desirable that she had gladly faked his test and sworn to its accuracy.

"What about the carjacker that he let walk out of his court on unsupervised probation?" I asked. "Anybody here have a connection to the young woman he murdered?"

Neither Lillian nor Martha could think of anyone.

"Besides," said Martha, "he seems to have passed all the blame for that on to the DA who didn't alert him to the guy's probation violations."

"Although he would have known about it if he'd bothered to read the file," said Lillian, echoing what others had said about the dead judge.

"I saw you talking to Bill Hasselberger last night, Deborah. I hope he's got a good alibi because heaven knows there was no love lost between him and Jeffreys."

"Who's Bill Hasselberger?" asked Martha.

"Former judge who's back in private practice down here now," I explained. "Jeffreys unseated him in what sounds like a dirty campaign."

"It was," said Lillian, "but I was thinking about his little godchild."

"Godchild?"

"The talk is that Jeffreys took money to give primary custody of the little boy to the husband and the child got hold of the stepmother's cigarette lighter and—"

"You're kidding," I said. "That was Bill Hasselberger's godchild? Judge Ouellette told us about that at our committee meeting today, but she didn't say that he was connected to Hasselberger. God! Jeffreys was a judicial disaster, wasn't he? How the hell did he get elected?"

"You ask that with all the incompetent crooks in office?" Martha asked sardonically. "Maybe voters thought he'd be a good man to have a beer with." She took a final swallow of her drink and set the glass back on the table.

Lillian smiled and assured us that Hasselberger was not a violent man.

Me? I was suddenly remembering that he did not have an alibi if it relied on my cousin Reid. There was a half-hour unaccounted for.

If he and Jeffreys had met on Front Street?

If words had been exchanged and Jeffreys had flipped him off?

If Hasselberger had erupted in anger and followed him into the dark parking lot?

If—if—*if!*

Suddenly I was very tired of talking about it. I excused myself, threaded my way through the increasingly crowded room without getting waylaid, and took the stairs back down to my floor.

More than twenty-four hours had passed since Dwight and I had snapped at each other. If I was tired of talking about Pete Jeffreys's death, I was also tired of feeling miserable every time I thought of Dwight. Pocketing my pride, I switched on my phone, keyed up his number, and pressed the talk button.

Six rings, then, instead of his drawled "Leave a message," a mechanical voice gave me the usual options.

Huh?

Thinking I had somehow misdialed, I tried again.

Same results, so I said I was at the beach and to call me. No way was I going to try to make up with him through voice mail.

I scrolled through my contacts list, but I had never entered Will's number, so I couldn't call him either.

Several messages were waiting for my attention. My best friend Portland wanted to tell me that little Carolyn Deborah had just cut her second tooth, my sister-in-law Doris reminded me that I'd promised to bring potato salad to the cookout to celebrate Robert's birthday next Saturday, and there were four messages from Reid.

The first had been recorded a little after four. "Hey Deborah, call me, okay?"

The second and third came at ten-minute intervals. The last had been less than fifteen minutes earlier. "Dammit, Deborah! Call me. *Now!*"

He answered on the first ring. "Well, it's about damn time."

Before I could ask him what was wrong, he said, "Did you talk to someone from the Wilmington police today? That detective that's investigating Jeffreys's murder?"

"Detective Edwards?"

"Yeah. Are you the one that put him onto Bill and me?"

"What do you mean put him onto y'all? It's a murder investigation, Reid. He was asking everyone for the names of who was there last night. I listed you and everybody else at your table and I'm certainly not the only one who saw you. Why?"

"Did you tell him Bill left a half-hour before me?"

"No, but is there any reason why I shouldn't?"

"Well..."

By now Reid had climbed down off his high horse and was ready to lead me into green pastures. I recognized that new tone from times past when he wanted to wheedle me into doing him a favor he knew I wouldn't want to.

"You lied to a police detective?"

"We didn't lie," Reid assured me. "He interviewed us here at Bill's house and I guess he sort of assumed we drove down to Jonah's in the same car and came home at the same time. He didn't ask us specifically and we didn't volunteer."

"That's about the dumbest thing you've ever done," I said. "Well, the fourth-dumbest thing," I amended, instantly remembering his history of leaping without looking. "Call him back and tell him the truth."

"We didn't lie," Reid said stubbornly. "Besides, you know good and well I didn't kill Pete Jeffreys and neither did Bill."

"Did you know that Jeffreys took a bribe to give custody of Bill's godson to the father?"

"Huh?"

"And that the child got so badly burned in the step-mother's care that he's had to have plastic surgery?"

Silence.

"*And* that he lost a couple of fingers?"

"I—okay, yes, I knew, but that doesn't mean—Look, Deborah. If we tell that detective that there's an unsubstantiated half-hour around the time it happened and that Bill had good cause to hate that bastard, he's going to land on Bill without looking further."

"You don't know that," I argued. "And how'd that half-hour get in there, anyway?"

There was a long pause, and I swear I could almost feel Reid turning red.

"Reid?"

"If you must know," he said in a sheepish voice, "I was hoping to get lucky. There was this little blonde at the bar..."

Of course there was. And of course, he didn't like to admit she must have turned him down.

"So promise you won't rat us out?"

"I won't lie for you," I warned him.

"I'm not asking you to lie. Just don't tell before you're specifically asked, okay?"

I thought about the look on Hasselberger's face when I told him and Reid of Jeffreys's death.

"*That was genuine surprise,*" said the preacher.

"*Or damn good acting,*" said the pragmatist.

Men don't talk about things that matter as easily as women do, but why hadn't he mentioned his godson when he was railing against Jeffreys this morning?

"Deborah?"

"Okay," I said, hoping I was making the right choice.

CHAPTER
13

The case was adjourned.

—Pliny (AD 62–113)

Chelsea Ann and I stopped at a restaurant on the other side of the causeway. We ordered shrimp cocktails, split a steak dinner, and still had time to stop for coffee at a little place on Market Street before strolling over to the shooting site.

On the way we passed a life-size bronze statue erected to the memory of one George Davis. According to the legend on the granite base, this son of Wilmington had been a senator and attorney general of the Confederate States of America. Bareheaded, he wore a nineteenth-century frock coat and his right arm extended in an upward gesture as if hailing a hansom cab or signaling his butler to fetch him another mint julep. He might have looked more statesmanlike had some smart-ass not wedged a beer can between those bronze fingers.

Halfway down the next block stood the building that doubled as the exterior of the club owned by the Stone

Hamilton character. The street was loosely blocked off with ropes and a few sawhorses, but even though Hamilton and Jill Mercer were standing on the sidewalk in the glow of spotlights when we arrived, I was surprised to see barely a handful of onlookers. Either all the tourists had gone home or else Wilmington had become blasé about cameras and TV stars in its midst.

Evidently this was to be a shot that established their leaving the club. We were too far away to hear their lines, but they seemed to exchange a few parting words, then Mercer walked away and Hamilton stepped off the curb and strolled toward a camera mounted on a dolly.

For some reason, it was deemed necessary to film that little snippet several times. Between takes Mercer spotted me and waved, but Stackhouse was too busy coordinating everything to glance around.

Eventually her part was deemed a wrap and she came over, held up the rope, and gestured for me to join her. Gone were the ball cap and mousy appearance from this afternoon. Now her long auburn hair rippled across one bare shoulder. Her eyes smoldered beneath long false lashes, and expertly applied mascara enhanced their beauty. The enhancement hadn't stopped with her makeup. What had been a flat chest earlier in the day now looked at least two cup sizes larger.

She laughed as she caught me staring. "Push-ups and padding. What you see ain't what you get."

I introduced Chelsea Ann, who had barely taken her eyes off Stone Hamilton. We watched as the main camera rolled backward across the street while Hamilton walked toward it. Suddenly a bright light flashed across his face and he squinted as if in surprise and apprehension.

"This is where he's supposed to realize that a car's about to hit him," Jill Mercer explained.

After another twenty minutes of duplicating that bit—who knew that watching the filming of a show could be so boring?—the main camera withdrew to the far sidewalk and someone cued a dark car parked near the end of the block. Its lights came on and it trundled slowly down the street.

"They'll speed it up and add screeching brakes when they edit it," Jill said.

The fourth time the car came rolling toward the point of impact, Hamilton had been replaced by a stunt double who met the front right headlight and appeared to be tossed like a beach ball. It was only as he was getting up that I noticed the mats that had been laid along the sidewalk behind him to cushion his fall.

As soon as Stackhouse was satisfied with the take, the mats were removed and Hamilton lay down on the bare concrete and tried to arrange his limbs to look like an unconscious hit-and-run victim.

Once he was still, Stackhouse shouted, "Hey, Jilly! Where the hell are you?"

"Oops!" said Mercer. "That's my cue."

She hastened back into the scene crying, "Don! Don!"

As she dropped to her knees beside his sprawled body, extras spilled from the doorway of the "club" and one of them shouted, "Call 911!" Another, "Did anyone see the car?"

The camera rolled in to focus on Mercer's distraught face next to Hamilton's as she implored him to hang on.

* * *

It was after midnight before we got that drink at a real club a few blocks over. Stone Hamilton had begged off—"I gotta go walk my dog," he told us—to Chelsea Ann's disappointment.

While Stackhouse flirted with Chelsea Ann and took notes on everything she had found wrong with the program's courtroom scenes, I learned that Jill Mercer's soft Southern accent originated right here in North Carolina.

"I was born in Elizabeth City and studied acting at ECU, a few years after Emily Proctor graduated. She was my idol and it still amazes me that I've pretty much matched her role for role," she said proudly.

We traded courtroom stories, real and fictional, which led to Pete Jeffreys's murder the night before.

"Did the police question y'all?" I asked.

She looked puzzled. "No. Why would they?"

"Because of the run-in Stone Hamilton had with him."

"What run-in?"

So I told her how Jeffreys had kicked the boxer, claiming that it had lunged at him. "And he was strangled with a woven nylon dog leash just like the one Hamilton had for his dog."

"Mo would never go for someone unprovoked," she said.

"Mo?"

"Stone's boxer. For Muhammad Ali. You think Jamie Lee Curtis was sappy over that chihuahua? Stone's worse about Mo. He's got a short temper, too, but if he didn't deck the judge right then and there, he certainly wouldn't go after him later."

"He didn't mention it to you?"

"No, but we're not that tight, y'know? His girlfriend

crews on the *Dead in the Water* set, so he mostly hangs
with them when we're not working."

Suddenly she laughed, then immediately apologized.
"I'm sorry. I don't mean to make light of your friend's
death, but if you and I were anything like Judge Darcy
Jones, we'd have this thing wrapped up by the time they
rolled the final commercial."

I smiled. "And the killer would be—?"

"Oh, the sleazy prosecutor or the bailiff or some an-
onymous nobody at the back of her courtroom."

We batted outrageous scenarios back and forth a while
longer, but when Stackhouse proposed another round of
drinks, I shook my head. "It's been a long day and we
have to be up early in the morning."

Back at the hotel, Chelsea Ann and I both went straight
to our rooms. Even though I was tired, I couldn't resist
going out on the balcony. The moon was three nights
from full and was already on its downward slide over
the top of the hotel, but it lit up the beach. From where
I stood, I could see that the tide was quite low and the
waves rolled in on long slow parallels that held me hyp-
notized till I realized that I was almost asleep standing
up.

Before I fell off the balcony, I went inside and un-
dressed, brushed my teeth, and smoothed cleansing cream
on my face. That woke me enough to remember that I had
been catching up on my voice mail when Reid's call interrupted. I rooted my phone out of my purse, switched it
on, and listened to one of my nieces asking if it was okay
to bring some of her friends over to swim off my pier that
afternoon. Because she and her cousins had been the one

to build it, they had an open invitation to use it any time, so this was just a courtesy call.

Still no call from Dwight, but one from my sister-in-law Minnie reminded me of a political lunch we were supposed to attend on Friday and there was a second call from one of those unfamiliar and unidentified numbers.

I punched the button to play the message and adrenaline shot through my veins the instant I heard Dwight's voice.

"Deb'rah? You get my last message? If you didn't, call me back on this number, okay?"

I didn't wait for him to repeat the number, but scrolled straight back to the first message that had come in from that number yesterday afternoon.

"Hey, shug. We got here just fine, but when we stopped for lunch, I dropped my phone in the parking lot and by the time I missed it, somebody'd run over it." I heard his rueful laugh. "You were right. We should've packed a lunch. Sandy's lending me hers while we're here. They think the SIM card's okay, so I'll wait till I get home to buy a new phone. Call me back at this number, okay?"

I played that message three times and heard absolutely nothing in his voice to indicate that he was still mad or that he thought I might be. All my angst for nothing?

Relief flooded through me as I remembered the many times I had snarled at him back when he was more like another brother than a future love. Half the time he never realized I was mad at him. The other half he just shrugged it off. He knew me too well: if I was seriously angry, I'd let him know; otherwise, I'd get over it as soon as I cooled down enough to think it over.

Was it really that simple? I played the message again.
Yesohyesohyes!

He and I and Cal were still going to have to sit down
and thresh out the ground rules again, but for now, the
huge weight that had burdened my shoulders for two days
melted away like ice cubes in a glass of warm sweet tea. I
was no longer exhausted. I wanted to rush downstairs and
dance naked on the beach. I wanted to ring room service
and order champagne. Most of all, I wanted to hurry the
night along so that morning would come quickly.

I slid between the sheets and fell asleep hugging one
of the oversized pillows and whispering happy nothings
in its nonexistent ear.

CHAPTER
14

*Under the name of things personal are included all
sorts of things moveable... by the common law, of all
a man's goods and chattels... But things personal, by
our law, do not only include things moveable, but also
something more.*

—*Sir William Blackstone (1723–1780)*

Monday dawned blue-skies bright with crystalline
air that for June was almost humidity-free. Sunlight sparkled on the turquoise water and turned the
soaring gulls a dazzling white. Another day in paradise,
made even more beautiful by calling Dwight as soon as I
awoke. We talked for almost an hour. He planned to go on
to his seminar this morning while Cal went camping with
Paul Radcliff and his boys. Paul and his wife Sandy had
known Dwight and his first wife from their tour of duty in
Washington. Paul is now chief of police in Shaysville,
which was how he and Dwight have kept in touch over
the years.

"What about the house?" I asked.

"There were some family pieces that Jonna's mother wanted back," he said, "and you remember Eleanor Prentice, Mrs. Shay's cousin?"

The only normal member of that whole family? Of course I remembered her.

"Her daughter will take the china. It's been in the family a couple of generations and I didn't think we wanted it."

"God, no," I said. In addition to the casual dinnerware we'd received as wedding gifts, we also had my own mother's Royal Doulton in enough place settings to serve a formal dinner to twenty.

"How's Cal handling things?" I asked.

"Okay. He cried a little when we got to Jonna's room, but Eleanor had emptied out all her closets and drawers and stripped the bed so it wasn't as bad as it could have been, I guess. About the only thing he really talked about was that the house and yard looked smaller than he remembered."

Time does that, I thought—magnifies in memory the well-loved places of childhood.

"Will's on his way back with a truckload of things he'll put in his next auction. The housing market here's a lot worse than ours, but the real estate agent's going to try renting the house to someone with an option to buy. With gas prices what they are, she thinks people are going to want to live in town again instead of miles out in the country."

"There was nothing in the house Cal wanted to keep?"

"Not really. We pretty much cleaned out his room when we moved him down in January. There was a little wooden box that Jonna used to toss her spare change in and a souvenir mug from Six Flags, stuff like that. None of the furniture. So how's your conference going?"

"It doesn't officially start till this afternoon," I said, stalling as I tried to decide how to tell him that there might be a murderer among us. "The chief judges meet at three and there's a reception tonight in honor of Judge Fitzhume."

In the end, because there was no way to avoid it, I told him as calmly and unemotionally as I could about Pete Jeffreys's death.

He was concerned that I was the one who had discovered his body in case Jeffreys had been someone I liked and respected. Not that my likes or dislikes would ever affect the way he works his cases.

"Who's in charge?" he asked.

"The lead detective's a guy named Gary Edwards. He says he's met you and to tell you hey when I talked to you."

"Tell him I said hey back if you happen to see him again. He struck me as pretty solid. You aren't messing around in his case, are you?"

Before he could tell me to stay out of Edwards's investigation or start worrying that I might be in danger, I said, "Too bad you're not here. They've remodeled the hotel and there's a Jacuzzi in every room now."

He chuckled. "Well, damn! If I didn't have to teach that class, I'd be right down."

"On the other hand," I said, tossing another ball into the air, "I don't know as I'd want to expose you to so much temptation. Guess who Chelsea Ann and I had drinks with last night? Jill Mercer and the director of *Port City Blues*."

The distractions worked. The rest of the phone call was devoted to last night's filming of a hit-and-run scene and that yes, Jill Mercer seemed to be as nice as she was beautiful. I didn't tell him about the push-up bra and padding. Some illusions should not be shattered, I decided, smugly aware that I hadn't needed padding since I was twelve.

After the call, I indulged myself by going back to bed for another hour, then called room service for a pot of coffee, a bowl of fruit, and a flaky croissant with blackberry jam, which I ate on my balcony while reading *The Star-News*'s update on the investigation. The story had moved off the front pages, shrunk to two short paragraphs, and was captioned "No Leads in Death of Judge."

True or not, I had no reason to call Detective Edwards. No startling revelations had been whispered into my shell-like ears in the last twenty-four hours. There was that bit about Jamerson Labs, but that was old news. Yes, Martha Fitzhume was still carrying a grudge because her cousin's daughter was screwed when Jeffreys bribed a lab tech to alter her ex's paternity test. Once that tech came clean in my court, though, all her cases were reexamined and, so far as I knew, new tests had set everything straight.

Bill Hasselberger was a possibility if he was emotionally close to his godson. Say he had brooded excessively over the child's burn injuries to the point that the sight of Jeffreys was enough to push him over the edge into murder. That missing half-hour certainly gave him enough time. It couldn't have taken more than five minutes to follow Jeffreys to his car, loop that leash around his neck, then throw him into the river.

I still thought it was odd that neither he nor Reid had

mentioned the boy when they were cataloging Jeffreys's sins on Sunday.

Of course, the murder didn't necessarily have anything to do with Jeffreys's bungled court decisions. Maybe it played out on a more basic level. Judges have a certain amount of power and more than one old, fat, ugly man has proved that power is an aphrodisiac. I might have been turned off by Jeffreys's smirk, but I'm willing to bet that he saw plenty of action around his district. Maybe it was time to talk to Roberta Ouellette again and see if I could pry loose some names that would link back to the trial lawyers who were meeting forty minutes away.

Only not now. This was my last day of hedonistic freedom and I was going to put Pete Jeffreys out of my mind and enjoy it.

A half-hour later I was sitting under a coral umbrella out on the sand. A warm breeze blew in from the water that gradually retreated as I smoothed sunscreen on every bare area I could reach. According to the lifeguard when I passed his stand, high tide was at ten and it would be at its lowest around four. Castles built at the waterline now would last for many hours, but nobody was working on one and my yellow sand bucket and red plastic shovel were thirty years gone. I don't quite understand the allure of a pool at the beach, but the SandCastle's was crowded with kids and adults while the ocean went begging.

I waded out till I was hip-deep, then dived into the next wave as it was cresting and swam out beyond the breakers so that I could float on the gentle swells without being dumped back on the shore. The water was as warm as a bath and the salt was sweet on my lips.

After almost a hour, when my fingers had turned to

prunes, I paddled back toward the shore and wound up a bit further from the hotel than I had started. As I emerged from the water, there sitting on the sand at play with his children was Allen Stancil.

"Hey, darlin'," he called, holding out a towel to me. "Come and meet my young'uns."

Useless to tell him not to call me darlin'. And churlish to walk past the little girl who was giving me a shy smile.

Instead I took the towel, dropped to my knees and smiled back. "You must be Tiffany Jane."

"Yes, ma'am," she said, ducking her blonde head. She wore a pink bathing suit printed with green and yellow starfish.

"And this little man's Tyler," Allen told me.

The toddler looked to be about sixteen months old and his disposable swim diaper sported starfish and seashells. He was having a grand time knocking over his sister's sand towers as soon as they were built.

I finished drying my hair and handed the towel back to Allen. "I thought you were only here for the weekend."

"Naw, we're staying till Wednesday. Wendy Nicole found us a good deal on the Internet. Bet you pay as much for your room as I'm paying for a whole suite." His eyes suddenly narrowed. "You with that bunch of judges down the hall from me? Sixth floor?"

I pled guilty.

"Y'all sure are noisy. Kept Tiffany Jane awake till after midnight."

"They were talking in their outdoor voices," the child said disapprovingly.

"Not me," I said. "Not last night anyhow."

Allen cut his eyes at me and white teeth flashed an

amused smile beneath his dark beard. "Examining a witness in another room, darlin'?"

"What's a witness?" his daughter asked.

Before I could tell Allen that my comings and goings were none of his business, he grabbed my left hand.

"Is that a wedding ring?" he asked in astonishment. "Don't tell me you went and married that rabbit sheriff after all?"

The last time our paths crossed, I had indeed been involved with a game warden from further up the coast, but he was ancient history.

"No."

"That SBI guy who was always hanging around?"

"Dwight Bryant," I said. "Last Christmas."

I didn't have to explain who Dwight was. They've known each other off and on since childhood. Whenever Allen ran away from home and fetched up at a neighbor's house, he and his cousin became part of the gang of boys that hung out at our house to play whatever ball was in season at the time. Too, he had been a "person of interest" when our paths last crossed and Dwight had called him in for questioning.

"Well, I'll be damned! Ol' Dwight? Maybe if I'd had a badge on my shirt, you and me'd still be married."

"We were never married," I reminded him. "And the only badge anybody'd ever give you is maybe a dogcatcher's."

Tiffany Jane sat back on her heels. "Did you catch dogs, Daddy? And put them in jail?"

"Naw, honey. She's just joking."

At that moment young Tyler's face brightened and the little girl cried, "Aunt Sally!"

Both children ran toward a bone-skinny woman who carried a large white plastic bag from one of the hamburger chains. An inch or two over five feet, she had lemon-yellow hair gathered up into a topknot tied with a peach-colored ribbon. Her sun visor was lime-green and so were her scoop-necked tank top and the frames of her oversized sunglasses. With her peach-colored slacks and stacked orange sandals, she was a walking fruit salad.

From a distance, with that sassy walk, she looked forty. As she got closer, I saw that she was past fifty. Her skin had the leathery look of someone who had either worked out in the sun all her life or else had her own tanning bed. "Time for lunch," she called. "Y'all hungry?" Her voice had the husky timbre of an addicted smoker.

As the children danced around her, she sat down under Allen's umbrella and spread the towels for a picnic.

The children immediately tore into the bag of food and the smell of french fries, onions, and pickles floated toward me and made my mouth water despite my full breakfast only two hours earlier. She unwrapped the hamburgers and poured juice into a sippy cup for the toddler, then paused to give me a quizzical look over the top of her colorful sunglasses.

"Hey there," she said, reaching out a hand that felt like thin dry twigs. "I'm Sally Stancil."

"I'm sorry," Allen said. "Sally, this here's Judge Deborah Knott."

"Judge? Really?" Her sunglasses slipped further down her thin nose and she looked me up and down. I automatically straightened my shoulders and sucked in my tummy, aware that my red bathing suit showed every extra ounce that I must have gained this weekend. Allen's second ex-wife (and the woman he'd still been married to when he married me) lifted a well-plucked eyebrow. "Idn't she the one almost cut off your balls?"

Happily, the children were too involved with their food to pick up on her question and Allen said, "Aw, that was just a little misunderstanding."

Sally Stancil gave me a friendly smile of solidarity. "He's a hound dog, idn't he? You want a hamburger, honey? I got extra."

"No thanks," I told her and stood to walk back to my own umbrella. "Nice meeting you," I said and waved goodbye to the little girl. The boy was carefully lining up french fries on his paper plate.

Allen jumped to his feet and followed me down the beach. "Sally's gonna take 'em on up to her room for a nap soon as they finish eating, so how 'bout we go someplace where we can set down and have a real lunch? Ain't no reason we can't be friends, right?"

I looked up into his hopeful brown eyes. His neatly trimmed beard and mustache had almost as much salt as pepper these days, but if you overlooked the scars and tattoos, he still exuded a rough-hewn sexy charm and he really did seem to have finally settled down to a law-abiding life. I mean, how much more respectable can you get than installing seamless rain gutters?

"Friends? Yes," I said and shook his work-hardened hand, "but I already made plans for lunch. Sorry."

It was a lie, of course, but he pretended to believe me.

"Okay, then, darlin'. Catch you later, maybe."

* * *

Inside the hotel, I stopped by the registration desk in the lobby to pick up my name tag and the thick packet of conference material.

Counting everyone who's come out of retirement to take up the slack when emergencies arise, North Carolina has around three hundred district court judges, all of whom are required to attend at least one educational conference a year. Some go only to the fall conference up in the mountains, others only to the summer one here in Wrightsville, while still others opt for offerings at the School of Government in Chapel Hill. But the beach is usually pretty popular and the elevator I rode up in was jammed with colleagues who had just checked in. I knew most of them by sight, but none were special friends, so it was "How's the beach?" and "How was your drive over?"

It reminded me that this was, after all, a professional conference and I was glad I'd pulled on a shirt and shorts over my bathing suit before leaving the beach. Back in my room, I showered and shampooed all the salt out of my sandy blonde hair, then lay down across the bed intending to look through the packet and familiarize myself with the issues that would be discussed. After a morning of sun and surf, though, good intentions fought with a pleasant inertia and inertia won hands down.

It was almost two o'clock before I was vertical again and ready to put on one of my favorite summer dresses. Made of soft blue cotton, the peasant skirt was topped by a matching tunic with bands of white embroidery around the keyhole neckline and along the edges of the three-quarter-length sleeves. I cinched my waist with a white straw belt and fastened a bracelet around my wrist that Mother had given Aunt Zell to keep until my wedding.

Each slender gold link held a tiny blue enameled forget-me-not. As if I would ever forget her, with or without the bracelet.

"Sue said it could be your something blue," Aunt Zell had told me.

Mother had loved Dwight and I would never stop wishing she could have known that we would wind up together. That last summer, when she was telling me all her secrets, I had asked how she had come to marry Daddy.

"It was his fiddle," she said. "He played himself right into my heart." Then she clutched my hand and said, "Oh Deborah, honey. Try to marry a man who can make you laugh." She paused and looked at me thoughtfully. "I wonder if you've met him yet?"

Well, of course, I thought I had, but that little romance went bust before the leaves turned. Dwight was in the Army back then, stationed overseas when Mother died, and nowhere on my radar.

I brushed my hair, dabbed moisturizer on my face, then applied lipstick and mascara with a light hand. My skirt had such deep pockets that I could do without a purse. Keys (car and room), lipstick, a thin wallet, and I was ready to roll.

CHAPTER
15

. . . If calculated deceit is involved, an action for fraud is in order.

—Ulpian (ca. AD 170–228)

The door to Room 628 was once again on the latch, but the voices and laughter were more subdued. Everyone using their indoor voices. I wondered if Allen or his ex-wife had come down and asked for quiet during the children's naps. Like me, some twenty-five or thirty people were skipping lunch for a handful of nuts, chips, the fruit tray, and a soft drink. A few were nursing beers or a glass of wine, but the hard stuff sat unopened on the sideboard.

Hard politics had been abandoned, too. I had spotted Roberta Ouellette, the judge from Jeffreys's district, out on the balcony in conversation with Addie Rawls from District 11 and some man who had his back to the door, so I circled past various animated groups, exchanging smiles and handshakes as I went. The snatches of conversations I overheard seemed to be about vacation plans, children and their college applications, the speeding ticket one judge had gotten while passing through the district of his mortal enemy, and an impassioned defense of her beloved Cleveland Indians by Shelly Holt, who will quit the bench in a heartbeat and run for baseball commissioner if it ever becomes an elective position.

Becky Blackmore, also from Wilmington, was using a ballpoint pen on Mark Galloway's hand to illustrate the symbols certain gang members tattoo on their knuckles while Joe Setzer and Hank Willis wished him luck in washing them off before he had to pass sentence on a Crip or Blood.

Just as I was about walk through the open French doors, I recognized the other judge who was talking to Roberta.

Last spring, a year ago, while still reeling from my breakup with the game warden, I was specialed into Asheboro to adjudicate the equitable distribution of marital property between two high-profile couples, a pair of prominent attorneys and two well-connected potters from nearby Seagrove.[*] I was invited to the local bar association dinner and it was there that I met Will Blackstone, a newly appointed judge. No relation to the famous jurist of the eighteenth century, he quickly told me. We were both at loose ends and when he asked me to dinner a few nights later and followed it up with an offer to show me his pottery collection, I accepted even though I figured that showing me his pottery would be the Seagrove equivalent of showing me his etchings.

Three minutes after he left to slip into something more

*See *Uncommon Clay*

comfortable, he was back wearing nothing but his brand-new judicial robe and a bronze-colored condom. I told him I'd get my own robe from my car and we could do the kinky judge-on-judge scenario he had planned. While he mixed us another round of drinks, I hopped in my car and drove away as fast as I could. I do have some judicial standards, thank you very much, and I knew I'd never be able to wear that robe again had I gone along with that session.

I decided that I could catch Roberta later. No way did I want to make small talk with Will Blackstone.

Steve Shaber was restocking the ice buckets when I reached the door. "Hey, didn't you just get here?" he asked. "Was it something I said?"

"Something you didn't say," I told him. "Like where you and Judge Cannell stashed the caviar and smoked salmon."

He gave a look of mock indignation. "You mean you didn't see them right beside the goose-liver pâté and the Dom Pérignon?"

"Well, I did see the champagne, but those plastic flutes are so tacky I couldn't bring myself to pour any."

He laughed and told me to come back later. "We'll have room service send up a case of Baccarat crystal just for you."

Down in the lobby I had paused to watch some children play with the creatures in the touching tank when Chelsea Ann, Rosemary, and Dave strolled in.

"Oh, good!" said Rosemary. "We were going to come find you. See if you wanted to come to Airlie Gardens with us."

"Airlie Gardens?" asked Martha Fitzhume, who was seated in one of the overstuffed lobby chairs. "May I come, too? I've never visited it and Fitz is meeting with the other chief judges this afternoon, so it would be a good opportunity. Unless five of us are too many for one car?"

"Not a bit," said Rosemary. "Dave's already begged off. Gardens always bore him." Her husband gave a what-can-I-tell-you? shrug.

"There's a tearoom I've been wanting to try, as well," Rosemary said. "So why don't we do the garden, get tea, and then plan to be back here when the chiefs' meeting breaks up around six?" She glanced at her watch. "That'll give us almost three hours. You don't mind, do you, darling?"

"Not a bit, honey." He leaned in to give her a husbandly peck on the cheek. "Y'all have fun and don't worry about me. I'll find something to do."

Airlie Gardens is one of Wilmington's jewels. Like many public gardens, this one started as the hobby and playpretty of a rich woman. Originally part of a huge estate, the gardens now cover sixty-seven acres, ten of them in freshwater lakes and water gardens. One bed of typical Southern perennials flows beautifully into another. Despite the late spring, most of the azaleas had finished blooming, but enough blooms were left to let us imagine the massed glory of a month earlier. Dark green camellia bushes with their shiny leaves formed a backdrop for daylilies of every size and color except blue. I made a mental note not to ever bring Dwight here. Bad as he is for planting trees and bushes, he'd go nuts for the huge, centuries-old live oaks that punctuated the wide lawns, and I could see him enlisting my brothers and their backhoes and trucks to try and transplant a couple to our place.

What really caught our fancy though was the Bottle Chapel, a whimsical gazebo-like structure built of stucco and hundreds of colored glass bottles as a tribute to Minnie Evans, a visionary artist who once worked at the gardens as a gatekeeper and who sold her pictures on the side for a few dollars each. They go for thousands today. Cobalt blue, ruby red, and funky shapes of clear glass caught the sun in an exuberant brilliance.

Less than an hour after we got there, though, Martha was clearly winded and we wound up accepting a ride back to the car from a passing golf cart. "This getting old is for the birds," she complained as she climbed out of the cart.

Rosemary glanced at her watch and said, "Instead of having tea out somewhere, let's go back to the hotel. Dave bought a huge box of pastries for our breakfast this morning and we barely put a dent in them. We can sit on the balcony and put our feet up. Besides, I want to show you the beautiful roses he brought me."

Martha laughed. "No diamond earrings? No pearls? That man's got a lot to learn about getting out of the doghouse."

"Well," said Rosemary, trying to look modest. "He did say something about a new car."

At the hotel, we trailed Rosemary down the hall to the room she now shared with Dave. She waited for us at the door, key card in hand, and when we had caught up with her, she swiped the card and pushed open the door.

From within came the sound of a bubbling Jacuzzi, a squeal of panic, frantic splashing, and Dave's "What the hell—?"

Rosemary stepped inside, then stopped short. The entryway and the sliding closet doors were faced with mirrors and the Jacuzzi sat in a mirrored alcove just beyond. Martha Fitzhume was in front of me, but reflected in the mirror were multiple images of a head of bright red hair as it disappeared beneath the soap bubbles. Dave was chest-deep in bubbles and his face was almost the same shade of red.

"You bastard!" Rosemary wailed. "I do *not* believe this!"

Unable to hold her breath any longer, Jenna the wannabe SBI agent surfaced long enough to see the shock on our faces and immediately submerged again.

Martha put her arm around Rosemary. "Come on, sugar. Unless you want us to drown 'em both for you, you don't need to stay here."

As she herded us out, I couldn't resist one backward look. Dave's face said it all: punitive alimony, generous child support, and at least half of everything he currently owned.

CHAPTER
16

An obligation to do the impossible is null and void.

—Celsus (ca. AD 67–130)

We went back to Chelsea Ann's room. Martha sent me up to hers for a bottle of bourbon while she filled the ice bucket, and Rosemary retreated to the bathroom to get control of her tears.

"I'm so sorry, sugar," Martha said when Rosemary emerged with red-rimmed eyes. "Y'all looked so happy yesterday morning out there on his balcony. I can't think why in the world he'd mess around with that idiot child when he has a beautiful smart wife like you. And right when you'd taken him back."

"Oh, come on, Martha," Rosemary said, taking a deep swallow of the drink I'd handed her. "A fresh firm young body over this forty-three-year-old wreck? You know exactly why."

"Only because he's a sex addict," Chelsea Ann said loyally.

Rosemary clasped her sister's hand. "Thanks for not saying you told me so."

"Yeah, well, the afternoon's still young, kid."

Martha poured herself a drink, put her feet up, and leaned back against the pillows on one of the beds. "Make a note of the date and time, ladies. We'll all come to court for you. Vacuum his assets, right?"

"Right!" we chorused and clinked our glasses in solidarity.

"Want me to have that little bitch fired?" asked Martha.

Rosemary shook her head. "It's not her fault. If I could fall for his lies, if he could make me believe he was a changed man, what chance did that dumb kid have?"

Martha waved the bottle in my direction, but I had volunteered to drive her and Fitz to the reception later, so I passed. Not Rosemary, though.

After an hour, she was well on her way to being thoroughly sloshed when she handed her key card to Chelsea Ann. "Would you and Deborah mind going up and getting my things? I don't think I can stand to see him again right now."

We agreed, but when we got to Dave's room, he didn't respond to our knock. Chelsea Ann used the key card and cautiously cracked the door. "Dave?"

No answer.

We stepped inside and almost tripped over the wet towels that were flung on the floor. The Jacuzzi had been drained, although several long red hairs decorated the bottom. The closet doors were open, but nothing was inside except for two of Rosemary's dresses. No masculine toiletries in the bathroom. No sign of his clothes in the dresser, no second suitcase.

"The bastard's checked out," Chelsea Ann said. "Good."

A large vase of roses had begun to drop their crimson petals on the desktop. Probably bought on sale at a grocery store. I dumped them in the nearest wastebasket.

We carried Rosemary's things back to Chelsea Ann's room and Rosemary called down to the front desk to confirm what we suspected. Yes, ma'am. Judge Emerson had checked out twenty minutes ago. Did Mrs. Emerson want to keep the room? It was paid for till eleven the next morning.

"No, thank you," Rosemary said.

Martha was determined to punish him every way possible. "Who's his chief over there? Joe Turner? I shall make a point of telling him that Dave cannot claim credit for attending this conference," she said magisterially, as she rose to go get ready for the evening reception.

"Could you give Fitz my regrets?" Rosemary asked plaintively. "I don't think I feel like going out again this evening."

"Of course, sugar," Martha said. "Charge your room service to Dave's tab, then you get a good night's sleep and just think about all that lovely alimony you're gonna collect."

Because I had volunteered to drive the Fitzhumes, Chelsea Ann asked if she could hitch a ride as well, and we agreed to meet in the lobby at 6:30.

I called Dwight, who was on his way out to supper with some other deputies, then scribbled a few words on a note card so that I could remember the sequence of the funny story I wanted to tell on Fitz at his roast tonight. Fresh lipstick and I was good to go.

* * *

The sun was more than an hour from setting as we crossed the parking lot to my car. I had planned to pull up to the door, but the others trailed after me. I had just pressed my remote to unlock the door and turned back to see where Martha and Fitz were when a red car dug out from its parking spot several spaces over and hurtled toward us.

For one bewildering moment I felt as if I were back on last night's sidewalk, watching them film the hit-and-run scene for *Port City Blues*. Same screeching tires, same noisy acceleration, same female scream, only this time I was the one screaming. The car's right bumper hit Fitz and tossed him in the air like a sack of potatoes. He landed against Martha, who went sprawling to the pavement, too, her white suit suddenly splashed with blood.

Without touching the brakes, the driver careened down the drive and out onto the street that ran the length of the island, narrowly missing the gateposts.

Even as I ran to Martha and Fitz, cell phones were flipping open all around me, their frantic owners pushing the 911 buttons.

Martha was dazed and bleeding profusely from a scrape on her cheek and another on her hand. She tried to push herself upright, unaware that it was Fitz's body that kept her pinned to the pavement. He was unconscious but breathing. I grabbed a roll of paper towels and a bottle of water from the trunk of my car and we made wet pads to ease Martha's wounds and stanch the blood. We were afraid to move Fitz before medical help arrived but Chelsea Ann slipped off her jacket and made a cushion for Martha's head. Between us, we managed to keep her calm.

It seemed hours before we heard ambulance and police

sirens, although another glance at my watch showed that only twelve minutes had elapsed.

Two patrol cruisers got there first. One uniformed officer and a security guard from the hotel held back the onlookers while a second officer began questioning us for details on the car.

All I could say was that it was an older red car. A hatch-back.

"There was something about the wheels," Chelsea Ann said.

"Yes!" I exclaimed, remembering now. "The hubcaps were spinners."

My nephew Reese is crazy about his truck and one of the many chrome extras he's bought for it is a set of hubcaps that keep spinning even after the truck stops.

An ambulance from the New Hanover Regional Medical Center swung into the parking lot and was directed over to us. The paramedics hopped out, checked Fitz's vital signs, and immediately put a cervical collar on his neck, then lifted him onto a stretcher. I heard one of them mutter, "BP's tanking and one lung's collapsed."

They fitted him with an oxygen mask before loading him into the ambulance—Martha, too.

Strong-willed, imperious Martha looked at me beseechingly. "Deborah?"

"Don't worry," I said. "We'll be right behind you."

"Ma'am, I'll need your statement," said one of the officers. "You can't leave."

"The hell I can't," I told him and slammed the car door on his protests.

As the ambulance rolled down the drive, I slid my key into the ignition, pausing only when Chelsea Ann yanked open the other door and jumped in. Flooring the gas pedal, I caught up with the ambulance and hung tight. Even after they turned the sirens back on and sped through red lights, I sailed through with them.

"Omigawd!" Chelsea Ann shrieked when I swerved around a pickup and almost T-boned a blue convertible full of white-faced college kids.

I saw that she had retrieved Martha's purse. "Is her phone there?"

A moment of rummaging and she came up with it in her hand. "What's their son's name? Chad?"

"Sounds right," I said.

Moments later, she had scrolled through Martha's contact list and found the son's number on speed dial.

Weaving in and out of the vacation traffic that clogged the island's main two-lane street, I listened with only half an ear as Chelsea Ann explained who she was and what had happened.

By the time she finished, we had crossed the causeway and were streaking down the four-lane highway that was the quickest route to the hospital on 17th Street. Adrenaline was still pumping through my system when we finally turned into the appropriately named Ambulance Drive and pulled up at the emergency entrance.

I let Chelsea Ann off to stay with Martha and went to find a parking space.

Fitz was nowhere in sight when I got back to the emergency entrance, but I was told I could go back to where Martha's cuts and scrapes were being treated. Either it was a slow Monday evening or the hospital was exceptionally well staffed for her to be seen so quickly.

Happily, her injuries seemed to be superficial. The gash on her hand needed only a few butterfly bandages to close it up. Her face would be red and bruised for several days, but she was quickly regaining her equilibrium. I hoped the nurses realized that it was only a matter of time before her polite requests to know what was happening with Fitz turned into a full-scale reminder of a patient's legal rights and the rights of a spouse to be kept informed. Yet all they could tell her was that he had been taken directly to surgery.

Their son Chad called twice during his drive up from South Carolina. He had immediately phoned his sisters, which meant that Martha soon had one frantic daughter calling from California and another from Rome. Each clamored to know if she should catch the next flight out. Martha was usually so decisive that this not knowing what to tell them left her impatient and frustrated; but until he was out of the operating room, there was nothing she could do.

Friends from the conference came to sit with us in the ICU waiting room, and the judges from Fitz's district brought pizza and milled about to lend support. Poor Fitz got his roast in absentia as we tried to keep our spirits up by remembering funny things he had said or done in his long career on the bench. It wasn't a wake, but it was damn close to it. And through it all we kept circling back to why the accident had happened and why didn't the driver stop?

Drugs? Alcohol? Or was it that someone had suddenly recognized that Fitz was the one who gave him jail time or ruled against him in court and impulsively decided to get even? Most defendants who come to district court wind up admitting sheepishly that yes, they are indeed guilty of the offenses with which they've been charged, and if they are angry, it's usually toward their accusers or the police. Nevertheless, I have been threatened by an occasional belligerent, as have most judges. So far as I know, though, those threats have seldom been carried out. All the same, it's been known to happen in other states.

"Fitz with an enemy? Nonsense!" Martha said firmly. "If it was deliberate—and mind you, I say *if*—then he must have mistaken Fitz for someone else."

Nevertheless, a vengeful defendant was one of several theories that kept us going round and round like blind mice hunting for a way out of the maze.

I was almost grateful for the distraction when Detective Gary Edwards arrived shortly after seven with a Wrightsville police officer in tow for courtesy's sake and asked to question us. Chelsea Ann and I were the only two there who had seen it happen.

"Let me buy y'all a cup of coffee or something," Edwards said, and the four of us went down to the hospital cafeteria where they were still serving supper. Once we were seated with coffee that wasn't as bad as I expected, Edwards tore open a packet of sugar, emptied it into his mug, and told us that one of the doormen had watched the whole thing. "He says it looked like the driver was deliberately aiming for the Fitzhumes. What was your impression?"

"Well, there was certainly enough room for him to have missed them if it wasn't accidental," I said, and Chelsea Ann agreed.

"He didn't slow down at all. In fact, I think he was still accelerating. I feel like kicking myself though."

"Why?" Edwards asked. "You couldn't have stopped him."

"No, but I could have gotten his license plate," I fumed. "Last night, we watched them film a hit-and-run for that TV show."

"*Port City Blues*," Chelsea Ann murmured, daintily adding creamer to her coffee.

"The script called for someone to yell, 'Did you get the license number?' and nobody had. I thought that surely in real life someone would at least get the first few letters. But when Fitz and Martha went down, it drove everything else out of my head. Why—why—*why* didn't I at least whip out my cell phone and take a picture?"

"Someone did," Edwards said, "but it's blurry and the car was too far away to get a good fix on it. Our computer techs are trying to enhance it enough to get a partial plate, but I'm not counting on it. Someone thought it was a two-door Geo Metro and at least ten years old. That sound about right to y'all?"

Chelsea Ann and I looked at each other and shrugged. Neither of us cares enough about cars to tell a Toyota from a Nissan.

I took a swallow of the coffee and tried to concentrate. "A hatchback for sure," I said, at last, "and yes, just two doors. Bright red and shiny like it'd been waxed recently, but I sort of think it had some serious dings."

"What about the driver?"

We both shook our heads. We had an impression that it was a man behind the wheel, yet couldn't say for sure. We were both too focused on Fitz and Martha.

"I think he was wearing a ball cap," Chelsea Ann said.

"I couldn't see him at all," I said. "He was driving into

the sun when he came at us and it glinted off the windshield. Maybe he really didn't see Fitz and then was too scared to stop."

"Maybe," Edwards said. "Or maybe somebody's got it in for a bunch of you guys. Is there a connection between Fitzhume and Jeffreys?"

We couldn't think of one. "They're in totally different districts. Fitz has been on the bench for twenty-five years and Jeffreys only for a year or two."

Edwards sighed and downed the rest of his coffee. "Well if you think of anything…"

We assured him we would.

Throughout the whole session, the Wrightsville officer had remained silent. Now he told Edwards that it looked to him as if the hit and run was related to the murder, so Wilmington could have it. "Just keep us informed, okay?"

When he was gone, Edwards looked around the cafeteria. "You know, the food's not half bad here. I think I might as well grab a bite to eat while I have a chance. What about y'all?"

Chelsea Ann looked torn and I realized that his 'y'all' was only for politeness. Even though there was a hollow space in my stomach, I stood up and told her to stay. "I won't leave without you."

"You sure? 'Cause I can wait."

It only took one more "I'm sure" from me to convince her it was okay to do what she wanted, which was stay there and get to know Detective Edwards on a nonprofessional basis.

* * *

Nothing had changed in the ICU waiting room except that a dispirited lethargy seemed to have settled over those who remained. I picked the pepperoni off of a slice of cold pizza and ate part of it.

Martha's son arrived just before nine. A few minutes later, a surgeon came to the waiting room in bloodstained scrubs and asked to speak to them privately.

"Whatever you have to say can be said before my friends," Martha told him. She held herself erect as if braced for the worst. "Don't sugarcoat it, Doctor. Is he going to be all right? Yes or no?"

"We don't know. There was internal bleeding. A rib punctured his right lung and his hip was fractured. We had to remove his spleen. He took a serious blow to the head but luckily there doesn't seem to be much swelling of his brain. We'll monitor for blood clots, of course. He'll probably be in and out of consciousness for the next couple of days. After that?" The surgeon shook his head. "We just don't know. His age is against him, but if he makes it through the next few days, then his chances improve."

She took it like the stoic she is. "Can we see him now?"

"It'll take them another fifteen or twenty minutes to get him hooked up to the monitors, and we've put him on a ventilator to help with his breathing," the surgeon said. "I'll tell the nurses to call you when they've finished."

Martha reached out and touched his arm. "We've been married forty-two years, Doctor. Thank you for giving him back to me."

He started to say not to thank him yet, but Martha's eyes held his in such fierce determination that he squeezed her hand. "I hope I have, ma'am. I hope I have."

CHAPTER
17

A judge who takes money [for a decision] against the life or property of a man is deprived of his property and deported to an island.

—*Paulus (early 3rd century AD)*

Even though Fitz could not respond, once Martha had seen him and touched him, she let their son Chad persuade her to return to the hotel for the night. She planned to transfer to a hotel nearer the hospital the next day.

As we waited with her at the entrance for Chad to bring the car around, I said, "You have my number, so call if there's anything at all that we can do."

Martha's not normally a physically demonstrative person, but I got a warm hug and a "Thanks, sugar" before her son whisked her away.

Chelsea Ann was silent on our drive through Wilmington's dark tree-lined streets. Away from the center of town, all was quiet until after we crossed the causeway that led over to the beach where vacationers were hanging out at the main intersection, spilling out into the street from the clubs.

"So what's the verdict?" I asked her as we maneuvered around the cars full of vacationing teenagers that were cruising back and forth.

She didn't pretend not to understand. "I don't know, Deborah. Another lawman?"

Her ex-husband was an ATF agent.

"I've been down that road before. Gary Edwards seems like a real sweetie. Cute, smart. But I'm in Raleigh and he's down here. When would we really get to know each other?"

"It's only a ninety-minute drive," I reminded her.

"And we both know that a lawman's life is not his own. Look how often Dwight has to bail on you and he's right there in Dobbs."

"Sam's erratic schedule wasn't why y'all split up," I said.

"No, but it certainly didn't help that he never seemed to be around when I wanted him," she argued. "Oh, well, why am I even talking like this? It's not as if Gary's even asked me out yet."

"And if he does?"

She grinned. "Oh, what the heck? I'll probably go. Why not? How I Spent My Summer Vacation. Better a summer fling with him than with a married judge, right?"

Which led us back to earlier speculations about a pair of fifty-something colleagues. He is from the mountains, she's from the Triangle. Both married, yet they never bring their spouses to the conferences. They discovered each other three years ago when they sat together during the sessions and talked animatedly during the breaks. At every conference since, they sit on opposite sides of the room, they don't speak during the morning breaks, and they don't go out to lunch together; but it's been noticed that they don't stay at the conference hotels and that one car pulls into the parking lot within minutes of the other. They both plead poverty and kids in college as a reason to book somewhere cheaper, yet somehow it's never at the motel where all the other budget-minded judges stay.

"Like judges have more personal judgment than ordinary mortals," my internal preacher murmured.

The pragmatist nodded. *"And like nobody noticed when you and Chuck Teach—"*

"Never mind," I told them firmly.

"It's not Sam I miss so much," Chelsea Ann said, interrupting my thoughts. "It's having someone put his arms around me and kiss me like I'm special and necessary to him that I miss. I miss being in love, Deborah. Forty-two years. That's what Martha and Fitz have had. That's what I want."

Me, too, I thought and patted the hand-carved knob on my gear shift that Dwight had given me so I'd always have a handy piece of wood to touch for luck.

When we reached the hotel, the moon was a huge silvery blue disc playing hide-and-seek with fluffy white clouds that barely dimmed its brightness.

I was feeling the need for some fresh air after our hours in the hospital. "Want to take a walk on the beach?" I asked.

She shook her head. "Sorry, I'm really tired. And Rosemary's probably going to want to talk."

We rode up in the elevator together and I went straight

to my room, but all I had to do was open the French doors and step out into that amazing moonlight and it was too much to resist. I quickly changed into a long-sleeved tee, slacks, and sneakers, and was soon back downstairs.

Although the bar was now closed, out on the terrace there were still people seated at the small tables or in rocking chairs. Nursing their final drinks, they spoke in low tones, as if equally reluctant to go inside and end this lovely night. One or two spoke to me when I passed but I wasn't looking for company and cut across the pool area and down the planked walkway to the steps that led to the beach. A young couple—honeymooners?—were making out in one of the hot tubs, oblivious to the world and certainly to me.

I walked down the steps to the sand. A whiff of cigarette smoke drifted past on the warm night air and I looked around for the source, but the beach was deserted so far as I could tell.

I took off my sneakers and tucked them under the steps beside the lifeguard stand. The tide was low again and a wide band of hard sand made walking easy. Not that I was out to do a marathon or anything. Although the moon was so near full that nothing could completely blot out its light, more clouds had drifted in from the west and they hid its face for minutes at a time.

As I walked, I thought about how complicated it all was. Life. Love. Why some marriages worked and others failed. Chelsea Ann was a funny, impulsively warm-hearted friend and I still liked her ex-husband Sam. I had known them both long enough to remember when they had genuinely loved each other. Where had their love gone?

And Rosemary and Dave. Almost twenty years down

the drain. But that I could understand. She had thanked her sister for not saying "I told you so," after Chelsea Ann berated her for telling that cute little waitress that Dave could give her the names of some SBI agents, but *sheesh*! It's all very noble to forgive your cheating husband, but you don't immediately turn around and give him the contact numbers of a Playboy bunny, do you?

And dear Martha and Fitz. If she should lose him, it would be through no fault of her own.

I paused to wait for the moon to come back out from behind a cloud that was as dark as my worry for Fitz. There wasn't a mean bone in his body, so why the hell would anyone deliberately try to kill him? And could Pete Jeffreys's death possibly be linked?

By now, pleasantly tired, I had retraced my steps until I was almost back in front of the lifeguard stand. I sat down on the dry sand and rested my chin on my knees as I stared out at the slow-rolling waves and rewound the tape on Saturday night.

I saw Jeffreys's run-in with Stone Hamilton's dog, I saw Martha's refusal to shake his hand coupled with Fitz's amiable clasp, I watched him speak to Allen Stancil, then introduce Cynthia Blankenthorpe to Allen. I saw Reid and his friend Bill's distaste for Jeffreys and the way Jeffreys snubbed me after I'd shared a drink with those two. I heard Blankenthorpe's annoyance at being stuck with his bill when she knew he'd just made a cash withdrawal of three hundred dollars at an ATM.

So where was the connection to the hit-and-run, assuming there was a connection?

No one admitted seeing Jeffreys after Fitz saw him entering the men's room alone and—

"*Hey, wait a minute!*" cried the pragmatist. "*Quick! Hit the pause button.*"

"*Those were not Fitz's exact words,*" the preacher agreed, peering at the screen.

Before I could figure out what had snagged my subconscious attention, a voice said, "Deborah? Deborah Knott?" and I jumped three feet.

"Sorry," the man said. "I didn't mean to spook you."

The moon had once again emerged from the clouds, and there was plenty of light to recognize Judge Will Blackstone, who continued to apologize for startling me.

"That's okay. I just didn't hear you come up."

"Somebody told me you were here and I've spent all day looking you. You're not avoiding me, are you?" he asked.

"Of course not. Good to see you," I murmured inanely, the automatic pleasantry out of my mouth before I could stop it. At the moment, he was the last person it'd be good to see.

I started to stand, but he sat down heavily, clutching at my arm as he went so that I was unbalanced and almost landed on top of him, which set off another flurry of apologies from both of us.

"And I wanted to be so cool," he laughed. He got to his feet and helped me up. "I hoped to see you at the fall conference so I could apologize for what happened last spring. I guess I came on too strong, too fast."

"Yeah, well, I think we both misjudged the situation."

He laughed at my unintended pun and held out his hand. "No hard feelings?"

"No hard feelings."

We shook on it and Blackstone said, "Good. This conference is weird enough without that. First Pete Jeffreys and now Judge Fitzhume."

"That's right. You're over there near the Triad. Did you know Jeffreys?"

"We were at a new-judges school together, but I can't say we were friends or anything. I thought he was rather lightweight and, not to speak ill of the dead or anything, a little bent."

"Yeah, that does seem to be the consensus, doesn't it?"

"Fitzhume, on the other hand—you were there, weren't you? When someone ran him down?"

I nodded.

"Is he going to be okay?"

I told him what the surgeon had said and while we talked we ambled back across the wide expanse of sand, winding up at the lifeguard stand and the steps where I'd left my shoes.

"Well..." I said as I sat down on a step to put them on.

"You're not going in, are you?"

"It's getting late and our first session's at eight-thirty, remember?"

"It's not that late," he argued as he sat down beside me. "And just look at that moon."

He leaned back on his elbows and turned his face up to the sky. "Do you ever get dizzy when you look up like this and the clouds are moving so fast over the face of the moon?"

Amused, I followed his example and yes, it was disorienting the way light and shadow came together and broke apart until it seemed as if it were the moon that was racing across the dark star-studded blue and not the clouds. So absorbed by that beauty was I that before I knew what was happening, Will Blackstone had slipped an arm around me and kissed me gently on the cheek.

"Hey!" I jerked away indignantly and sprang to my feet.

"I'm sorry," he said with a boyish grin. "You looked so beautiful with the moon in your eyes and on your hair that I couldn't resist. Please, can't we start over again?"

"No, Will, I'm—"

"You said no hard feelings, but I still have feelings for you. And whether or not you admit it now, you had feelings for me last spring. You didn't come home with me just to see my pottery collection."

"That was then, this is now. Besides, I'm married."

It was as if he didn't hear me. I stepped back when he stood up, but he put his arms around me. His breath was hot against my face as he tried to kiss me and I caught a whiff of whiskey.

"Are you crazy?" I cried, trying to pull away. "Let me go! *Now!*"

"Don't be like that, Deborah, honey." His arms tightened around me. "You know you like me. You were the one came on to me first, remember?"

His arms were starting to remind me of octopus tentacles. No matter how I struggled, as soon as I got one hand free, another arm seemed to grab me there and hold me fast. Just as I was ready to put a knee in his groin or bite his nose, a large dark shape landed on his back and the three of us went sprawling. Blackwood jumped up with his fists flailing, then I heard an *oompf* as he took a punch in the stomach and another to his eye.

He collapsed to the ground, gasping for breath, and Allen Stancil said, "Want me to go ahead and kill 'im for you, darlin'?"

"No, that's okay," I told him.

Blackstone groaned and fumbled for his cell phone. "I'm calling 911, you asshole. You don't know it, but you just assaulted a judge."

"And what were you doing?" Allen asked ominously. "Didn't you hear this judge say no?"

He grabbed the phone and started to throw it in the ocean, then paused and offered it to me. "Less'n you want to call the police yourself, darlin'?"

Testosterone was so thick in the air I almost choked on it.

"Could you both just calm down?" I took the phone and handed it back to Blackstone. "I'm sorry if we got our signals crossed last year, Will, but get over it. Chalk it up to experience and let's both act like professionals and forget that tonight ever happened, okay?"

"My nose is bleeding," he muttered sulkily.

I had no tissues on me and looked at Allen. He hesitated, then pulled a small packet from his pocket and held it out to Blackstone with an odd look on his face.

"What the hell is that?" Blackstone asked suspiciously.

"It's—um—uh—a diaper wipe." Allen sounded embarrassed. "But it'll take care of blood, too."

"*A diaper wipe?*" Blackstone sneered. He clearly wanted to refuse, but a fresh trickle of blood snaked down his lip. He grabbed the packet, tore it open, shook out the moist towelette, and held it to his nose.

"Look, Will," I said, but he waved me off before I could continue to make nice.

"You're right, Judge Knott." His voice was icy cold. "This night never happened." He glared at Allen. "You can thank her that I'm not going to press charges against you." Then, with as much dignity as he could muster, he marched up the steps and back toward the hotel.

"Bastard," Allen said cheerfully, rubbing the knuckles of his right hand.

"Did you really have to hit him that hard?" I asked. "Twice?"

"He won't taking no for an answer, was he? Seems like you oughta be thanking me."

"Why? I can take care of myself."

"Yeah? Didn't look that way to me."

"Where did you fly in from anyhow?"

"I'm an angel, darlin'. Your guardian angel, didn't you know that? So how come he thought he could snuggle up to you?"

"It's a long story," I said wearily.

"Well, less'n you want to go in while he's still roaming around looking for ice, you got time to tell me one." He stopped at the foot of the lifeguard stand and started up the ladder. "Just let me get my cigarettes."

So that was the smoke I'd smelled earlier and it was how he'd landed on Blackstone's back. I followed him up the ladder. If we were going to kill some time, might as well have a gull's-eye view of the water.

With a roof and railings, the structure was more like a deer stand than a single chair on stilts, which was why I hadn't noticed him sitting up here so still and quiet.

"Lots of room here on the bench," Allen said, when I sat down on the floor with my back against a post.

"I'm fine here, thank you. Why didn't you say something when I passed below you before?"

"I sorta thought you wanted to be alone for a while.

Figured I'd catch you on your way in and then that SOB showed up right behind you. Hunkered down over there and waited for you to come back."

For some reason that freaked me out a little. I was ready to see the encounter as the result of one too many drinks, but to follow me from the hotel and wait to see whether I was alone or meeting someone? Maybe I was luckier than I realized that Allen had been watching.

He lit his cigarette, inhaled deeply, and leaned back. "So what was that about pottery, darlin'?"

"Don't call me—" I caught myself and bit back the rest of my words. It would be ungrateful not to cut him a little slack right now. Instead, I told him about my first run-in with Blackstone, exaggerating enough to have him shaking his head in amusement at the end.

"I could almost feel sorry for that poor slob."

"Don't waste your tears," I said. "Now it's your turn. Tell me everything you know about Pete Jeffreys."

"You asking as a judge or off the record?"

"Off the record," I assured him. A man who carries diaper wipes in his pocket has to be a good daddy and who knew what kind of mother his third ex-wife was.

(*"Or fourth,"* whispered the preacher. *"If we count you."*)

Hesitantly at first, and then more confidently, he fleshed out the story of the Jamerson Labs tech that he'd seduced and how she'd told him Jeffreys had tempted her to fake some of the blood tests for his clients.

"He was real sneaky about it. Never right-out asked her to do it and never paid her a dime himself, but the men she helped sure did. So then when he got to be a judge and I was fighting Katy for my young'uns, I figured he might see things my way if I offered to put new gutters on his house, if you know what I mean."

I knew what he meant. "How much did it cost you?"

He shrugged. "I'd've paid a lot more."

In the end, he didn't add a thing of substance to what I'd already heard. The clients Jeffreys had nudged toward Jamerson Labs, the burned child, the murdered college kid, the DWI dismissals, the solicitation for campaign donations in open court?

Yesterday's news.

Without a complaint from the attorneys who'd heard the solicitation or a confession from those he'd taken bribes from, the rest was circumstantial and nothing for which he could be held criminally culpable. But a pattern was emerging and it would have been only a matter of time before he came to the attention of the State Bar, which could and would have censured him and called on the chief justice to remove him from the bench.

"When he brought Judge Blankenthorpe over to meet you that night, what was that about?"

"Showing off. Acting like I was a millionaire who give him some big bucks for his campaign and maybe he could talk me into throwing a little her way when she has to run. Like I give a good goddamn for a judge that's got nothing to do with me." He cocked his head at me. "So when you running again, darlin'?"

CHAPTER
18

A court is defined to be a place wherein justice is judicially administered.

—*Sir William Blackstone (1723–1780)*

Drifting off to sleep a little later, I drowsily found myself remembering Fitz's exact words at lunch yesterday. He had talked about almost bumping into Pete Jeffreys at the restroom door. When I asked if anyone else was there, he had said, "Nobody I knew, but—"

It was at that point that the very sexy and very stupid Jenna had returned with our drinks. By the time she got our orders sorted out, the conversation had moved on.

"*But*"?

How would Fitz have finished that sentence if she hadn't distracted him?

"But someone else was there"?

Someone he didn't know but who recognized him?

Someone who realized Fitz hadn't yet mentioned him and who was afraid that he might if the police questioned everyone again?

Someone who thought he could get rid of the only person who could link him to Jeffreys's death?

I looked at the illuminated dial of the clock radio on the nightstand. It only confirmed what I knew: that it was much too late to call Detective Edwards. I lay back down and closed my eyes.

Sleep eventually came, but it was filled with restless, uneasy dreams in which the hit-and-run became the running of the bulls in Pamplona. Instead of a red car, Fitz was gored and tossed through the air by a huge red bull to fall broken and trampled on the ground.

It was a relief to wake up before the alarm went off at seven. Before Dwight was awake, too. I apologized for calling so early.

"That's okay," he said through a half-muffled yawn. "I need to be up."

He was sympathetic about Fitz. Even though they've never met, he's heard me mention the Fitzhumes often enough to know how concerned I was. I told him my theory about why Fitz was hit and for once he didn't suggest that I mind my own business.

"Did you tell Edwards?" he asked.

"Not yet. I only remembered it after midnight when I was already in bed."

"You'd better call him right away. He might want to put a guard on your friend's hospital room."

"He's not in a room. He's in intensive care."

"Good. He should be safe there for the time being."

"You really think—?"

"Hell, Deb'rah, I don't know. But if it was me, I'd rather not chance it. Besides, maybe he said something to his wife. Edwards needs to be told. *Now*."

He said it so forcefully that immediately after we finished talking, I scrolled through my contact list for Gary Edwards's number.

It rang four times before a groggy male voice said, "Edwards here."

Again I found myself apologizing for calling so early, "But I thought you ought to know," I said and told him what I'd told Dwight.

Sleepy as he was, he immediately connected the dots and thanked me for calling. "And yeah, I'll put a man on ICU."

"Any luck in finding the car?" I asked.

"Not yet. We were able to make out a couple of the numbers and we're running it through our databases. No matches so far."

We hung up and I hesitated over my next call. I didn't want to chance waking Martha in case she had been able to sleep, but I was too worried about Fitz to let it go. There was a phone book in the drawer of the nightstand and I found a number for the hospital, dialed it, and asked for intensive care.

The ICU nurse who answered was very pleasant, but very firm that she could not give me any information about Fitz.

"Even if I tell you I'm his niece?"

"Are you his niece?"

"Yes," I lied.

She clearly didn't believe me, but she must have heard the worry in my voice because she kindly told me that there was no change in his condition.

"No change is good, right?" I said. "Means he's not deteriorating?"

"I'm sorry, ma'am. Even if you are his niece, you'll have to speak to his doctor about that."

Click.

That's okay, I thought, as I showered and dressed. No change means no change for the worse. I'd take that as a positive sign.

Downstairs, a breakfast buffet of sweet rolls and fresh fruit had been set up for us in the large lobby outside the main halls. In normal times the place buzzes with cheerful talk, bursts of laughter, and lots of politicking and logrolling. In normal times sunlight shines through the floor-to-ceiling windows that line the east side of that wide corridor. Today the mood was as glum as the weather.

The light clouds that raced across the moon last night had stalled and thickened into dark gray. There had been thunder and lightning before dawn, and now the rain had settled in as if it meant to keep falling for forty days and forty nights.

At 8:30, balancing coffee cups and plates of fruit, we took our seats at the long rows of narrow tables as our president, Joe Buckner from Chapel Hill, called us to order. He gave us the update on Fitz: "He's in intensive care at New Hanover Regional downtown. His condition's stable, but serious. No visitors and no flowers, but Martha asks that you keep him in your hearts and in your prayers, which we certainly do."

As for Pete Jeffreys, there were no suspects yet in his death, "And again, our hearts and prayers go out to his family."

"Does he have any?" I whispered to Chelsea Ann, who was seated beside me at a front table.

"Ex-wife, but no kids," she whispered back. "Don't know about siblings or parents."

Buckner recognized the recently retired and recently appointed emergency judges and asked the chief district judges to introduce to us those newly on the bench in their districts.

Next came Chief Justice Sarah Parker of our supreme court, who spoke to our salary needs and the bills that were currently before the general assembly in Raleigh. I wondered if that young reporter from the local NPR station had interviewed her yet. She also touched on the problems of alcoholism and depression among some judges and attorneys, but commended our court system for its professionalism and overall lack of corruption.

I hope she's right and that judges like Pete Jeffreys are a tiny, tiny minority.

Justice Parker was followed by John Smith, the director of the Administrative Office of the Courts, who spoke about the updated technology being put into place, everything from e-filing to e-citations.

Finally, the executive director of judicial standards spoke to us on campaign ethics and what we could and couldn't do.

When the mid-morning break arrived, I was more than ready for it.

CHAPTER
19

The burden of proof is upon the party affirming, not on the party denying.

—*Justinian (AD 483–565)*

DETECTIVE GARY EDWARDS (TUESDAY MORNING, JUNE 17)

As soon as he got off the phone with Judge Knott, Detective Edwards called headquarters and arranged to have an officer stationed by Judge Fitzhume's bed.

Next, he called the SandCastle Hotel and asked to speak to Mrs. Fitzhume.

"I'm sorry," said the desk clerk, "but Mrs. Fitzhume checked out about ten minutes ago."

Edwards identified himself, then asked, "Did she happen to say if she was on her way to the hospital?"

"No, sir, but I do know that she was moving over to a hotel in town to be nearer the hospital. The Hilton."

A call to the Hilton confirmed that she had reserved a room, but had not yet checked in.

As he showered and shaved, Edwards decided that Martha Fitzhume would no doubt go to the hospital first, so he stopped by the department, where he picked up the list of names he had compiled earlier and checked to see if any progress had been made on identifying the license plate on the red Geo Metro.

"It looks like the plate was deliberately smeared with mud or something," the squad's computer jock told him. "It also looks like one of those specialty plates, but I haven't been able to match it yet."

North Carolina issues dozens of different license plates to special interest groups. From its many colleges to the Sons of Confederate Veterans to horseless carriage enthusiasts, each group has a plate with a different design. Most of them carry the state name in blue along the bottom, and while Edwards could make out a fuzzy—TH CAROLINA when he peered at the screen, the design was unfamiliar. Nor did it fit any of the electronic templates that had been tried so far.

"Any chance that those first three letters at the bottom are S-O-U instead of N-O-R?" he asked. Wilmington was only about seventy miles from the border.

"Hey, that's a thought," the younger man said, and his fingers flew over the keys.

"Buzz me if you get anything," Edwards said, and headed over to the hospital through a steady rain that was causing deep puddles in low areas of the street. An oncoming car threw up such a sheet of water, he had to brake until the wipers cleared the windshield enough for him to see through the gray morning light.

Inside the medical center, the sharp hospital smell hit him as soon as he passed the main reception desk and turned down a wide hall, a chemical blend of cleaning agents, antiseptics, and bleached linens. The smell always upped his anxiety level, rousing dormant childhood memories of his younger sister, who had died of leukemia when he was twelve. Not for the first time, he found himself wondering if he would feel differently about hospitals if he and his ex had had a baby. Would a joyous birth balance out death? He was forty-four years old and glumly aware that every year increased the odds that he might never know.

At the intensive care unit, Martha Fitzhume and her son were emerging through the door that led to the ICU pods when he arrived. He spoke to the uniformed officer and then to the judge's wife. There were dark circles under her keen blue eyes and she looked drawn and tired, yet she recognized him immediately and her voice was strong when she asked, "Have you found the car, Detective Edwards?"

"Sorry, ma'am. Not yet. How's Judge Fitzhume?"

"No change," the son said, positioning a chair for her. He had his mother's bony face and nose and there were a few gray hairs at his temples.

"You're mistaken, Chad. When I spoke to him and squeezed his hand, it felt as if he squeezed back."

"I know you want to believe that, Mom, but are you sure you didn't imagine it?"

"I do know the difference," she said crisply, but did not argue the point. "Why are you here, Detective? And why is that rather large officer here, too? Is he guarding Fitz?"

"It's just standard procedure, ma'am."

"Oh, please," she said. "Credit me with a few brains."

Chad Fitzhume grinned and shook his head.

Edwards smiled, too. He'd always had a weak spot for opinionated old women who spoke their minds. "You're right, ma'am. We may be closing in on the reason why your husband was run down."

"Reason can have nothing to do with it," she said tartly. "Explain."

Trying to match her straightforwardness, Edwards repeated his conversation with Judge Knott less than an hour ago.

She frowned, reliving the lunch in her mind, then nodded. "Deborah's right. That's exactly what Fitz said, and I should have picked up on it myself. I wish I could say that we discussed it again later, but we didn't."

Edwards drew a list of names from an inner pocket of his tan sports jacket. "I questioned everyone from the conference who was in the restaurant that night. Fourteen judges, five attorneys, and assorted spouses or friends. Twenty-seven names in all. I'd like you to go over the list and mark anybody you think your husband would not have known if he saw him in the restroom."

"Men only, I suppose?"

"No, because maybe it was a woman he saw as he came out."

She put on a pair of reading glasses and asked for a pen, then very carefully went down the list, commenting as the pen point touched and then marked through names. In the end there were three names left: one wife, one attorney, and two male judges.

Judge and Mrs. Albert Beecher, Judge James Feinstein, and Bill Hasselberger.

Hasselberger he remembered because he was an attorney, not a judge, but the other three had not stood out from the group when he questioned them earlier.

"These are the ones I don't know, at least not by name," said Mrs. Fitzhume. "Fitz might, though. Albert Beecher was appointed to the bench last month and we haven't met him or his wife. Some of the others on the list I know only by sight, but if I could recognize them on the street, then they should have looked familiar to him, don't you think? Or are you just clutching at straws?"

Before he could answer, his phone buzzed and he excused himself to walk a few steps away. "Edwards here."

"You were right," said the voice in his ear. "It's South Carolina. Want to hear something funny? It's a 'Share the Road' plate."

"Too bad the judge wasn't riding a bicycle," Edwards said grimly.

"I got enough numbers to cross-match it to a Sidney Kyle Armstrong of Myrtle Beach, age twenty-six. I ran the name through our records here and there's a speeding violation from last December that has a local address on it and South Carolina's going to E us the picture from his driver's license."

Edwards jotted down the address that had been written on the speeding ticket, a building off Market Street. The name Armstrong sounded familiar, but he could not put a face to it. Turning back to the Fitzhumes, he asked, "Does the name Sidney Armstrong mean anything to you?"

Mother and son both shook their heads.

"You sure? Sidney Kyle Armstrong? Twenty-six years old?"

"Kyle?" said Martha Fitzhume. "One of the waiters at Jonah's was named Kyle. He's an actor, but he's only eighteen or nineteen and I didn't get his last name."

Edwards riffled through his notes and there it was. He had interviewed the slender young man at the restaurant on Sunday. Like Mrs. Fitzhume, he had pegged the guy as being in his late teens. Judge Knott was there to look for a lost earring, and after denying it emphatically, this Kyle kid finally admitted seeing Jeffreys when Judge Knott and the headwaiter practically drew him a picture.

"Would your husband have noticed him?" he asked, knowing that most people never really look at a waiter's face.

"Yes, of course. He waited on our table."

"What you have to understand, Detective Edwards," said Chad Fitzhume, "is that if a waiter says, 'Hi, my name's Kyle and I'll be your server,' she'll introduce herself and then find out how long he's been working there, his favorite dish on the menu, the name of his first puppy, and what he's doing with his life."

"My son exaggerates, Detective Edwards, but Kyle did tell us about his acting career. Surely he wasn't the driver of that car?"

"The car's registered to him," Edwards said and rose to leave.

"I trust you will keep me informed," she said, and gestured to the uniformed officer, who obediently came over to her. "I'm Martha Fitzhume, Officer. And you are?"

Edwards suppressed a grin as he stepped into the elevator and turned his thoughts back to Judge Fitzhume's unfinished words.

"I didn't see anyone I knew, but—" Fitzhume had said.
"But our waiter was there"?

Is that how he would have ended that sentence had he not been interrupted?

It occurred to Edwards that Kyle Armstrong had been standing nearby when Deborah Knott said something about Fitzhume being the last to see him as they passed in the doorway of the restroom. The very next afternoon, he ran down the judge.

But how would Armstrong know where to find him? Figuring out which hotel was hosting the conference would be easy, but how could he possibly know that the judge he wanted would be crossing the parking lot at 6:30? A lucky guess? A stakeout?

Well that was something he could ask the twerp when they picked him up. He called for his partner to meet him at Jonah's and gladly left the hospital and its depressing smells behind.

As Detectives Edwards and Wall entered the restaurant, the perky young waitress at the reception stand said, "Two? Inside or out?" Then she giggled at her own question. "Sorry. It's just automatic to ask. Obviously you don't want to sit out in the rain."

"Naw, we left our umbrellas in the car," said Andy Wall, shaking raindrops from his iron-gray hair. He was eight months away from retirement and not out to risk anything by calling her honey or flirting with her as he once would have, even though she was terminally cute with those two ponytails on either side of her head that bounced when she moved.

As did other things.

They identified themselves and her blue eyes widened. "Oh, wow, yeah. I heard that one of our customers was killed and dumped in the river. I had the weekend off and missed it all."

"We need to speak to Kyle Armstrong again. Is he here?" Edwards asked.

"I don't think he's working lunch," she said. "Let me check."

She returned a few moments later, followed by a stocky middle-aged man in a short-sleeved white shirt and a loosened tie that he was tightening as he walked toward them.

"I'm the manager here," he said. "How can I help you?"

"We'd like to speak to one of your waiters," Edwards said. "Kyle Armstrong?"

"He doesn't come in till four. *If* he comes in."

"If?"

"He was supposed to work the dinner shift last night, and he never showed up. Kids today! They work when they want to, take off when they want to, never think twice about if they're screwing up everybody else's workload. He don't show up at four on the dot, though, his ass is so fired."

"Does he still live at—" Edwards fumbled in his pocket for the scrap of paper he'd written the address on and read it off.

The manager shrugged. "So far as I know. What's this about? More questions about Saturday night?"

"Something like that," Edwards said.

"Y'all come back now," said the bouncy waitress as they trudged back out into the rain.

* * *

"Kyle?" said the young man who opened the door to the walk-up apartment two blocks off Market Street. "He moved out in February."

A very pregnant brunette appeared at his elbow. "Y'all looking for Kyle? He's got a place near the Cotton Exchange."

No, she did not know the address, but it was one block up Walnut Street and there was a hardware store on the ground floor.

"He still have that red Geo?" Edwards asked.

"So far as I know," the former roommate replied.

They circled the block before pulling up in front of the circa-1920 brick building. No sign of a red Geo. As always, it was a toss-up as to whether to risk getting soaked or struggle with an umbrella. This time they found a parking space right in front, close enough that they could make a dash for it.

The tiny lobby showed remnants of bygone glory. The outer door was bronze, tarnished now, as were the filigreed mailboxes, but still bronze. The grungy floor was white marble with a long crack across the middle. Three names were listed for Apartment F: G. Smith, K. Armstrong, and R. Loring. No response when they pressed the buzzer, but the inner door wasn't locked and they were able to walk up the four flights without challenge.

It took several loud knocks to get a response.

"Yeah?" said the beefy thirty-something man who opened the door in boxer shorts and a faded blue BORN TO

RUMBLE T-shirt. They had evidently awakened him from a very deep sleep and he stared at them with bleary eyes. "Whas'up?"

"Smith?"

"Loring. Who're y'all?"

Andy Wall flashed his badge. "We're looking for Kyle Armstrong."

"He ain't here, man. He's gone."

"When do you expect him back?" asked Edwards.

"I told you. He's cleared out. Split. And don't ask me where 'cause he was gone when I got back."

Loring told them he was a long-haul trucker. He had gotten in from Arizona around two a.m. to find all of Kyle's things gone from his side of the room. "Clothes, CD player, clock radio, toothbrush, razor, his stupid bicycle, everything."

"When?" they asked.

"How the hell do I know when he left? I told you. I just got in."

"What about your other roommate?"

"George?" He shrugged. "His shit's still here, so I guess he's at work. He's a carpenter on that TV show."

"*Dead in the Water*?"

"Naw, the other one."

"*Port City Blues*?"

"Yeah, that's it."

They put out a BOLO for one Sidney Kyle Armstrong, driving a red Geo Metro, and drove out to the sprawling Screen Gems complex on North 23rd Street. At the gate, they were directed to the *Port City Blues* sound stage. Inside the building, they passed a set that looked like the interior of a nightclub and another that duplicated a courtroom. The place seemed almost deserted.

"They're shooting on location today," a passing technician told them. "Taking advantage of the rainy day."

"We're looking for a George Smith."

He pointed them to a door that led outside to a picnic table and benches under a metal roof. Three young men sheltered there out of the rain to smoke their cigarettes. As always, Gary Edwards found himself half envying them. He had been quit for eight months, three days, and sixteen hours and he still missed the way that first drag hit his lungs with its jolt of fresh nicotine.

He correctly assumed the smoker with the leather tool belt was George Smith. As soon as Andy Wall flashed his badge, the other two men ditched their cigarettes and went back inside.

"Kyle's split?" Smith asked. "You sure about that?"

"That's what your other roommate says."

"Ronnie's back?"

For a moment Edwards wondered if there was something besides tobacco in that cigarette. "Don't you guys talk to each other?"

Smith shrugged. "It's not like we're best friends. I'm usually in bed by the time Kyle gets home and I'm gone in the morning before he wakes up. My name's the one on the lease and I need two roommates to split the rent. Ronnie's gone so much it doesn't bother him to share the second bedroom and Kyle's saving his money to get a nose job. He thinks that's why he can't land a role. Like a new nose is gonna put his name in lights."

"He say anything to you about the judge that was murdered Saturday night?"

"Nope." Smith took a final drag on his cigarette and ground it out in a can of sand that sat on the table. "I think the last time we even saw each other might've been last week sometime. He didn't say anything about moving out. You sure he's gone?"

"That's what your friend Ronnie said. Took all his clothes and his bicycle."

"Well, hell. Now I've gotta find another guy to move in."

They left him lighting up another cigarette.

CHAPTER
20

*The deified Hadrian stated… "You have to determine
what in your best judgment you are to believe or what
you think has not been proved to your satisfaction."*

—*Justinian (AD 483–565)*

At our mid-morning break, I decided it'd be quicker to
run up to my room than wait in line to use the ladies'
room. Out in the main lobby, the SandCastle's child-
friendly policy was getting a full test as rain continued to
fall. There was an arts-and-crafts playroom downstairs on
the ground level next to the exercise room, but judging
from the grumbling I heard in the elevator, both were
filled to capacity.

When I came back downstairs, a staff member had
been stationed next to the touching tank to keep bored
preteens from getting too rough with the sand dollars and
starfish, while another tried to keep toddlers from banging
their action figures on the glass aquarium that lined the
hall to the restaurant. At the concierge's desk, discount
vouchers were being offered to beleaguered parents to
tempt them to try some off-premises attractions.

I saw Bernie Rawlings's pudgy daughter being hauled out through the revolving door by Bernie's equally pudgy wife. Both were red-faced and angry and I heard the child shriek, "But I don't wanna go on a stupid trolley ride! I wanna watch *SpongeBob*!"

There was one oasis of quiet in the lobby, though. Rosemary Emerson sat on a couch with four or five small children clustered around. They leaned against her or perched on the arms and back of the couch to hear her read *Horton Hatches the Egg*, while their mothers relaxed nearby with coffee or soft drinks.

She glanced up from the book to smile at me as I passed and she looked rested and ready to cope with anything.

No way could I be that cool if Dwight dumped me.

The buffet table had been cleared away from the lobby outside our meeting room and the food replaced with tubs of iced drinks and urns for coffee or hot tea. The area was crowded elbow to elbow and I was working my way down for a final cup of coffee when someone from the next district stopped me. She'd heard about my marriage for the first time that morning and wanted to give good wishes. "And he comes with a little boy?"

I smiled and nodded. "He turned nine last month."

"Good luck," she said. "My husband brought a twelve-year-old daughter to our marriage."

"You have my sympathy," I said, remembering the unremitting antagonism shown by my game warden's resentful teenage daughter.

"Fortunately, she's sixteen now and has started to think I'm pretty cool because I'm not on her case about her boyfriend and her clothes the way my husband and his ex seem to be."

We agreed that boys were probably easier than girls.

"And cats are easier still," said Aubrey Hamilton, a judge from up near Virginia. She wore a black pantsuit that sported a generous scattering of cat hairs.

I laughed. "At least kids don't shed on you," I said.

"There *is* that," she conceded.

I started to edge past her to get to the coffee when over her shoulder I saw Will Blackstone approaching the urns from the opposite direction. His handsome face sported a black eye of epic proportions and he seemed to be getting jovial remarks from those around him.

I decided a bottle of water from the tub of ice at my elbow would do just fine and hastily returned to my seat next to Chelsea Ann, who was laughing with Beth Keever seated on the other side of her.

"We were talking about Judge Blackstone," she said. "You know him?"

"We've met," I said cautiously.

"Have you seen that black eye he's wearing?"

Judge Keever leaned in with an amused smile. "He *says* he fell in the shower last night and hit his eye on the sink. He's even making noises about a lawsuit against the hotel because of the slippery tub, but John Smith saw him come in off the beach last night with a bloody nose so I don't think that dog'll hunt."

To change the subject, I said, "I saw Rosemary out in the lobby. She seems pretty relaxed."

Chelsea Ann nodded. "It amazes me, too, how well she's taking it. I guess she was more ready to move on than she realized. I do wish it'd stop raining, though, so she could get out on the beach while we're tied up in here. Want to go out somewhere for lunch?"

"Sure," I said and we turned our attention to the podium as a professor from the School of Government put up the first slide for our update on criminal law.

When we broke for lunch, Detective Gary Edwards was loitering outside. He wanted to talk and I wanted to hear what news, if any, there was in his investigation, but hunger battled with curiosity.

"I'm really sorry," I told him, "but I skipped supper last night and only had a slice of melon for breakfast, so I'm too hungry to skip another meal."

"Well, if it's breakfast you want instead of lunch, let me take you to the best breakfast place out this way. I could use some myself."

His invitation included Chelsea Ann, who looked interested. "You're talking about the Causeway, right?"

He nodded.

"Why don't y'all go on ahead? I have to find my sister. See what she wants to do. Maybe we'll catch up with you later."

It was still raining heavily, but Edwards had parked under the portico so I didn't need an umbrella. Twelve minutes later we were seated on mismatched chairs in just about the scruffiest restaurant I've ever walked into.

Its main attempt at a unified decor were the aqua oilcloths imprinted with shellfish that encased the tabletops. The grungy walls and wooden booths cried out for paint, as did the low ceiling. We had passed through clouds of smoke from the cigarette addicts who filled the porch tables. Inside, the air was redolent of hot grease, bacon, and fried fish. On a chalkboard, the day's leading offering was eggs and grouper.

I was afraid to ask what the sanitary rating might be, but as crowded as it was on this rainy Monday, I knew the food had to be special.

"Only the breakfast menu," Edwards said. "Everything else is ordinary."

I quickly settled on scrambled eggs and country sausage—air-dried links with a flavor like nothing else.

"Grits or hash browns?" asked our waitress, a seen-everything brunette on the wrong side of forty. She did not have a cigarette dangling from her lips, but judging by the cloud of nicotine that enveloped her, a lit one waited for her somewhere.

"Grits, please."

"Biscuits or toast?"

"Biscuits."

Edwards wanted the salt-cured ham and redeye gravy with his eggs and we both ordered coffee.

I was amazed by the prices listed on the menu. Even with a generous tip, I'd get serious change back from a ten-dollar bill.

"And it'll be a ten-dollar bill," Edwards told me. "They don't take plastic."

On the drive over, he had told me that Martha was encouraged by the thought that Fitz had squeezed her hand. He also told me that the car that had hit him was registered to Kyle Armstrong, the waiter from Jonah's, and that he appeared to have fled the town with all his belongings.

As we waited for our food to come, he asked if I'd noticed Kyle paying much attention to Jeffreys.

I shook my head. "Martha's the one who pays attention to waiters, not me, I'm afraid. Although he did desert us when Stone Hamilton came in, but it wasn't his table and we got him back. Speaking of Hamilton, what about the dog leash?"

"He showed us his and it wasn't a brand-new one, either. We're thinking now that the leash that strangled Jeffreys was a piece of litter. Somebody's dog probably chewed the lead off and they just threw it away. It was frayed and sun-bleached and caked with dirt, like it'd been outdoors for a while. One of the waitresses said she saw a faded blue length lying in the bushes out front when she came to work. The killer must have just grabbed up the handiest thing possible to choke him with."

"You're saying that if someone hadn't littered, Jeffreys might still be alive?"

"Not necessarily. If it hadn't been the leash, he could've had his head smashed in with a rock or something. It might not have been premeditated, but we're pretty sure it was done by someone who did mean to kill him."

Our breakfast plates arrived and everything was wonderful. It's always risky to order soft-scrambled eggs because they often come out as dry and tasteless as if they'd been sitting on a steam table for an hour. These were moist and creamy with streaks of yolk still visible amid the white. The biscuits were hot and flaky, the grits were perfectly seasoned, and the sausage tasted homemade.

"Mmmm!" I said blissfully.

Edwards grinned as he poured redeye gravy over his grits and dug into his own ham and eggs. "Told you they know how to do breakfast."

The waitress came back to refill our mugs. "Y'all need anything else, just holler," she said.

After a couple of mouthfuls to ease my hunger pangs, I said, "The thing that sounds odd about all this is that Jeffreys wasn't all that tall, but he was well built and looked like he worked out."

Edwards lifted an eyebrow at that.

"I saw him on the beach that afternoon," I explained. "In a bathing suit."

"Your point is?"

"Well, Kyle Armstrong didn't strike me as somebody who spent any time in a gym. He's almost skinny, in fact. Would he have been strong enough to strangle Pete Jeffreys and then throw him in the river?"

"Maybe. He seems to be a cyclist." Edwards told me about the waiter's specialized license plate and that he owned a bicycle. "Cyclists can be stronger than they look."

"Like Cynthia Blankenthorpe," I mused. "She's a cyclist, too. Brought her bike down with her and rode from the hotel to the Cotton Exchange in all that heat Sunday."

A sudden thought struck me. "Did you see her hands?"

"What about them?"

"One of them had four deep scratches on the back. She said it was from a run-in with a yucca plant, but . . ."

"But you're wondering if it could have been Jeffreys when he was struggling to get free?"

"Did anybody check his fingernails?"

"You've been watching too much *CSI*," he said with a wry grin. "But yes. We did bag the hands. They were in water for at least an hour though, and our ME didn't get anything useful from the fingernail scrapings. Besides,

Judge Blankenthorpe was in somebody's view from the time Jeffreys left their table till she rode back to the hotel with the Fitzhumes. And that reminds me."

He pulled out a list of names and handed it to me. "You know those four that aren't marked through?"

I put a dab of blackberry jam on my biscuit and took a bite as I looked at the list. "I know Bill Hasselberger and Judge Feinstein. Not the Beechers. He's brand-new to the bench, appointed last month, I think."

"Mrs. Fitzhume says these are the ones at Jonah's Saturday night that she wouldn't recognize and doesn't think her husband would either. What's your opinion?"

"She's probably right about the Beechers," I said slowly, stalling for time by cutting up my sausage and eating a piece with a forkful of egg. "I'm pretty sure that Fitz and Feinstein were on a committee together last year."

"What about Hasselberger? He's on your list of people at the restaurant next door. Along with your cousin."

I gave a reluctant nod. "But Fitz would probably recognize him. He was on the bench for four years till Jeffreys ran against him and took his seat."

"Really? Not much love lost there then, right?"

"No, but as you just said, he was at the restaurant next door. What would he be doing near the restroom inside Jonah's?"

At Jonah's, the men's restroom was diagonally to the right of the front door. What if that door opened about the time Fitz and Jeffreys were passing each other? Even if Bill Hasselberger had been walking past out on the sidewalk at that exact moment, would Fitz have noticed him enough to remark on it?

"Besides," I argued, "how could he be driving Kyle's car when it hit Fitz? And why would Kyle have cleared out if he's not the killer? I should think you'd be trying to find the connection between him and Jeffreys."

"Jeffreys was from the Triad and the car is registered to Armstrong's home address in Myrtle Beach." He pulled another crumpled sheet of paper from his jacket pocket. It looked like a computer printout. "Here's what we've learned so far: graduated high school in Myrtle Beach, then enrolled in the drama program at Cape Fear Community College downtown. Dropped out in the third semester. Lived with an aunt when he first came here—"

"Right!" I interjected. "That's what he said when Martha was telling us about his wanting to act. He said his aunt lived here and that she knew someone on the *Matlock* show. She got him into a courtroom scene as an extra when he was a child. Have you questioned her yet?"

"My partner's on his way out to Castle Hayne right now," he said, referring to the next town up from Wilmington, off I-40. "But there's nothing on this paper to indicate he was ever further into North Carolina than right here. Nowhere near the Triad. So unless Jeffreys came down here and royally pissed him off..."

He broke off in frustration and finished his ham and eggs.

"If it really was Kyle, wouldn't one of the other waiters notice if he wasn't on the floor?"

"They say not. He might not have been gone that long. Less than five minutes, ten at the most, to follow Jeffreys out to the parking lot, slip the leash around his neck as he was unlocking his car, then roll him over the edge of the bank and into the river."

"What about the other people in Jonah's that night?" I asked. "We weren't the only ones there."

"I know and I've got officers checking out the names we got off the credit card receipts to see if any of them noticed Jeffreys and Armstrong together. It's probably a waste of time. Once we get Armstrong and his car, we've got him on the hit-and-run and that should be enough to pry the rest of it out of him."

All the time we'd been there, he had kept glancing past me to the door.

"Guess she decided to go somewhere else to eat," he said as he called for our checks.

I glanced at my watch. Still thirty-five minutes till the next session was due to start.

"Sorry," I said.

He gave a fatalistic shrug. "I'm just spinning my wheels with her, aren't I?"

It was my turn to shrug. "I don't know. Honestly. She likes you. She just doesn't see much future if she's going back to Raleigh on Thursday."

"Raleigh's not so far."

"That's what I told her."

"Yeah?" He brightened. "Thanks."

We took our checks over to the cash register. When I opened my wallet to pay, I saw that I had nothing left but three fives and a few ones. Time to find an ATM.

It was a short drive back to the hotel, with the rain still coming down heavily enough to make potholes and low spots a real hazard. We saw two fender benders on the way.

I was still trying to work out the sequence of events. "Okay. Let's say Kyle recognizes Pete Jeffreys and he's there in the vestibule when Jeffreys comes out of the rest-room and leaves through the front door. Kyle follows him out to the parking lot, kills him, and then comes back inside before he's missed."

Edwards nodded as he swerved to miss a deep puddle and turned the windshield wipers up a notch.

"He may have noticed Fitz, but he didn't know his name till you and I were talking about it at Jonah's when I was there to look for my earring. Oh, God!" I said, suddenly stricken. "That's how he knew. It's my fault Fitz was run down. If I'd kept my mouth shut, he never would have known."

"Not necessarily," Edwards said kindly. "He worked your table. The Fitzhumes paid with a credit card, so he had to have seen it."

I could not excuse myself so easily. "Maybe so, but my telling you that Fitz was the last of our group to see Jeffreys put a big red bull's-eye on his back."

As he pulled up under the SandCastle's portico, Edwards said, "What I keep wondering is how someone other than you judges would have known that Judge Fitzhume would be walking across the parking lot when he was."

I had been wondering that myself and I thought I had the answer.

"Come on inside and I'll show you."

CHAPTER
21

I was aware of the difficult nature of the case.

Pliny (AD 62–113)

DETECTIVE GARY EDWARDS (TUESDAY MIDDAY, JUNE 17)

People had begun to filter back from lunch as Edwards followed Deborah Knott through the SandCastle's lobby to the registration table set up at the archway that led to the meeting rooms. At the near end stood an easel with a whiteboard where judges could leave each other messages. The schedules for each day's events were clipped to the top of the easel, and yesterday's schedule was still there. She pointed to the bottom of the sheet where large letters proclaimed that a reception honoring Judge Fitzhume would take place at 6:30 at a clubhouse on the other side of the island.

"That's been posted here all weekend," she said. "I don't suppose you have a picture of him?"

"Actually, I do," said Edwards. When Andy Wall had joined him at Jonah's, he had brought along an extra copy of the photo South Carolina's DMV had sent them.

He listened as the judge showed it to the women working the table and asked if they had seen him hanging around the whiteboard on Sunday or Monday.

Blank looks.

She described Kyle Armstrong's slender build and tentative manner in more detail and added, "He may be the one who ran Judge Fitzhume down," which made them look at the picture even more closely.

"Poor Judge Fitz!" said the woman who seemed to be in charge of handing out the conference packets and information sheets. "I wish we could help, but with so many people in and out, unless he came over and asked a specific question, he'd've had to be wearing a hot pink tutu for us to notice him. Do hope they catch him though."

Judge Knott handed him back the picture with a rueful smile. "I was so sure this was how he knew."

"It's still a logical premise," Edwards assured her.

"Is there anything else I can do for you right now?"

"Well, it'd be helpful if you could refresh my memory and point out the Beechers and Judge Feinstein."

"I think that's Judge Beecher at the end of the hall," she said and guided him through the judges who were gathering for the afternoon session.

As he trailed along behind her, he found himself thinking that Dwight Byrant was probably a lucky guy with his sexy, down-to-earth woman for a wife. Well liked by her peers, too, if one could judge by the warmth of the smiles that greeted her as they passed.

She paused a step away from a threesome who seemed

to be one-upping each other on how to get delinquent dads to pay their child support.

"—and I told him I didn't care how he paid his arrears but he was going to be doing community service eight hours a day for no pay till they were. Two days of picking up trash along the highway and he found the money."

"Yeah, I tell 'em, 'Hey, I don't have a problem. *You're* the one with a problem,'" said a satanically handsome judge with a neatly trimmed Vandyke. "Five times out of eight they'll come up with the money before you adjourn. Oh, hey there, Deborah! You want to talk to me?"

She smiled. "I always want to talk to you, Chuck, except that right now I want to meet Judge Beecher."

Now that she had identified him, Edwards remembered that he was the one who couldn't put many names on the diagram of Jonah's porch tables. A middle-aged white man with a shock of graying black hair and polished rimless glasses, Beecher took the hand she offered him with a ready-to-be-amused look on his face.

"I'm Deborah Knott, District Eleven-C," she said. "Welcome to the bench. How're you liking the view?"

He smiled. "A little scary. Sure is different, isn't it?"

"If you hold that thought, you'll do fine. You remember Detective Edwards, don't you?"

He nodded and Chuck Teach turned with a hopeful look. "Any news for us, Detective?"

"Soon, we hope," he said, deliberately vague. "Wonder if I could speak to you a minute, Judge Beecher."

As they moved off to one side, Judge Knott said she would try to find Feinstein for him.

"Have you and Judge Fitzhume met yet?" he asked.

Puzzled, Beecher shook his head. "No. I heard about

his accident, of course. You know if he's gonna be all
ight?"

"Too soon to say."

"Damn shame."

"He was at Jonah's Saturday night."

"That's what they tell me, but he must have been a few
ables away."

"You didn't see him in the restroom or outside it
around nine-thirty that night?"

"No, once we got to the restaurant, I didn't leave the
able till we were all ready to leave."

"What about your wife?"

"She went to the ladies' room around eight." He
ooked at Edwards sharply through those shiny glasses.
"You gonna tell me what this is about?"

"Just tying up some loose ends, sir. He seems to have
been the last one to definitely see Judge Jeffreys as he
vas leaving the men's room and we were hoping that you
could add to that."

"What time was that?"

"Around nine-thirty."

"Then I can't help you there, Detective. My wife
vasn't feeling well and we left shortly before nine."

"What about your waiter?"

"What about her?"

"Your waiter was a woman?"

Beecher nodded.

So much for that line of inquiry, Edwards thought as
Beecher rejoined the others. He realized that he was go-
ng to have to go back to the restaurant and pinpoint
precisely which tables Kyle Armstrong had served if he
vas going to have any luck linking the guy to Jeffreys.

Behind him, a voice said, "Detective Edwards? James Feinstein. Judge Knott said you wanted to speak to me?"

Again it was someone he had spoken to on Sunday and asked for his help on the seating diagrams. A wiry black man, mid-forties, with a long thin face and keen brown eyes set deep in their sockets. He wore a blue golf shirt tucked into khaki pants with creases so sharp he could have peeled an apple with them. Edwards remembered his first assessment of the man: someone who did not like to waste time and who did not easily suffer fools, a judge who knew the law inside out and probably would not have much sympathy for slackers who showed up in his courtroom.

"You wanted to ask if I know Judge Fitzhume?"

"Actually, sir, it was does he know you?"

"He does. Not in a social way. Our districts are widely separated, but we've served on a couple of committees together and have worked together for six or seven years."

"Did you speak to him Saturday night?"

"Briefly. He passed by me on the way to the restroom. At least I assume that's where he was headed. I stood up, we shook hands, said it was good to see each other. The usual. Then he went on and I sat back down. I didn't notice when he returned."

"What about Judge Jeffreys?"

Feinstein shook his head. "As I told you Sunday, I barely knew the man and I didn't pay any attention to him. Now if you'll excuse me?"

While they talked, the crowd had thinned and the judges ambled through the double doors and back into the meeting room.

Edwards looked around for Judge Knott and saw her

at the front of the room in animated conversation with Judge Chelsea Ann Pierce. It was still a few minutes before two—not enough time to say anything meaningful to Judge Pierce even if he could think of anything meaningful to say.

Several stragglers hurried into the room and the last one in closed the door behind him, effectively putting an end to that problem for the moment.

As he rounded the corner into the main lobby, he called to check in with Andy Wall, who answered on the first ring.

"Where are you?" Edwards asked. "Get anything from Armstrong's aunt?"

"I'm just leaving Castle Hayne," Wall replied. "And yeah, I got every clever thing our boy's said since he started talking. I've looked at scrapbooks of the school plays he was in. I've had to listen how Andy Griffith told her what a fine nephew she had and how he all but said that Ron Howard wouldn't have had a chance to play Opie if little Kyle had been old enough to try out for the role. I've heard how sensitive he is and how upset he was when he didn't get a part on—*Jesus H, lady!*"

There was a stream of steady swearing before Wall calmed down. "Sorry, pal. Some senior citizen, going about twenty miles an hour in this rain. She decided at the last minute that she really did want to get on the on-ramp here and almost rammed me."

"So did you get anything useful out of the Rudd woman or not?" Edwards asked impatiently.

"'Fraid not. He calls her every Sunday, but he didn't mention the murder and she was surprised to hear the judge had eaten at Jonah's Saturday night. She's also surprised that he's moved without telling her. I thought for a minute we were gonna get lucky when she gave me his cell phone number. That we could locate him through it."

"No?"

"Disconnected. But I've relayed the number to the office and Chip's gonna get the guy's records. And Mrs. Rudd did give me several good pictures of him. I asked her if she could think of who he might go to if he was in trouble. First she swears he'd come to her if he didn't go home to Myrtle Beach. But then she said that he might go to her place down near Southport. She's got a trailer down on the Intracoastal Waterway and her daughter lives there. She and Armstrong used to be good buddies before the daughter got sick."

Edwards heard the sarcasm in Wall's voice. "Sick?"

"She's an alkie. Can't hold a job and won't go into rehab, so Mrs. Rudd lets her stay in the trailer. She's grateful her daughter's not into crack or meth, but she can't stand to see her falling-down drunk, so she sends our boy down every week or so to take her a bag of groceries and some clean clothes. He was there Sunday evening, so what do you think? Should I run down and check it out? See if he's there or if he's told his cousin anything useful about the murder?"

"Might as well," Edwards said. Southport was less than forty minutes away. "I'll check out Jonah's again. See if I can pick up anything new there. And maybe Judge Knott will find the connection between him and Jeffreys. Somebody, somewhere's bound to have noticed something they haven't told us yet."

"Don't hold your breath," his partner said pessimistically.

CHAPTER
22

The proconsul will look into the truth of the facts you allege and will make it his care that no injustice is perpetrated.

—Caesar Augustus (63 BC–AD 14)

DETECTIVE GARY EDWARDS (TUESDAY AFTERNOON, JUNE 17)

Driving back into Wilmington, Edwards thought that the sky might be brightening up to the west even though the rain was as heavy as it had been when he crossed the causeway earlier in the day.

Despite the rain, determined tourists were thick along the Riverwalk. A long line of umbrellas waited in front of the information booth at Market and Water Streets and another line had formed at the trolley car stop. The shops down at Chandler's Wharf were busy, too, as people darted from one storefront to another as if trying to run between the raindrops. The parking lot at Jonah's was full and he had to drive well past the row of waterfront restaurants before he found an empty space.

His black umbrella had a broken rib, but it kept the worst of the rain off as he splashed across the cobblestones to Jonah's. He stood it in a corner of the porch, not much caring if it got stolen or not, and went inside, where the smell of deep-fried shrimp and hushpuppies almost made him forget the big breakfast he'd eaten earlier.

Between the air-conditioned interior and the warm summer rain outside, the windows overlooking the Riverwalk were too fogged up for him to see the water.

Although it was now almost 2:30, the restaurant's main room was at least half full of customers who dawdled over coffee or dessert before plunging back out into the rain. At the bar, more people nursed beer mugs or wineglasses and watched a baseball game being played somewhere under clear blue skies while four or five members of the waitstaff and the bartender chatted off to the side, all the time keeping a watchful eye on their stations in case someone should call for the bill.

The manager was there at the reception stand when Edwards entered and he gave the detective a sour look. "What now?"

"I'm still trying to find Kyle Armstrong. You hear from him yet?"

He waited till the manager finished his rant about inconsiderate, unreliable help and then said, "He seems to have skipped town. You have any idea why?"

The manager gave him a shrewd look. "Hey, you don't think he had anything to do with that judge getting killed, do you?"

"What do you think?"

"Kyle? Naw. It's gotta be a coincidence. He's been

talking about Hollywood from the day I first hired him. Maybe he finally just up and went."

"Maybe," Edwards said. "When's payday?"

"Friday."

"So you still owe him money for the weekend?"

"Two shifts. Yeah. Saturday dinner and Sunday lunch."

"Seems to me if I was taking off for LA, I'd get every penny owing me first."

"That's you," the manager said. "Kyle's a space cadet."

"All the same, I want to talk to everybody who was here Saturday night, starting with you."

"Me? I wasn't on the floor and I left around eight."

"Yeah? You didn't come out to welcome the judges or ask them how everything was?"

"I'm not that kind of a manager. I make sure everything's running smoothly behind the scenes and leave the front to whoever's working this reception stand. Unless there's a major problem, I don't come out."

While the manager continued to insist he did not normally interact with the customers, Edwards glanced around and decided that the empty side room was as good a place as any to conduct his interviews. It was separated from the main room by a waist-high wall topped by glass windows that went up to the ceiling so that there was plenty of light and he would not be overheard by the diners. "How about we talk in there?"

"It's set up for a tour group that's coming in at five," said the manager, "but yeah, I reckon you can use it, long as you don't mess it up too much. Who you want to start with?"

"Who do you have?"

The manager looked around. "There's Mandy, but she was off this weekend. Mel was here. I think she and Kyle got into it a little. Hank was working reception. Art, Clarence, and Mike, of course, at the bar."

"Tell me about Mel. How long's she been working here?"

"Just since the season started. Same for most of them. Kyle's been here about three years. He and Mike both. They work year-round."

"You say Kyle and this Mel mixed it up? Why?"

"Who knows? I'll send her in and you can ask her yourself, okay?"

"No, let me talk first to the guy that was working reception. Hank? He the one I spoke to Sunday?"

The manager nodded.

"Yeah, we worked the lunch shift Sunday," said the waiter. "You came to ask us about the judge that got killed Saturday night, remember? He sat at Kyle's table."

Hank Barlow was as earnest as Edwards remembered from Sunday: clean-cut, neatly trimmed hair, polished shoes, crisp shirt. There were dark circles under his eyes today and he smothered a yawn as he sat down.

"Sorry. I thought I could sleep in this morning, but Sam called and said they were shorthanded and now it sounds like Kyle might not make it in this afternoon. Sam says you told him Kyle's left Wilmington?"

Edwards realized he should have told the manager to keep his mouth shut about that. Too late now.

"Did he tell you he was moving?"

Barlow shook his head and explained that this was his first summer working down here at the coast. "We usually head for the mountains but Mel thought the beach would make a good change."

"You go to school in Greensboro, right?"

"Yeah, UNCG."

"You or this Mel ever hear of Judge Jeffreys before Saturday night?"

Hank shook his head.

"What about Kyle? He in school?"

"Not that I know of."

"Are you guys friends? Hang out together?"

"Not really. I only met him last month. We drove out to the beach when I first got here, and we've gone for drinks at one of the clubs once or twice with some of the others, but he...well, all he wants to talk about is acting—what shows he's trying to get on, how they screwed up his tryout, or how people are always doing him dirt. It's all about him."

"Think back to Sunday morning," Edwards said. "Did you get the impression that he didn't want to admit that he had waited on Judge Jeffreys?" The younger man considered it and then shook his head. "Not really. I don't think people register on his radar unless they're connected to the movie or television industry."

"And the last time you saw him?"

"He got off Sunday afternoon at four. I was supposed to get off then, too, but I told Mandy I'd cover her dinner shift so she could go to a friend's wedding. I had a half-hour break, though, and Kyle asked me to give him a lift back to his place so that—"

"You gave him a lift? He didn't have his car?"

"No. He usually rides his bike over unless it's raining but the front tire had a slow leak and he didn't want to ride on it until he could fix it. He said he was going to patch it first and then he was going to drive down to Southport to see his cousin."

"Cousin?"

"Yeah. I think she's an invalid or something. He made it sound like it was a real drag, but at the same time like he ought to get a pat on the back for doing something nice for her."

"You really don't like him very much, do you?"

"He's okay. Just immature."

Edwards almost had to smile. Kyle Armstrong was nearly five years older than this serious young man.

"I dropped him at his place on Walnut Street a little after four and that's the last time I saw him."

"Who else doesn't like him here?"

"I don't think any of us particularly *dis*like him unless it's Mel. We all tend to help each other out in a pinch, but Kyle's pretty lazy unless it's somebody in television and then he's right there, Mr. Helpful and 'Can I get you water and do you want a lemon in it, sir?' He tried that Saturday night when Stone Hamilton and his friends were here. It was Mel's table and she almost had to beat him back with a stick to get him to butt out."

"Yeah," said Mel Garrett, the waitress who'd worked Stone Hamilton's table Saturday night. A rising senior at UNCG like Hank, she had jet-black hair streaked with fuchsia and a dirty mouth that she tried to control after apologizing for laying the F-word on him. ("Sam keeps telling me I've got to dial it back.") Like all the others, she knew that Armstrong had waited on the murdered judge and that he was now missing. It seemed to confirm her already negative opinion of him. "The little bastard's always trying to horn in if you get any of the Screen Gems people. And yeah, he has a temper on him. Sneaky as hell, too. You piss him off and he'll screw up your order if he can. Shift yours down on the list or mix up the drinks so your tables start complaining about the lousy service and stiff you on the tips."

"I've had to watch him," said the bartender. Of all the waitstaff, he had worked at Jonah's the longest. Almost three years now. Kyle had started a month or two after him. The rest came and went with the seasons. "I caught him trying to palm one of my tips and I told him if he ever did it again, I'd beat the crap out of him. But he'll sneak and mix up the drinks on a waiter's tray if he's ticked off at them."

"No," said Art Taylor, an English major at George Mason University, who had also worked the porch Saturday night. "I can't say I noticed that he paid much attention to that judge or any of the others either. Of course, I wasn't paying much attention to *him*."

"Sorry," said the other waiter, a pre-law student at Wake Forest, who had been on duty during the relevant time. "My tables were all in the bar area Saturday night. If Kyle was upset about anything, I didn't see it. Actually, I thought he was in a pretty good mood. Excited because a new casting director was here. I think he even got the director's card. And yeah, I did hit on him a week or two after I started work here. I thought he was going to punch me out. Talk about denial! Just as well though. He doesn't care about anybody except himself. No room between him and the mirror, if you know what I mean."

There was one more waitress who had worked the dinner shift Saturday night, but she would not be in till four. Edwards filled the time with questions for the rest of the staff even though they had not been on duty then.

Those who had spoken to Armstrong on Sunday were all under the impression that he had barely noticed Jeffreys.

"Could he be lying?" Edwards asked.

"Well, he *is* an actor," one young man said.

"He's not *that* good an actor," said another.

The bouncy little blonde who had been there when he came in that morning said that she had been off all weekend and that she didn't have much to do with Kyle anyhow. The only thing they ever talked about were their bicycles.

"Bicycles?"

"Yeah." Her twin blonde ponytails were tied with purple beads that bobbled up and down when she nodded her head. "I brought mine over with me from Charlotte. Thought it would help me stay in shape, y'know?"

And a very nice shape it was, thought Edwards, keeping a perfectly straight face.

"Does Kyle like to ride, too?"

"He thinks it's good exercise. Builds up his muscles. In fact, his bike is out there on the rack right now."

"Could you show me?" Edwards asked.

"Sure. Just let me tell Hank in case my table wants their check while I'm gone."

* * *

Out front, Jonah's porch took a jog at the far end where azaleas were thickly planted. Rainwater ran off the porch roof and splashed onto a bike rack that was almost hidden among the wet bushes. Tethered to the rack by a chain and padlock was an older model all-terrain bike with wide tires and a shiny green frame.

"I noticed it when I got here this morning," she said.

"I thought he didn't come to work yesterday."

"He didn't."

"But the bike—?"

"I figured he caught a ride home from work Sunday and just hasn't had a chance to come back for it."

"No. Hank Barlow said he drove Kyle and the bike both to his apartment Sunday because it had a leak in the tire. So Kyle must have ridden it back here sometime between Sunday evening and this morning."

"Whatever," the young woman said, evidently becoming bored with his speculation and heading back inside.

Edwards followed. "When did you last see him?" he asked.

"Friday maybe? When the shifts changed? He usually works the four-to-eleven dinner shift and I work the eleven-to-four lunch shift. Weekends can get a little crazy, y'know? Sam barks a lot but as long as everything's covered and we keep up with our hours, he doesn't really care if we switch off or double up. My girlfriend got married down in Southport this weekend, and Kyle and the others covered for me so that I could be off. He was supposed to work the dinner shift yesterday and he never showed. I thought maybe he'd gotten his time mixed up. Is he in trouble?"

"I'm afraid so. You and he friends?" She shrugged and her twin ponytails swayed back and forth. "I guess. As much as anybody here. He isn't much of a people person, y'know? Besides, I've got a boyfriend and Kyle...? I don't think he's into girls very much."

"Gay?"

"I don't know about gay. Just not very interested either way. He really, really wants to get into television. That's pretty much all he talks about, but he's not doing much to make it happen, y'know? Doesn't take classes. Doesn't try out for an internship. He does go on casting calls, and then he'll spend the rest of the week griping because someone always beats him out." She hesitated and her pretty little brow furrowed. "It's weird, though."

"What?" Edwards asked.

"He's really fussy about this bike. Keeps the frame waxed and everything oiled so it won't rust, y'know? It's not like him to leave it out in the rain without a cover on it."

Upon being asked, no one admitted seeing Kyle or his bike after Hank Barlow dropped him off in front of his apartment before coming back to work the Sunday evening shift.

When the final member of Saturday night's waitstaff checked in shortly before four, she could add nothing to what had already been said.

In the end, Edwards was left with the picture of a fiercely closeted, narcissistic loner and not a single hint as to why he would have killed Judge Peter Jeffreys.

CHAPTER
23

*To be learned in the law (jurisprudentia) is the know-
ledge of things divine and human, the science of the
just and the unjust.*

—Ulpian (ca. AD 170–228)

**DETECTIVE ANDY WALL (TUESDAY AFTERNOON,
JUNE 17)**

Using his car's GPS system and the address Kyle
Armstrong's aunt had given him, Andy Wall navig-
ated the narrow roads that branched away from River
Road, deeper into a swampy area of Brunswick County,
and turned at last into a rutted drive that curved through
a tunnel of live oaks and yaupon made even darker by
the rain clouds overhead. The branches scraped along
the side of the car and made him wince for the paint
job.

If the GPS had not sounded so sure of itself when
it said "Arrive at destination on right," he would have

backed out and tried somewhere else. Eventually the tunnel opened up into sky and water and a grassy yard in bad need of mowing, and he caught his breath. This was exactly the sort of lot he hoped to buy when he retired next spring: isolated, no near neighbors, on the Intracoastal Waterway so that his boat would have easy access to the Atlantic, yet sheltered from the worst of hurricanes and high water by one of the barrier islands.

A single-wide house trailer sat squarely in the middle of the yard and was shaded by five or six live oaks. If this were his lot, though, his first act of ownership would be to tow that trailer to the nearest landfill. There was a burn barrel off to the side, but trash was everywhere—cans, plastic bottles, sodden cardboard boxes, fast-food cartons. Dozens of flimsy plastic bags had caught in the bushes around the edges of the yard, and the trailer itself had a forlorn dilapidated air of neglect. The storm door had either fallen or been torn off its hinges and now stood propped against the side, a couple of screens lay on the ground, and one broken window had been patched with duct tape.

No red Geo. No car of any kind and no sign of life.

He drove across the yard, following faint signs of car ruts right up to the door, where he rolled down his window and blew his horn.

No response, but at least he was on the leeward side of the wind so that rain did not beat in on him.

He blew the horn again and this time he leaned on it for a full thirty seconds. Out on the waterway, a hundred or so feet away, a huge white yacht sounded its own horn as it passed, evidently thinking the detective's land blast was some sort of greeting.

Wall waited till the yacht had moved out of sight, then blew his horn again. At last the door cracked open and a gray-faced woman peered out at him with bleary eyes. Mrs. Rudd had told him that her daughter was the same age as Kyle Armstrong.

Twenty-six.

This woman looked to be at least forty.

"Ms. Rudd?" he called. "Ms. Audrey Rudd?"

"Yeah. Who're you? Mama send you? You got somethin' for me?"

As he got out of the car and started up the shallow wooden steps, she drew back and began to close the door. He quickly pulled out his badge. "Detective Wall, Ms. Rudd. I need to ask you some questions about your cousin. Kyle Armstrong."

"Kyle? What about him?"

"Could I come in and talk to you a minute?"

She shook her head. "No, you don' wanna come in here."

From the odor of stale bourbon and general decay that met his nose, he was ready to agree with her. There was an overhang above the door. Too small to be called a proper porch roof, it did keep the worst of the rain off and he decided it was better to get a little wet than to have his clothes permeated with a smell it would take dry cleaning to get rid of.

"Can you tell me when you last saw your cousin, Ms. Rudd?"

She looked at him blankly. "He's not here."

"I know, but he was here this weekend, right?"

"Mama give you some money to give me?" With dirty fingernails she scratched at her scalp and her unbuttoned shirt fell open to reveal a chest so thin that every detail of her collarbone and upper rib cage could be seen above a pair of flaccid breasts. It could have been the chest of a starving refugee in Darfur.

"No, Ms. Rudd," he said gently. Disgust mingled with pity. "But she told me she sent you some food and things when your cousin came a couple of days ago."

"Oh, yeah...tha's right. Kyle."

"Did he talk to you about his job? About the restaurant?"

"Jonah's. He's a waiter at Jonah's."

Wall took a deep breath and willed himself to be patient. "That's right, Ms. Rudd. He works at Jonah's. Did he talk to you about it when he was here?"

"I gotta sit down," she said and pushed past him to lower herself to the top step.

She seemed oblivious to the rain and he realized that she was probably too deep into her alcoholic haze to give him anything useful. Nevertheless...

"Where was he going when he left here, Audrey? Did he say?"

She lifted her face to the warm rain and smiled; and for a moment, he could almost see the young woman inside this physical wreck.

"What did he tell you, Audrey?"

After a long career on the force, he should not have been shocked by the string of profanities that spewed from her mouth, but he was. Equally unexpected was the way her face crumpled with grief.

"Tha's what he said I was," she wept. "Tha's what he called me. And then he got in his car and said he was never coming back. Never—ever—*ever*."

"Let me help you back in the house," he said, taking her arm. "You're getting soaked."

She flinched away from him. "Go away!" she sobbed. "Leave me alone."

She drew her skeletal legs up under her chin and buried her face in her arms. The rain beat against her bowed head and turned her unkempt hair into snakelike strands that seemed to writhe in the wind and wet.

With nothing to be gained by staying, Andy Wall got back in his car, turned it around, and drove out of the yard. Just before the tunnel of yaupon and live oaks closed in around him, he glanced back in his rearview mirror. Another big expensive boat was passing, but she hadn't moved.

He gave a weary sigh, knowing that one of these days the Brunswick County sheriff's office would get a call that buzzards were circling this trailer and "y'all really need to send somebody out here to take a look."

CHAPTER
24

*Whenever a judicial investigation cannot be made
without injury, the course should be adopted which is
productive of the least unfairness.*

—*Javolenus (ca. AD 86)*

**Detective Gary Edwards (Tuesday afternoon,
June 17)**

Between the rain and the tourists, it took Detective
Edwards longer than usual to clear downtown traffic
and get onto the MLK Parkway, the quickest route out to
Wrightsville Beach. Once on it, he had just set the cruise
control when the lanes ahead started to back up. Bad
wreck or fender bender? He queried the dispatcher, but
nothing had been reported yet, so he inched along, playing the usual mind game: get off at the next exit or hope it
would soon clear? Happily, the cause was around the very
next bend—a shiny new Prius hybrid with warning lights
flashing. Its hapless driver and passenger were pushing it

onto the shoulder. No smashed fender, no second car involved.

Edwards put on his own flashers and pulled alongside the tall white-haired man who was puffing from exertion, and lowered his window. "Out of gas?"

"Yeah, dammit! It was supposed to get at least another twelve miles."

"Need help?"

"Not unless you've got a gas can," the man said, wiping rain from his face with his wet shirtsleeve. "It's okay. I've called somebody."

Edwards notified the dispatcher in case anyone else called in about the delay and waited with his lights flashing till they had the car completely off the highway and well onto the shoulder before he accelerated past. He grinned as he remembered a friend up in Raleigh who had called Triple A when his new hybrid conked out on him several miles from home. Jim was embarrassed as hell when the wrecker showed up and its driver declared that there was nothing mechanically wrong with the car, only that it was out of gas, several miles per gallon short of what his indignant friend expected. The driver gave him a gallon of gas, more than enough to get him to the next station, but Jim was sure it would be enough to get him back to his favorite service station.

It wasn't.

It should comfort Jim to learn he was not the only one who suffered from a syndrome Edwards was starting to call hybrid overoptimism.

According to the conference schedule Judge Knott had shown him, the judges were due to adjourn for the day at 5:30, so there was no need to speed along Eastwood, which naturally ensured that he would catch green lights all the way. As he pulled into the parking lot at the SandCastle Hotel, his pager went off.

"Hey, Gary," Andy Wall said. "Just got a call. They've located our red Geo with the South Carolina 'Share the Road' plate."

"Yeah. Where?"

"North of town on I-40. The Castle Hayne exit. Sounds like it ran off the westbound ramp and crashed into some trees. They haven't ID'd the driver yet, but he's dead."

Expediting with lights and siren, Gary Edwards got to the Castle Hayne exit only a few minutes after Andy Wall. Whether it was the rain or the inconvenient location, the usual curiosity seekers were missing when he arrived. He parked his car behind one of the cruisers and half-walked, half-slid down the steep incline to the crash site, unimpeded by rubberneckers. The grass was so wet and slippery that he almost lost his balance a couple of times before reaching level ground. Despite his umbrella's broken rib, it served its purpose with a certain dignity; but the troopers who wore standard rain gear seemed much amused by Andy Wall, who sheltered beneath a dainty floral umbrella with a pink ruffle that lent a rosy glow to his face.

It was so reminiscent of the parasols carried by the Azalea Queen's court that Edwards couldn't resist. "Gee, Andy, I thought the Azalea Festival was two months ago."

"Don't you start, too," he groused. "My wife took my umbrella this morning and this is the only one I could find."

"So what've we got?"

"The troopers think he must've gone off during last

night's heaviest rain," Wall told him as they looked down on the twisted and crumpled pile of red metal, all that remained of the little red hatchback.

"Yeah," said the nearer officer. "Looks like he misjudged the angle of the curve and was accelerating instead of braking. Either that or the brakes didn't catch and he just hydroplaned over. No skid marks. Not that we'd expect them with all the rain we've had."

They automatically glanced upward. The rain had finally begun to ease off and they could see a patch of blue through an opening in the western clouds. Wall furled his frothy umbrella and used it as a walking stick as they eased themselves down closer to the car, half hidden in a tangle of yaupon and sturdy pines.

A lifeless body was tightly pinned between the steering wheel and the roof. Through the crushed windshield they could make out part of the face, which was cut and torn.

"Not much blood," Edwards observed.

"Probably washed away by the rain," said Wall, looking at the headshots Mrs. Rudd had given him, the wannabe actor's publicity photos. "Is it Armstrong?"

"Looks like him to me," Edwards said as he tried to reconcile this battered face to the man he had met briefly on Sunday. In the pictures Armstrong's chin was as weak as he remembered, but thrust forward like this, in three-quarter profile, it managed to convey a certain sensitive strength.

Too bad, thought Edwards, that he had heard nothing today to indicate an ounce of sensitivity for others. To strangle a man, dump his body in a crab-infested river, and then run down another man in front of his wife?

"He hit that tree with one hell of a force," the trooper said. "It's gonna take the jaws to get him out in one piece. Wasn't wearing a seat belt, either."

"You really think a seat belt would've helped?" Edwards asked.

The trooper nodded. "Naw, probably not."

The bushes were strewn with sodden clothes, CDs, and bits of speakers and players from the waiter's sound system. It looked as if he had piled all his worldly goods into the back of the car without any rhyme or reason in his haste to leave town.

"Probably planned to stay with his aunt overnight," said Wall, who had given him a condensed version of his trip out to see Armstrong's cousin. "Maybe he wanted to hit her up for some cash before clearing out. She told me that she helps him out when he comes up short."

"Who found him?"

"The traffic helicopter called it in," answered the trooper. "Saw the wreckage and asked if we knew about it. Detective Wall here says you think this is yesterday's hit-and-run?"

"Yeah. So pay attention to the front right fender, okay? And copy us on all the pictures and reports."

The rain had stopped completely by the time they climbed back up the slope, but the ground was so muddy that the pink umbrella was a wreck where Wall had jabbed it in the ground to help haul himself up.

"One good thing," Wall said. "He's saved the state the cost of putting him on trial and then keeping him in prison for the next thirty years."

"Yeah," Edwards agreed. "Just hope we find out why he killed Jeffreys before they pull us off the case. I can understand running down Fitzhume. He was afraid the judge could place the two of them in the restroom right before the murder, but what was his beef with Jeffreys in the first place?"

"Who knows?" Wall said, and glanced at his watch. "I'll run by the office and get the paperwork started and then call it a day. What about you?"

"I think I'll stop by the hospital and tell Mrs. Fitzhume and then maybe ride back out to the beach, see if Judge Knott's learned of a link between Armstrong and Jeffreys."

Andy Wall smiled at the younger man. "And maybe ask her friend out to dinner now that the case is practically closed?"

"Maybe."

CHAPTER
25

*It is declared...that all marriages contracted by law-
ful persons in the face of the church, and consum-
mated with bodily knowledge, and fruit of children,
shall be indissoluble.*

—*Sir William Blackstone (1723–1780)*

Our last session of the day was a lively update on family law by Cheryl Howell, a brainy blonde professor
from the School of Government.

Just as Nina Totenberg can clarify and explain to her
NPR audience the most arcane rulings of the Supreme
Court, so Cheryl manages to make the acts of our legislature sound almost logical. There are times, though,
when the lack of clarity in the specific language of a
statute causes a disconnect between what the new legisla-
tion is supposed to do and what it actually appears to do.
Last year we spent an inordinate amount of time on civil
no-contact orders (restraining orders in cases other than
domestic violence situations). Stalking had earlier been
defined as, and I quote, "Following on more than one occasion or otherwise harassing."

What we needed to know was if the "more than one occasion" applied to harassing or only to the act of following. Could we issue a civil restraining order after one harassment or must it be at least twice?

At such times, even Cheryl throws up her hands and says, "You'll just have to use your best judgment on this until it comes before the high court and they make a ruling on it."

It's the ever-recurring sticky flypaper between what is meant and what is said, which is why we have a Supreme Court still parsing the words of our Constitution more than two hundred years later. Did the framers mean that every citizen could own an assault rifle? Does free speech include hate speech? Does freedom *of* religion include freedom *from* religion?

On a more mundane level, today's thorny issue was parent versus nonparent custody and visitation, as modified by the appellate court's recent rulings on third-party custody—in other words, the rights, if any, of stepparents, grandparents, blood relations, or any other third parties who have been ceded (or *thought* they had been ceded) a parent-like relationship to the child by its natural parent.

It's hard enough making custody and visitation decisions when you start with a traditional two-parent family unit and the third party is a grandparent. Stir in lovers who claim they did all the parenting, or a sibling who's been raising the children for years, or same-sex couples who are breaking up with the same regularity as heterosexual couples, and you've got a witch's brew of tricky complications.

We were still arguing about certain aspects of the case studies Cheryl had brought us and comparing how we had ruled on similar issues as we spilled out into the lobby at 5:30 and headed up to Room 628 for drinks.

The rain had finally stopped and when the balcony doors were thrown wide, everyone crowded outside to ooh over a vivid rainbow that seemed to touch down in the ocean.

Chuck Teach pointed to that spot and said, "Somebody get me a boat. That pot of gold can't be more than twenty feet under the water."

"Anybody heard from Martha?" I asked.

"Yeah, I talked to her at the break," said Andy Corbett, the chief judge over in the next district from mine. "No change. Fitz is still in a coma and still in intensive care."

Across the room, Roberta Ouellette was opening a can of soda and I went over to her. She gave a friendly smile and said, "Interesting session, wasn't it? But I'm sorry. I do think that a blood relationship gives automatic standing and if grandparents want to see their grandchildren on a regular basis and they aren't pedophiles or raving lunatics, I'm going to keep trying to let them. Children can't have too much love in their lives."

"I agree," I said, adding a light splash of bourbon to my own diet cola. "And what about godparents? There's often no blood relationship."

"True," she sighed. "But again, don't you find that a little judicial reasoning can sometimes mitigate a vindictive parent's desire to cut all ties to the past relationship?"

We took our drinks out to the terrace and leaned against the railing to enjoy the return of sunshine. Big patches of blue sky appeared amid the retreating clouds and our rainbow had faded into nothingness.

"When you were telling us how Pete Jeffreys gave custody of that burned child to his father and stepmother, you didn't mention that he was Bill Hasselberger's godson," I said.

Ouellette looked surprised and pleased. "Bill Hasselberger? You know Bill?"

I nodded. "He and a cousin of mine were at Jonah's the other night. Or rather, on the porch of the restaurant next door to Jonah's."

"What's he doing now, do you know? I've lost track of him since he left the bench."

"He's in private practice down here. Has a house in Wilmington."

"Bless his heart. It really all came down on him, didn't it? Losing his election, losing his wife. But I didn't know that little boy was his godson."

"I don't think he talks about it much. But what about the other cases Jeffreys mishandled?" I asked. "You're from the Triad area. Anybody here have a personal involvement with, say, the carjacker or the DWI cases that got dismissed?"

She gave me an amused smile. "Have you traded your robe for a detective's badge?"

"Nope," I said cheerfully. "Just terminally curious as to why someone killed him down here rather than in Greensboro."

Her smile turned serious. "You honestly think it was one of us?"

"Not really." I hesitated. Detective Edwards hadn't told me not to mention the waiter, and if he'd told Martha Fitzhume, then it was a safe bet everyone else would soon know. "Does the name Kyle Armstrong mean anything to you?"

Ouellette shook her head. "Who's he?"

"A waiter at Jonah's. Owns the car that ran Fitz down."

She frowned. "He killed Judge Jeffreys and then tried to kill Judge Fitzhume? Why?"

"I was hoping you might've have heard of a connection to them."

She turned the name over again. "Kyle Armstrong? Sorry. Have you tried Joe Turner or Bill Neely?"

Both were chief judges in neighboring Triad districts. I'd actually spoken to both of them during the afternoon break and had gotten equally blank looks. But the Triad stretches from Winston to Greensboro to High Point and holds over a million people. Even though the judicial community is relatively small and gossipy, how likely was it that any judge would know another's enemy? Especially if that enemy was a seemingly innocuous waiter with aspirations to stardom?

All sorts of fantastic scenarios scrolled through my head. Maybe there wasn't a connection between Jeffreys and the waiter. Maybe it really was a local, someone like Hasselberger, who killed Jeffreys in the heat of the moment and then stole Armstrong's car to run down Fitz. If the waiter was a cyclist, wouldn't he normally leave his car parked somewhere for days on end and ride his bike back and forth to work? I myself have never actually hotwired a car, but most of my brothers know how.

As does Allen.

Allen?

"*Oh, please!*" said the preacher, who was getting tired of this fruitless round and round. "*He had his children with him that night, remember?*"

"*Yeah, but he left early enough that he could have*

brought the children back here to the hotel and then returned to the parking lot," said the pragmatist, who couldn't leave it alone. *"If Fitz saw him, Allen could've read the schedule at his leisure and would've known when Fitz would be crossing the parking lot."*

"And what's his motive for killing Jeffreys?"

"How the hell do I know? I'm looking at opportunity right now."

"Half of Wilmington had opportunity. Give me a motive."

By now Roberta Ouellette had been swept into a conversation with Shelley Desvouges and Yates Dobson, who were looking at pictures of Aubrey Hamilton's cats. I dumped my unfinished drink and decided to get out of the hotel for a while.

When I stepped out of the elevator into the hotel lobby, I saw Detective Gary Edwards standing by the touching tank that had been abandoned by the child guests now that the sun was out again.

He smiled at me and returned a sand dollar to the tank. 'I was hoping I'd see you."

"Wish I had some information for you," I said, "but if there's a connection between Kyle Armstrong and Pete Jeffreys, I can't find it. Any luck locating him or his car?"

"Unfortunately." With a grim face he told me that Kyle Armstrong was dead.

I was shocked. "What happened?"

"Looks like he loaded up all his things and was going to skip town when he ran off an exit ramp near Castle Hayne and crashed into a tree. If you and Chel—I mean, Judge Pierce—haven't picked up on anything substantive, I doubt if we'll ever learn why he killed the judge."

"So that's it? You're closing the case?"

"As soon as we get the autopsy results and write the report." His eyes strayed past my shoulder and his face lit up.

I turned and saw Chelsea Ann emerge from the elevator, her blonde curls shiny, fresh lipstick and eye shadow, a lowcut yellow dress with a swirly skirt. She carried my white cotton sweater over one arm.

"Hope you don't mind if I borrow it for one more night," she said, smiling up at Edwards. "Gary and I are going to take a dinner cruise."

"Have fun," I said.

Other colleagues came by on their way out to dinner or to gatherings further down the island and several invited me to join them, but I had other plans.

I stopped by an ATM to replenish the cash in my wallet and twenty minutes later I was in the ICU waiting room at the New Hanover Medical Center. I was not the first judge to come by that evening, but none of them had been able to persuade Martha Fitzhume to break her vigil. She had been there since sunrise, almost as if it were her personal willpower that was keeping Fitz alive. I was encouraged to hear that his condition had been upgraded from *critical* to *serious* even though he was still in a coma.

Martha herself was moving a little stiffly after the tumble she had taken. One of the nurses had given her an antiseptic ointment for the scrape on her face and it was starting to fade a bit, but there were dark circles under her eyes.

She told me that Gary Edwards had been by earlier and had told her of Kyle Armstrong's death.

"Maybe I'll be able to pray for him later," Martha said. "Right now I'm still so angry for what he did to Fitz that there's not an ounce of pity in my heart."

"Come on, Martha," I said. "You need to get out of here for an hour and breathe a little fresh air. The rain's stopped and it's a beautiful evening. Come have supper with me. We'll go eat a crab in Fitz's honor."

That got a smile and her son chimed in.

"Yeah, Mom. Go. You could use a break and I'll be right here till you get back."

"I don't know, Chad. What if he—?" She stood up as if to come, then sat back down a moment later. "I don't think I should. I'm not very hungry."

Chad shook his head. "C'mon, Mom. It's not going to help Dad for you to keep skipping meals."

I was surprised and saddened to see her this indecisive. It was so unlike Martha to dither. She stood again. "You'll call me if there's any change?"

"I'll call," he said patiently.

"All right then. Let me just take one more look at him," she said. "Do you want to see him, Deborah?"

It was as bad as I'd imagined. Poor Fitz had a huge bruise on the side of his pale face and there seemed to be a dozen different tubes and wires attached to his body—drainage tubes from his surgery, an IV drip to keep him hydrated, catheter, heart monitor, and God knows what else.

"His color's so much better tonight," Martha said to the nurse. "Don't you think?"

"I do," the nurse said kindly.

Martha walked over to him, took his hand, and in a normal tone of voice said, "Deborah's here to see you, sweetheart. Can you open your eyes and say hey to her?"

To my total amazement, not to mention Martha's, Fitz's eyelids fluttered and actually opened. He tried to speak but his words were unintelligible. He squeezed Martha's hand and tried again.

"It's okay, sweetheart," Martha crooned with tears in her eyes. "You're in the hospital. You got hit by a car but you're going to be all right."

The nurse who was monitoring him came over to the other side and fiddled with the dials on the equipment. "How you doing, Judge Fitzhume?"

More slurred syllables, then his eyes closed again and his grip loosened.

"His blood pressure and pulse rate are looking better," the nurse said. "And his heartbeat's almost back to normal."

Martha was more reluctant than ever to leave, but the nurse finally convinced her that Fitz needed to rest undisturbed after his first exertion. "For all we know about comas, he could be wide awake tomorrow morning or it may take him another few weeks, but I think the doctor will say this is encouraging."

It was a little after seven before we got to a nearby seafood restaurant recommended by the nurse.

When we were seated and a waiter came over to bring us our menus, Martha didn't look up while he told us that his name was Michael and that he'd be our waiter and if there was anything special we needed—

"I'll have a vodka collins," she interrupted coldly. "What about you, Deborah?"

"A glass of Riesling, please."

When he had gone away to get our drinks, Martha said, "Between Kyle the actor and Jenna the slut, I'm through making nice to waiters. From now on, I don't give a damn where they go to school or what they want to do when they finish growing up. If you hear me ask this Michael one single thing other than if the soft-shelled crabs are fresh or frozen, please kick me."

I laughed. The old Martha was back.

We were assured that the crabs were indeed fresh and we both ordered them. When they came, Martha dug into hers with relish.

"I guess I was hungrier than I realized," she said sheepishly.

Fitz's attempt to speak had her almost giddy with relief.

"I don't mind telling you, Deborah. I've been really, really scared."

"Of course you were. Who wouldn't be?"

"I know that Fitz and I are down to the short rows—no, don't look at me like that. Death is a fact of life, sugar. I'm not being morbid and I don't need you or anybody else to pat my hand and tell me that these are the best years. They're not. The best years were when the kids were little and there was a lifetime of those golden possibilities ahead for Fitz and me. Things to do, places to go, young bodies and young muscles to go and do with. No arthritis, no daily pills, life stretching out endlessly before us." She finished her vodka collins in two swallows. "No, these sure as hell are *not* the best years. All the same, they're *our* years and every minute is still precious.

Everything ends. That's life. But for that—that *creature* to try and kill Fitz to cover up what he'd done? I hope he's roasting in hell."

Michael breezed over about then. "Everything all right here?" he asked cheerily.

Martha held up her empty glass. "Another one of these, please."

They both glanced at my wineglass. It was still half full.

"I'm driving," I said.

When we finished eating and the bill came, Martha insisted on paying.

"Then I'll leave the tip," I said.

I opened my wallet to fish out some bills and a small slip of paper floated to the floor. It was the ATM receipt.

Martha saw me frown and asked, "Something wrong, sugar?"

"Not really," I answered.

What I had remembered could wait. No point in wrecking Chelsea Ann's evening by calling Detective Edwards in the middle of their supper cruise, and it probably wasn't important anyhow.

CHAPTER
26

One must look…to the simple credibility of the witnesses and to the testimony in which the light of truth most probably resides.

—*Justinian (AD 483–565)*

At the hospital, I went back in with Martha on the off chance that Fitz was wide awake and I could ask him about who he'd seen Saturday night.

He wasn't. But his doctor had been by and had, as the nurse predicted, told Chad that he was much encouraged by the slight improvement in Fitz's vital signs.

Reid was there in the ICU waiting room with Chad and a couple of Fitz's colleagues from the district who had known Chad since he was a teenager, when his father first came on the bench.

While Martha immediately went in to see Fitz, Chad said, "I asked the doctor if there was any chance that Dad would remember what happened to him." A law professor at USC, he had naturally been very interested in learning that Fitz had probably been targeted because he could have named Kyle Armstrong as the last person to see Jeffreys alive. "He won't remember the accident itself, of course."

"No," I agreed. "It all happened so fast and besides, he had his back to the car. He never saw it coming. What about earlier, though?"

"Very iffy, according to the doctor. He might remember everything up to the moment of impact or he might not remember anything past last month." He gave an unhappy palms-up shrug. "Or for the last ten years for that matter, but I don't want Mom worrying about that possibility till he's conscious and we can know for sure where we stand."

I walked out of the hospital with Reid. The trial lawyers' conference had ended that afternoon and he was on his way back to Dobbs. It was still early, however, and he was in no particular hurry. There was no one waiting for him at the moment.

"There's a place down on the river. Why don't I buy you a drink before I hit the road?"

"Okay," I said. "I'll follow you."

I'm not particularly squeamish, but I admit I had a moment's hesitation when Reid pulled into the parking lot where Pete Jeffreys had been killed Saturday night. I did park right at the front, though, instead of following Reid to the far end under the mulberry trees. Nor did I look for signs of police activity when we passed the spot on the riverbank where I had found the body.

Small tables were scattered around the rear entrance to a bar a hundred feet or so further up the Riverwalk from Jonah's. A live jazz piano was playing inside and the mellow notes spilled out to the half dozen people who were there to enjoy the music and the soft evening air. Small boats passed back and forth on the river and we could see the lights of an oil tanker moored upriver across the way. The moon had not yet cleared the roofline of the buildings on our side of the river, but it already illuminated the marshy opposite bank where dilapidated pilings marked a line of once-busy piers. Downriver, more lights crossed the high arching bridge. A funky aroma rose from the water itself, a combination of tidal flats, mud, and decaying vegetation, a yeasty summer smell that almost made me want to wade out and set some crab pots.

I sighed and settled happily into a roomy wicker chair and when someone came out to take our order, I said, "Regular coffee, please. No cream or sugar."

"Really?" asked Reid.

"Really."

"Well, in that case..." He smiled up at the waitress. "I don't suppose you have desserts?"

"Just pie. Pecan and key lime."

"Deborah?"

"Not for me."

"Okay. Espresso and a piece of pecan pie."

After the waitress left us, Reid said, "Thanks for not telling that detective about Bill's godson."

"No need to thank me. I would have had to if it wasn't pretty clear that our waiter was the one who killed Jeffreys."

"Yeah, well, I knew Bill couldn't kill anybody and once they find that guy—"

"Didn't you hear?" I asked.

"Hear what?"

"He crashed off I-40 up near Castle Hayne in the rain last night and killed himself."

"No kidding!"

I told him as much as I knew from Detective Edwards's brief account. "But they still don't know *why* he killed Pete Jeffreys, not that I think that's going to keep them awake at night. There doesn't seem to be any link between them. Jeffreys was from the Triad and evidently Armstrong was never further east in the state than Kinston. Any chance your friend Bill knows?"

"I doubt it."

The pie and coffees came. The pie had been warmed and topped with a scoop of vanilla maple ice cream. The smell of that nutty custard mingled with vanilla made my mouth water. Reid offered me a bite—"It's as good as Aunt Zell's"—but I'd eaten hushpuppies *and* fried crabs that night and I managed to resist.

As I sipped my coffee and the pianist inside segued from "Once Upon a Summertime" to a bluesy "Moon River," Reid talked about his long friendship with Hasselberger, Hasselberger's decency, his sense of humor.

"Is he good with his hands?" I asked casually.

"How do you mean?"

"You know. Can he build shelves? Rewire a lamp? Tune his car?"

Reid laughed. "I think he may know how to top off the windshield washer fluid, but I wouldn't count on it. He's like me. His favorite tools are a phone and the yellow pages."

I smiled. Reid's ineptitude with anything mechanical is legendary in our family. My brothers, who amongst them will tackle anything from a toaster to a hay baler, just shake their heads.

So there went the nebulous theory that Hasselberger

might have hot-wired Armstrong's Geo and gone gunning for Fitz. Even if the police were satisfied that Armstrong had acted alone, the final nail in that particular coffin came when Reid mentioned some mutual friends he and Hasselberger had gone out to supper with down in Sunset Beach last night before driving back to Wilmington together long after 6:30.

As we walked back down the Riverwalk, we saw the cruise boat drifting up toward us and stopped to watch.

"Dotty and I did that once," he sighed, the moonlight making him nostalgic. "Dinner and dancing on the river."

He hadn't had anything to drink, so I didn't have to worry about him getting maudlin. Dotty was remarried now, but Reid would always mourn the end of their marriage even though it was his endless catting around that finally drove her to leave him.

We reached the parking lot and he pulled out his keys and jingled them in his hand. "So when's your conference end?"

"Thursday noon," I said.

"See you on Friday then?"

"Probably."

Reid's the closest thing I'll ever have to a younger brother, so I gave him a hug and told him to drive carefully.

The cruise ship passed and nosed into a dock further up the Riverwalk. I briefly considered circling around back to catch Edwards and Chelsea Ann as they came down the gangplank, but why interrupt their evening with something that probably had no significance?

I drove back to the SandCastle, parked the car, and went inside. Too restless to go straight to my room, yet not really in the mood for the shop talk that was bound to be going on up in 628, I went into the nearly deserted bar, ordered a nightcap, and took it outside to the terrace. Except for a couple on the far end, I had the place to myself. The moon was so huge and bright that I could have read a newspaper. Instead I took a sip of my icy drink and called Dwight. He had been back in his room almost an hour, he said, and had almost fallen asleep watching a baseball game.

"How's your judge friend?" he asked. "Did they catch the driver that hit him?"

Once again, I found myself describing how Armstrong had died.

"Wraps it up nice and tidy, doesn't it?" he said drowsily.

"Except that no one knows why he killed Judge Jeffreys."

"Can't have everything."

I heard him yawn and said, "Go to sleep, darling."

"Yeah, I'm a little beat. There's one more session tomorrow morning. A breakfast meeting, then I'll pick up Cal and head home. I'll have to give this phone back to Sandy, so it'll be tomorrow evening before I can call you."

"That's fine," I said. "I just wish I was going to be there when you get home. I've missed you."

"Not half as much as I've missed you, shug. I've been thinking. If Mama can keep Cal, how about I hitch a ride down to Wilmington on Thursday?"

"Really?" My heart was suddenly turning somersaults.

"Well, I haven't seen you in that new red bathing suit yet," he drawled, and from there the conversation took a decidedly different turn.

* * *

After we finally said good night, I continued to sit there in the moonlight, nursing my drink because I was too lazy to go in and order another.

For once, indolence and sloth were rewarded. I heard low voices and glanced over to see Chelsea Ann and Gary Edwards walking toward me with their own nightcaps.

"I thought that was you," she said. She held Edwards's drink while he pulled two more rocking chairs closer to mine to form a rough semicircle.

"How was the cruise?" I asked.

"Awful," Edwards said.

Chelsea Ann gave his arm a light poke. "No, it wasn't. But we almost didn't go."

"Why not?"

"It seems that cruising the river in the moonlight isn't enough. They have special entertainment every night." She giggled. "Guess what tonight's was?"

I shook my head.

"A murder mystery," Edwards groaned.

"You're kidding."

"I wish I was. I thought there would be dancing. Instead it was bad actors waving guns or running around with bloody knives, while everyone roared with laughter. Like murder's a funny joke."

"We found a place out on a deck that was away from all the mayhem," Chelsea Ann said. "It was beautiful. Very relaxing. I'm glad we went."

I noticed that his hand had found hers.

"Well, not to spoil the mood here, but something occurred to me this evening," I told Edwards. "The money in Pete Jeffreys's wallet. Didn't you say it was over two hundred dollars?"

"Yeah. About two-sixty, I think. Why?"

"Well, Judge Blankenthorpe said they stopped at an ATM on their way to Jonah's and he got three hundred dollars. That's why she was so annoyed that he stuck her with his dinner check. She knew he had cash. Unless they stopped somewhere else along the way, what happened to that forty dollars?"

Edwards frowned. "Wouldn't have been robbery. A thief wouldn't have left that much cash and the credit cards."

"Here's what I was thinking could have happened. Say he started the evening with only ten or fifteen dollars in his wallet, which is why he stopped at an ATM. With a couple of drinks, his dinner would have run around fifty dollars. What if he ran into Kyle Armstrong in the restroom and that's when they got into it? Then, instead of going back to the table, he pulls out his wallet and hands Armstrong enough cash to cover his bill and storms out the door to the parking lot. Armstrong kills him, pockets the money and goes back in and acts like nothing's happened."

Edwards thought about it a minute, then nodded. "I like it. Especially if—hey! Was Jeffreys gay by any chance?"

I shrugged and Chelsea Ann was equally unsure. "I haven't heard that he was, but I didn't know him, why?"

"Because one of the other waiters at Jonah's is. He says he tried to hit on Armstrong last month and almost got punched in the nose. What if Jeffreys came on so strong to him in the men's room that he freaked out?"

"Yes!" I said as the last piece of the puzzle snapped into place. "Armstrong did strike me as somebody so caught up in his own image that he didn't have a real firm grasp on reality."

"And if that image was one of total masculinity?" said Chelsea Ann, who's seen as many impulsive and self-delusional people in her court as I have.

Edwards leaned back in his rocker and smiled at us. "Finally! A reasonable motive for why he killed a man we couldn't prove he'd met before. Thanks, Your Honor."

"Call me Deborah," I said with a meaningful glance at their entwined fingers. "For some reason, I have this weird premonition that our paths are going to keep crossing."

"By the way," Chelsea Ann said sweetly. "What time's our first session tomorrow?"

"Oh, yeah, right," I said as I finished the last drops of my drink and stood up. "Sorry to have to say good night, but I really need my beauty sleep."

Hey, I can take a hint as quick as anybody. Especially when it's a hit over the head with a sledgehammer.

CHAPTER
27

Commodus made terms...for he hated all exertion and was eager for the comforts of the city.

—Dio Cassius *(ca. AD 230)*

I awoke to sunshine Wednesday morning and with the same sort of happy anticipation I used to get as a child on the day before my birthday, when I knew that there would soon be presents to unwrap.

The idea made me smile and I wondered if Dwight would mind being compared to a birthday present.

"He'd like the unwrapping part," snickered the pragmatist.

"Don't you have to be downstairs in twenty minutes?" asked the preacher.

"Yikes!" I said and jumped out of bed.

Fortunately I'd showered last night, so I had time to snag a peach Danish and a cup of coffee before sliding into a seat between Shelly Holt and Becky Blackmore about half a minute before Beth Keever began her presentation on "Child Support: Deviation Review and Enforcement."

Four concurrent sessions ran from 8:30 to ten, then repeated from 10:30 to noon, with the afternoon free. We
were supposed to attend two of the eight sessions.

At the ten o'clock break, the lobby buzzed with news
that Jeffreys's killer had died in a car crash.

"Poetic justice that he tried to kill Fitz with his car and
wound up killing himself with it," said some.

"Remember when Jeffreys said his opponent was
gay?" Chuck Teach said. "I'm starting to wonder if guys
who make a big deal out of that aren't launching a pre-
emptive strike."

"The best defense is usually an offense," one of his
listeners agreed.

Another nodded. "Like my mama always said: you
point your finger at somebody, you got three fingers
pointing back at *you*."

Unspoken was the relief that the killer had been
someone else. Not one of us.

At 10:30, as I started into the room for "Criminal Senten-
cing Resources," I saw Will Blackstone and his bruised
face headed that way, too. As soon as our eyes met, he
abruptly changed course and detoured into the session on
gangs and gang crimes.

I decided not to take it personally.

Upon adjournment, I immediately drove over to the
hospital. I had told Martha that I would be by to take her
to lunch and when I arrived she was positively radiant.

"Come see Fitz!" she said and practically dragged me
into the unit.

He was awake and he smiled when he saw me. "Hey,
Deborah."

His voice was weak and he was still groggy from so many drugs, but it was definitely Fitz. When I leaned over to kiss him, he said, "Martha says y'all're going out to lunch?"

I nodded.

"Watch out for cars," he said drily.

If he hadn't been so encumbered with tubes and wires, I would have hugged him. "Want us to bring you a nice crisp softie?" I teased.

"I'd better take a rain check." His eyelids drooped. "Sorry. I can't seem to keep awake."

"You rest, sweetheart," Martha said, patting the hand that didn't have an IV attached to it. "Chad's right outside and we'll be back in an hour."

"Take your time," he murmured as his eyes closed again.

"They're going to move him into a room this afternoon," Martha said. "And if he continues to improve, we can transfer him to a hospital nearer home in a few days."

She told me that Gary Edwards had been by that morning to bring them up to date on Kyle Armstrong's death and his probable motive for killing Judge Jeffreys.

"All because the judge made a pass at him? I should think he would have been flattered. As I recall, Pete Jeffreys was rather handsome and Kyle was decidedly *not.*"

Unfortunately, Fitz had no real memory of going to the restroom or of seeing Jeffreys or the waiter. He rather thought that he had, but he couldn't be certain and Martha quit pushing him.

"What difference does it make now?" she asked.

* * *

After last night's fried food, we were both in the mood for a fresh green salad and some crusty bread. Martha knew of just the place over on Oleander Drive.

"Best of all, it's near a good used-book store," she said. "I want something to read besides last year's *Newsweek* and *Golf Digest*."

The restaurant was in a small shopping center and had a salad bar to die for. We piled on locally grown baby spinach, arugula, oak leaf lettuce, and mustard greens, topped them with cherry tomatoes that actually tasted vine-ripened, then took our plates out to a wisteria-shaded patio. It was a typical June day, warm but not too muggy. Yesterday's rain had washed the air so clean that it almost squeaked.

"I hope you appreciate how upscale North Carolina's getting to be," I said. "Did you notice that there wasn't a single shred of iceberg lettuce on that counter?"

"Fine with me," said Martha, who looked more rested today. "I ate enough for the whole South when I was growing up. So how's the conference going? Am I missing any good gossip?"

"Doesn't seem to be much," I told her.

"Really?" She looked at me skeptically over her sunglasses. "Joy Hamilton told me that one of the judges was walking around with a very suspicious black eye."

"Oh?"

"Will Blackstone. From 19-B, I think she said. I don't know him. Do you?"

"We've met," I admitted. "And he really does have a shiner. I heard he slipped and fell in the bathroom."

"Not what I heard," she sniffed. "Jane Harper said John Smith saw him come off the beach the other night with a bloody nose."

"Maybe he ran into a piling. Or a pelican." I dribbled some dressing over my salad and pushed back from the table. "I think I want some grated cheese. Bring you anything?"

"Well, as long as you're going, a few bacon bits would be nice."

By the time I got back to the table, she had forgotten all about Will Blackstone and his black eye.

After lunch, we drove a few short blocks to McAllister and Solomon, a used- and rare-book store on Wrightsville Avenue near 44th Street. If you're a book lover, this is probably the place for you. Certainly it was the place for Judge Audrey Hamilton, whom we met leaving the store with a half-dozen vintage mystery novels in her arms. I myself would rather see the movie than read the book, but Dwight's mother always has two or three books going at the same time and whenever we drive into Raleigh for lunch or shopping, she wants to stop by Reader's Corner or Quail Ridge Books and Music and look at every title on the shelves. I usually kill time stocking up on CDs and greeting cards.

While Martha cruised biography and history, I went looking for the children's section. My brother Zach had been mildly dyslexic, so Mother made him read aloud every night. I remember being transfixed by *Old Yeller*. Cal's a reader like his grandmother, and I thought he might enjoy it even though we could probably rent the video.

I didn't really expect to find a copy, but there it sat on a lower shelf. Unfortunately, it was a first edition and carried a seventy-dollar price tag. I sat down on a nearby stool and opened the pages to refresh my memory of Travis and his irritating younger brother, Arliss. Naturally I had identified with Arliss back then. My brothers thought I was a tagalong pain in the ass and didn't hide their opinion much better than Travis did. I flipped to the heartbreaking ending and found myself choking up as if I were four again and about to sob, "No, no, *NO!* He *can't* shoot Yeller!"

I had been aware that there were two people on the other side of the shelves from me, but the male voice was halfway through a quietly emotional reading of a poem before I came up from Yeller's death scene and registered his words:

> *...And I shall have some peace there, for peace*
> *   comes dropping slow,*
> *Dropping from the veils of the morning to where*
> *   the cricket sings;*
> *There midnight's all a glimmer, and noon a*
> *   purple glow,*
> *And evening full of the linnet's wings.*
> *I will arise and go now, for always night and*
> *   day*
> *I hear lake water lapping with low sounds by*
> *   the shore;*
> *While I stand on the roadway, or on the pave-*
> *   ments grey,*
> *I hear it in the deep heart's core...*

His voice broke then and after a moment the woman said, " *'I will arise now and go to Innisfree.'* Yes, I can see why she loved it."

A moment or two later they came around the corner. He was in jeans and a faded Obama T-shirt; she wore hip-hugging white shorts that showed off the jeweled ring in her navel and a bright pink bandeau that matched her hair. Their eyes were suspiciously moist as if the poem he'd read had moved them both to the brink of tears. They seemed startled to see me sitting there and I was equally startled to recognize them.

"Oh, hey," the young man said. "Did you ever find your earring?"

"Hank, right?" I slid the book back into its slot and stood up.

"Yes, ma'am." To the girl with him, he explained, "The judge here lost an earring the other night but no one turned it in."

"Deborah Knott," I said, extending my hand.

"Mel Garrett," she replied. "I work at Jonah's, too."

"I know. You waited on the Stone Hamilton table."

"Wow! Wicked good memory."

"Well, it *was* Stone Hamilton," I said. Not that her fuchsia-streaked hair wasn't also memorable. "I guess y'all heard about Kyle Armstrong?"

Both faces turned sober and Mel Garrett said, "I feel like the woman who worked alongside that serial killer—what was his name? The guy that killed all those sorority students?"

"Ted Bundy?"

"Yeah. Not that Kyle killed thirty women, but still. Two judges?"

From behind me, Martha said drily, "Only one judge. My husband's banged up, but he's going to live. Hello, Hank. How nice to see you again."

"It was your husband Kyle ran down?" asked the Garrett girl. Martha nodded and the girl tsk'd in commiseration. "I'm so sorry."

"Me, too, sugar."

"I knew he had a mean streak in him, but I didn't know it was that fu—frickin' wide. I'm really glad your husband's going to be okay."

We chatted a moment or two longer, then Martha paid for the two books she'd found, a biography of John Adams and the collected letters of E. B. White.

Hank and Mel came up behind us and she said, "You know, Judge, sometimes the cleaning people leave things they find in a box in back instead of bringing them to the desk. What did your earring look like?"

I described the red-and-white hoops and she said she'd check on it. "We're both on duty this evening if you're over that way and want to stop by."

"Thanks," I said. "I might do that."

After dropping Martha off at the hospital, I drove back to the SandCastle, where I fired up my laptop and made a note to buy an inexpensive copy of *Old Yeller* next time I was in Raleigh. I found a couple of messages that needed an answer, then checked out the headlines on *The New York Times* and *The Washington Post* to make sure the world was still turning on its axis. I always read *The News & Observer* all the way through when I'm home and keep my car radio tuned to NPR, but when I'm away like this it's the online *Times* and *Post*. If it's not splashed across their front pages, I figure I'm not missing anything.

And yeah, okay, whenever I'm on the *Post* site, I read Miss Manners, too. Doesn't everybody?

I was in the middle of answering email when Rosemary called. "Chelsea Ann's still on the hunt for that table but I'm tired of prowling through cluttered consignment shops. Want to come down to the beach with me?"

"Sounds like fun," I said.

She told me where she'd set up her umbrella and twenty minutes later I was seated on a towel next to hers, smoothing sunscreen on every bit of bare skin I could reach.

Rosemary had pulled her strawberry blonde hair back from her face with a black hairband that picked up the black leaves in her sarong-styled bathing suit. White flip-flops, white sunglasses, and a chunky white bracelet on her slender arm. She looked pretty fine for a woman entering middle age after dumping her husband.

"You doing okay?" I asked, and she didn't pretend I was asking after her health.

"I'm doing better than okay," she said with a genuine smile and showed me the title of the book she was reading: *The NC Divorce Litigator's Manual.*

"You're not going to represent yourself, are you?"

"I'm not that dumb," she said, and told me the name of the attorney she'd retained, one of the best divorce lawyers in the Triangle. "But I *am* going to petition for reinstatement in the State Bar even though that means taking fifteen hours of CLE classes. I've been thinking about it and I believe family law's what I want to practice. God knows I'm going to get a lot of practical pointers on equitable distribution of marital property and post-separation supplements in the next few months. Might as well take advantage of the experience." She gave an evil grin. "Lovely to think of Dave having to pay for my professional training."

"Too bad you have to start fresh proceedings," I said, lying back on my towel.

"Actually, I won't. We've agreed to let the original petitions go forward."

"Even though you technically condoned the first affair by coming down here and resuming marital relations?"

"He's decided it'd be better all around to get this over with as quickly as possible. After all, with you and Martha as witnesses to his fling with this waitress, it's going to end up in the same place."

There was so much complacency to her tone that I couldn't resist zinging her. "Tell me one thing, girlfriend."

"What?"

"Why did you condone Dave's last affair, then turn around and set him up with that waitress?"

"Excuse me?"

"You pushed Jenna on him at lunch Sunday and then you let him think you'd be gone all afternoon on Monday."

She sat up indignantly and pulled off her sunglasses to glare at me. "We *did* plan to be gone all afternoon. Airlie Gardens and then the Cottage Tea Room, but Martha got tired. Remember?"

"Oh, please, Rosemary." I rolled over onto my side and propped myself up on one arm. "The way you kept looking at your watch? The way you persuaded us that tea on the balcony would be more relaxing so that we'd get back much earlier? The way you made sure we were right behind you when you threw the door wide open?"

She stared at me in consternation, guilt all over her face.

"Sorry," I said. "I can't help myself. I notice things. And I was always good at simple math. Two plus two and all that."

"You didn't say anything to Martha or Chelsea Ann, did you?"

"Not yet."

"I really wish you wouldn't, Deborah."

"Then you did set him up?"

"The bastard set himself up. But yeah, Chelsea Ann was right. I just don't want to have to listen to her crowing about it the next forty years, okay? I really wanted to believe him, that he wanted to save our marriage, not throw twenty years down the slop chute. But it was all a farce. He didn't give up his little cupcake. He just put her on hold and she agreed because it would mean less for me and more for her if we had a no-fault divorce. Once he got me to publicly condone the affair by resuming marital relations, he'd be home free. He could claim that we had sincerely tried to reconcile, but 'O sorrow, sorrow, folks. It just didn't work out.' "

As she talked, I could see Rosemary getting angry all over again. Her cheeks flushed and her green eyes shot sparks when she mimicked Dave's voice.

"You know when you and the Fitzhumes saw us out on his balcony Sunday morning? That touching display of domestic harmony that he deliberately staged?"

I nodded.

"Twenty minutes later, I left him outside and went in

to get dressed. I didn't close the French doors all the way, but I'm sure the cocky bastard thought I'd gone into the bathroom to do my face. I came back into the room to get my purse that I'd left by the door and I heard him say, 'We're home free, baby. Three judges and a judge's wife just saw us connubilling.'"

"Connubilling?"

"His term for connubial behavior," Rosemary said drily.

"So as soon as Jenna presented herself, you hatched the plan?"

"Why not? It didn't take much pushing. She was hot to trot and he never turned down an easy roll in the hay." She grinned. "Or a splash in a Jacuzzi."

"So the real reason he's willing to let the original proceedings go forward is because he doesn't want the cupcake back in Durham to hear about it?"

"Oh, I imagine she'll hear about it," Rosemary said complacently. She held out her sunscreen to me. "Could you get my back?"

I laughed. "Seems to me like you've already got it."

CHAPTER
28

That which is faulty in the beginning cannot become valid with the passage of time.

—*Paulus (early AD 3rd century)*

I lay on my stomach, my head pillowed by my crossed arms, half drowsing, when Rosemary came back to our umbrella from her swim. As she toweled her hair dry, she said, "Will Blackstone was out there in the water, too. Have you seen his eye?"

"You know him?" I asked.

"Sure." She reached into her beach bag for a comb and began untangling her hair. "He and Dave worked on a report together two or three years ago. Teen courts and recidivism. He stayed over one weekend while they finished working on the statistics. Nice man."

"Did he say how he got the eye?" I asked innocently.

"Slipped getting out of the shower and banged into the sink, poor guy. He says everyone's teasing him that somebody's husband punched him out."

"Oh?"

"Well, if you know him, you know what a hunk he is.

Divorced. Unattached. And he does like to flirt. He even flirted with me just now. He's heard that Dave and I are headed for divorce and he said Dave must be crazy to go out for a hamburger when he had steak at home. Wasn't that sweet?"

"Joanne Woodward probably thought so."

"Huh?"

"I read somewhere that that's the reason Paul Newman gave for not cheating on her."

"Oh." She digested that for a moment, then, with a touch of defiance in her voice, said, "I still think it was sweet of Will. He asked me to have a drink with him later."

"You going?"

"Why not? Chelsea Ann's having dinner with that detective again tonight. You want to join us?"

The thought of watching Will Blackstone squirm through a round or two of margaritas was incredibly tempting, but I resisted. "I don't think so, thanks."

I wondered if Rosemary would let him put the moves on her. Will Blackstone and Dave Emerson struck me as two of a kind and some women do have a tendency to keep picking the same losers time after time.

"Not that it's any of your business," said the preacher.

"And not that you haven't picked your own share of losers," said the pragmatist.

I closed my eyes and thought about the various men I'd been involved with over the years. Were there similarities? One could say that Dwight and the game warden had a few things in common—both liked the outdoors, both wore badges and were comfortable with guns. Allen Stancil never wore a badge and his moral compass was several degrees to the left of theirs, but he and Dwight were built alike. On the other hand, those three were nothing at all like the rather bookish law student I'd lived with one winter in New York, neither physically *nor* mentally.

"*Maybe Lev Schuster was the skinny little exception that proves the rule*," whispered the pragmatist.

Beside me, Rosemary began to pack up her belongings. "You ready to go?" she asked. "I want to shower before Chelsea Ann gets back. Takes me a little longer these days to get all bright-eyed and bushy-tailed."

"Catch you later," I said. "I may still go for a swim."

I lay there for close to another hour mulling over the events of the week while the sun sank lower in the sky. Just before it touched the top of the hotel, I saw Allen's two children dart past me. Allen trundled along behind, loaded like a packhorse with thermal bags, towels, sand toys, and an umbrella.

"Need a hand?" I called.

"Three or four if you got 'em."

The umbrella slid out of his hand and I rescued it for him and helped him set up next to mine.

"Thanks, darlin'. You all by your lonesome this evening?"

"For the moment. Hey, Tiffany Jane. Hey, Tyler. Y'all having fun here?"

The little girl nodded shyly and the toddler gave me a goofy smile.

"Did you put sunscreen on them yet?" I asked.

"Well, damn!" he said. "I knowed I was forgetting something."

"That's okay. I have some." I rummaged in my bag and found the bottle. "Come here, honey, and let me rub it on you."

The child came and knelt on my towel and held her beautiful little face up for me to smooth on the cream. Allen was right. She really was going to break a heart or two before it was over. When I finished with her arms and shoulders, she took the bottle and said she could do her legs herself. "And Tyler, too."

"Tippy-canoe and Tyler, too," Allen teased, his white teeth flashing beneath his luxuriant mustache.

"Oh, Daddy!" she protested, having clearly heard him say this many times before.

"Why you reckon folks say that?" Allen asked me. "I can see how a tippy-canoe could be a problem, but what's with the Tyler, too?"

"It was an old campaign slogan. From back in the eighteen-hundreds, I think. Tippecanoe was the Indian nickname for some presidential candidate, and Tyler was running for vice president, but don't ask me who he was or if he won."

Well covered in sunscreen now, the children took their buckets and shovels down to the water's edge.

Allen sat cross-legged on his towel to keep an eye on them and popped the top on a can of light beer. "You want one?"

"No, thanks," I said. "What happened to your finger?"

I had just noticed that his right index finger was bandaged and seemed to have a splint on it.

"You know what happened, darlin'." He took a long swallow of beer. "You was there."

"You broke your finger when you punched Will Blackstone?"

"That his name? Sucker's got a damn hard head."

"And a very black eye, so you two are even."

I couldn't help laughing and he gave a rueful shrug. "He ain't bothered you again, did he?"

"No."

"Good."

My knight in shining armor.

"I heard that one of the waiters at Jonah's killed Judge Jeffreys?"

I nodded.

"And then he got hisself killed in a car crash?"

"Yeah. They think he was going too fast and hydroplaned off an exit ramp."

"Amateurs." His voice dripped with the scorn of a professional stock car driver for nonprofessionals who take unnecessary risks. "They know why he killed Jeffreys?"

"The theory is that Jeffreys propositioned him in the men's room and he freaked out."

Allen lowered his beer can and looked at me in puzzlement. "Pete Jeffreys gay? No way in hell."

"You can't always tell."

"The hell you can't. Well, maybe *you* can't, but I've got me a gaydar that's never been wrong. I can spot 'em ten miles away. And he won't no AC/DC neither. I'm telling you here and now, Pete Jeffreys was straighter'n a yardstick."

No matter how I argued that one could never be a hundred percent certain about another's sexuality, Allen was that tree planted by the water. He could not be moved.

In the end his conviction convinced me and I went back to the hotel to call Gary Edwards.

* * *

I hate to admit it," Edwards said when I finally got through to him, "but from all we've heard, your friend's probably right. Judge Blankenthorpe's sure he would never have sought a homosexual encounter and that's what we're getting from our inquiries in Greensboro."

"So you're back at the beginning with no motive?"

"And that's the way we'll probably leave it. Something's worrying the ME, but he's promised us a preliminary report tomorrow. Soon as that comes my boss and the DA will both be ready to call it closed."

"What's bothering him?" I asked.

"Not enough blood," Edwards said succinctly. "Bad as he was banged up, his clothes should have been soaked. Probably washed off in the rain . . . or . . ."

"Or what?" I asked. Yet even as I asked, it came to me. "Could he have already been dead before the car crashed?"

"Yeah. The ME wants to take another look at Armstrong's heart. See if maybe he had a heart attack first."

Possibilities suddenly started to shift and rearrange themselves in my head and a different pattern began to emerge. "There's one more thing," I said. "Something Judge Ouellette told me."

When I finished talking, there was a long silence on his end.

At last, I said, "You do remember that the conference ends at noon tomorrow and everyone scatters after that?"

"Yes, but—"

"Better me than Fitz," I told him firmly. "And if I'm wrong, I'll bring a crow with me the next time I come to Wilmington and you can watch me eat it."

He laughed. "You're on."

CHAPTER
29

*Our ancestors established the rule that all women, be-
cause of their weakness of intellect, should be under
the power of guardians.*

—*Cicero (BC 106–47)*

After showering, I dressed for comfort, not style:
black flats, loose black knit slacks with a white bel
a red knit halter top, and the earrings I'd made at the Co
ton Exchange. With luck, Mel Garrett would have foun
my red-and-white hoop. Enamel over some sort of gold
colored metal. They had probably cost less than twent
dollars, but their sentimental value was above rubies. M
favorite nephew had given them to me for my birthda
when he was sixteen and I was touched that he had no
ticed my fondness for red.

I stopped at a drugstore on the way into town an
bought several fat scented candles in preparation fo
Dwight's arrival tomorrow night. Candles add so much t
a Jacuzzi, don't you think? And with all the angled mir
rors around the tub, a few flames would look like dozen

I made sure that my phone was switched on before I put it in my pocket. Unless it's an emergency, Dwight is the world's slowest driver. Nevertheless, if he'd left his conference according to plan, he could be getting home any time now and I didn't want to miss his call.

When I got to Jonah's, it was almost eight-thirty and the dinner rush had wound down. Even in June, vacationers aren't standing in line to eat that late on a Tuesday night and Hank had time to chat for a few minutes while we waited for Mel Garrett to finish taking credit cards at her table.

"Sorry, Judge," she said when she came up to me. "The only earrings are a rhinestone stud and some cheap clip-ons. A hell of a lot of lipsticks, though, if you're missing one of those." Her own lipstick was a deep dark purple that gave her a vaguely goth look and complemented the streaks in her hair.

"Thanks, but no thanks," I said, looking out over the stepped-down dining areas. The sun had just set and bands of orange and gold burnished the river. "Not too crowded tonight."

"Yeah, weekdays, this town pretty much rolls up its sidewalks after nine."

"I guess y'all heard the motive the police have come up with for why Kyle killed Judge Jeffreys?"

"Not me," said Mel, leaning closer as I lowered my voice. "Hank?"

He looked up from running the credit cards she'd handed him and shook his head.

"They think the judge hit on him in the bathroom and that Kyle got insulted, freaked out and killed him in a blind rage."

"No shit!" said Mel, who seemed incapable of removing all the salt from her speech. I could almost see the wheels turning in her head as she fit my words with the guy she had met only a few weeks earlier when she and Hank first came to work at Jonah's. She liked it, though. She liked it a lot because her dark eyes gleamed when she said to Hank, "He would have gone off like a pistol, wouldn't he, Hank? Remember how he almost punched Biff in the nose for trying to flirt with him?"

"It did make him crazy when people took it for granted that he was gay," Hank said slowly, looking at me with those shrewd, intelligent eyes. "You're not buying it, though, are you?"

I shrugged. "Nobody at the conference knew Kyle, but several of my colleagues have known Judge Jeffreys for several years and no one believes he was wired that way."

"But they still think it was Kyle, right?" asked Mel, who seemed reluctant to let go of her coworker's guilt. "I mean it *was* his car that knocked down the other judge, right?"

"Right. But if he left his car on the street and rode his bicycle back and forth to work, someone could have hotwired it and had it back where it belonged before Kyle missed it."

"Oh, come on, Judge!" She pushed a fall of fuchsia hair back from her face with an impatient hand. "You saying it's a coincidence that Kyle decided to leave town this weekend?"

"Not at all. His death is too convenient for it to be a coincidence. Whoever killed Jeffreys probably killed Kyle, too, and then sent his car off that ramp."

"*Two* murders?" Her face mirrored her skepticism.

"Three if you count the attempt on Judge Fitzhume's life. Not that the police care. Far as they're concerned, this is an easy clearance. Case closed."

"I'm with the police," the girl said, her cheeks flushed with emotion. "Who cares why he did it?"

"Judge Knott cares," Hank said quietly as he handed Mel the black vinyl check holders for her table.

"Why? Kyle's no loss to the world and that judge isn't either. If it wasn't Kyle, then it has to be one of you guys."

"I'm afraid you're right," I said. "There's someone here in Wilmington with a huge grudge against Judge Jeffreys. He was at the restaurant next door and he could have been waiting for Jeffreys to leave. I'm betting that my friend—the one that got run down—saw them together. His memory's still shaky, but I'm going to walk him through every minute of Saturday night. The police may not be interested now, but if he remembers someone besides Kyle, they'll have to take another look and Kyle will be cleared."

"I don't give a flying flip about clearing Kyle," Mel said. "He was a total jerk."

As she got back to work, Hank said, "Don't mind her. She and Kyle never got along from day one. So did you want a table? Or are you joining some friends?"

I surveyed the room again and shook my head. "I don't see a soul I know."

"I can give you a table by the Riverwalk, and we've got an oyster po'boy special tonight," he said in a voice that would have tempted Eve to eat the apple.

I laughed. "Sold!"

He seated me at the far edge of the porch and sent a

different waitress over. As dusk settled over the River-walk, candles flickered in cut-glass holders on every table. I relaxed and ordered a glass of wine to go with my po'boy, then called my home number. My own voice answered after five rings. "Dwight? It's me," I said. "I thought you guys would be back by now. Call me when you get in, I don't care how late it is."

The oysters arrived, crisp and sizzling on a toasted but-tery roll and soft Bibb lettuce. As I ate, I noticed that there was another unaccompanied woman seated several tables away. Amid the chattering groups, she read a news-paper as she ate, the single woman's shield when eating out alone. I'm usually too interested in observing my fel-low diners to keep my eyes on a printed page, but tonight I couldn't quit thinking about why Pete Jeffreys had been killed.

If I was right, if it was because of a tragedy his judicial ruling had caused, then maybe he did deserve to die. As someone sworn to uphold the law, I can't condone it, but I'd be lying if I said I didn't understand the primal desire for revenge—that old reptilian brain stem reflex: an eye for an eye, a life for a life. You hurt me, I'll hurt you.

But poor self-centered, unfulfilled Kyle? Maybe he wasn't much of a loss to the world, but he didn't deserve to die as a by-product of someone else's revenge.

Nor did Fitz deserve to be tossed like a matador to land on the pavement with broken bones and injuries that would probably give him pain for the rest of his life, pain that would impact on the retirement he and Martha had earned.

How it would all play out, I couldn't tell. Dwight would not be happy with me if he learned that I'd put myself in the middle of a murder investigation, but if all went as planned, the killer would be booked and behind bars before Dwight got down here tomorrow and he would never have to know.

Look, it's not in the marriage vows that husbands and wives have to tell each other every little thing, is it?

I picked the oysters off the roll, drank the last of my wine and signaled to the waitress that I was ready for my check. When she brought me the check holder, I tucked a couple of bills inside and told her to keep the change.

"The conference adjourns at noon tomorrow so I guess I won't see you again," I said to Mel, who had come up to me now that I was leaving. She seemed to have gotten over her huff. "Where's Hank? I'd like to say goodbye."

"He got a phone call and said he had to leave early so I'm stuck with closing out the register for him. I'll tell him you said 'bye."

"Have y'all been together long?" I asked as we crossed the room to the vestibule and the reception stand.

"Oh, we're not together," she said. "Not like you mean. We're both majoring in hotel management at UNCG and we're wicked good friends, but he's not my boyfriend."

At the reception stand, I stopped short, struck by a sudden thought, and looked at her as she rang up a charge on the cash register. "You knew him, didn't you?"

"Knew who?"

"Judge Jeffreys. You said he wasn't a loss to the world. How would you know?"

For a fleeting moment Mel Garrett looked like an apprehensive schoolgirl and not the hard-edged, foul-mouthed sophisticate, and it confirmed my guess.

"You go to school in Greensboro where he held court, so you did know who he was. What did he do to you?"

"You're crazy!" she snarled, all her defenses back in place. "Go play detective somewhere else, okay?"

She whirled and stalked off past the bar to the kitchen beyond, and I knew it would be useless to go after her.

"*Give it a rest*," said the pragmatist, who was starting to have second thoughts about the conclusions I had reached earlier.

"*Yeah*," said the suddenly timorous preacher. "*Let Detective Edwards question her.*"

The parking lot closest to Jonah's where Jeffreys was killed had been full when I got there and I had parked in the overflow lot further down, beyond the last restaurant and well past where the Riverwalk stopped. The lot was nothing more than a dirt-and-gravel cleared space that dead-ended in overgrown rhododendrons, live oaks, and yaupon at the river's edge. Despite the moon, it was even more poorly lit than the front lot, full of deep shadows and menacing shapes. The branches of the unkempt bushes that lined the sides swayed in the light breeze that blew off the river, making the shadows seem alive with unseen, lurking forces.

While I hesitated, the taillights came on from a car near mine. It backed out of its slot and turned my way, nearly blinding me with its high beams. I had to press against the fence to let it pass. Behind me, a man and two laughing, chattering women emerged from the neighboring restaurant and got into a nearby car parked nose out. I breathed a little easier, but they drove away before I'd gotten halfway to my car and I was alone in the deserted lot with dark cars that probably belonged to restaurant workers who would not be coming out for another hour. It was suddenly very quiet, almost as if the rhododendrons were holding their breath. I heard a boat horn out on the river, the swoosh of traffic over the bridge, and from somewhere off to my left a car horn blew and a dog barked. My footsteps crunched against the gravel.

I passed a white car and something in the bushes loomed out at me with a crackling noise. I jumped back and almost lost my balance on the loose gravel. To my chagrin, it was only a dark plastic bag that a stray breeze had filled with air. I gave myself a mental shake for an imagination that seemed to be working overtime, seeing danger where none existed.

All the same, when I felt in my pocket for my keys and touched the button that unlocked my car door, I was comforted by its chirp and the blink of its taillights. Another minute and I would be safely inside with the doors locked.

I rounded the car next to mine and was reaching for the handle when a crouching figure leaped up and grabbed me.

I screamed and my fingers desperately pushed the little buttons on my key. The taillights flashed and the trunk popped up before I finally hit the one that set off the car alarm. The horn split the night air in several rhythmical blasts, then the keys were wrestled from my hand and with a muttered curse my attacker immediately found the right one to stop the horn. All this time my arm was twisted behind me in a grip that threatened to dislocate my shoulder.

Almost before I knew what was happening, I was

thrown into the trunk and the lid was slammed down on me. I ducked automatically, but it still gave me a bruising knock on the head. My arm burned with pain from the wrenching and I scraped my bare shoulder on a corner of the small metal toolbox I keep in the trunk, yet once I heard the car engine start and felt the car begin to back up, adrenaline stopped pumping. I quit being afraid and took several long, steadying breaths. Instead of being killed there and then, I was going to be taken to some isolated spot where I could be dealt with more easily.

Amateur! I thought scornfully, unconsciously mimicking Allen. This was something Dwight had made Cal and me practice till it came automatically even though I protested that neither of us was ever likely to get locked in the trunk of my car.

Cal thought it was fun.

I had broken two fingernails and banged my knee.

As the car finished reversing, but before it was put in forward drive, I yanked the release over the lock. The lid flew up and I rolled to the ground and away from the wheels.

With a squeal of the brakes, the car was immediately thrown back into reverse, but I was well out of the way of those crushing tires.

My assailant jerked open the car door and ran toward me. By then, I had pulled my .38 from the ankle holster I had strapped on before leaving the hotel parking lot, a gun Daddy had given me back when I was in private practice and driving around the state by myself late at night.

Moonlight silvered the barrel as I took aim. "Stop right there or I swear to God I'll shoot you where you stand."

A prowl car suddenly drew across the entrance to the

parking lot. Flashlights hit Hank Barlow's face from two directions. One of the lights belonged to the police officer who had been reading her newspaper while she ate a solitary dinner and kept her eye on me. The other belonged to Detective Gary Edwards.

The first question he asked me was, "You okay?"

The second was, "Do you have a license for that thing?" which was exactly what Dwight had asked the first time *he* saw it.

Why does a woman with a gun freak men out?

CHAPTER
30

Manslaughter on a sudden provocation differs from excusable homicide se defendendo *in this: that in one case there is an apparent necessity, for self-preservation, to kill the aggressor; in the other no necessity at all, being only a sudden act of revenge.*

—Sir William Blackstone (1723–1780)

By the time they got around to taking my statement, Hank Barlow had waived his rights to an attorney and made a full confession. It was as if he was glad to be done with all the violence and had a huge need to unburden his soul, holding nothing back. Afterwards, Edwards let me sit in on his interview with a tearful Mel Garrett, who confirmed the events and conjectures I had pieced together.

Much as we would like to be infallible, no judge gets it right every time and the consequences of compassion and of sloppiness are often indistinguishable.

When I sat court for Bernie Rawlings's brother up in Cedar Gap last fall, I saw a family snapshot of Kenneth

Rawlings with his wife and young son. His clerk told me that Mrs. Rawlings and their little boy were killed instantly when they were broadsided by a drunk driver, a driver Ken had sentenced to several days of community service when he appeared in court on his first DWI.

Pete Jeffreys had violated his oath of office in more ways than one, but the thing that got him killed was carelessly giving probation to a felon without noticing that he was currently in violation of an earlier probation—a stone-cold killer who went out and carjacked, raped, and murdered a young college student.

"Annie was my cousin," Mel Garrett said, fighting to hold back her tears. "She and Hank were supposed to get married last November. At Thanksgiving. I was going to be her maid of honor."

At our committee meeting on Sunday, Roberta Ouellette had said, "She was on her way back to class after a fitting of her wedding gown when he grabbed her."

Too bad none of us thought to ask the name of the groom-to-be.

"He told me that he and his girlfriend usually took summer jobs in the mountains," said Edwards, "but that you convinced him the beach would be a good change. I thought you were the girlfriend he was referring to."

Mel shook her head, her eyes as pink as the streaks in her jet-black hair. "Not me. Annie. She loved the mountains. After graduation, they were going to work at one of the inns till they could afford to buy an inn of their own. They had so many plans. When she got killed, Hank was so out of his mind with grief that we were all afraid that he might hurt himself. If he could have gotten his hands

on the asshole that killed her, he would have ripped his
bloody heart out.

"Then when the newspapers wrote about how he
should have been behind bars and not out on the street,
that the judge had screwed up, that really started to eat
at Hank. I thought getting him to come here this summer
instead of going to the mountains would help him, but
it was like that appointment in Samarra, wasn't it? He
comes here to get over Annie's death and the man who
caused it turns up here, too."

She pushed back the hair that had fallen over one eye
and looked Edwards straight in the face. "Honest to God,
I didn't know that the judge was here that night. All we
knew was his name, not what he looked like. That's why
I believed Hank when he swore he had nothing to do with
the murder. I was afraid that if I told about Annie, you'd
say he did it."

I remembered looking across the crowded dining
porch when Hank seated Allen and the children, how Pete
Jeffreys had come up to the table and Hank had stood
by patiently while Allen introduced the children to Judge
Jeffreys. "I'll bet that's how he knew who Jeffreys was,"
I said, and Edwards told me that Hank had confirmed it
when he confessed.

The rest was as I'd conjectured. He had followed Jeffreys into the restroom and accused him of causing his
fiancée's death. When Jeffreys tossed him enough money
to pay his bill and stormed out of the restaurant, Hank had
followed.

"I wanted him dead," Hank told them. "Dead like Annie. I was in such a rage that I just snatched up that strap
and strangled him. At that point, I didn't care if anyone

saw me or not. But once I'd thrown him into the river and nobody had seen me, I thought I might get away with it. Then you and Judge Knott came back to the restaurant Sunday morning and she mentioned the judge who saw me follow Jeffreys into the restroom. I knew I had to get rid of him before he said anything about me."

He had killed Kyle late Monday afternoon—a crushing blow on the head that he thought would not be noticed with all the other damages a car crash can inflict on a body, not realizing that blood doesn't spurt once the heart stops beating. And he had been incredibly lucky that neither roommate had walked in while he was packing up the would-be actor's things. After sending the car with Kyle's body off that exit ramp late last night, he had pedaled Kyle's bicycle back to Jonah's in the rain with all the loose ends neatly tidied away.

"Except that Judge Knott kept picking at them, unraveling them," Hank had said. "She was going to help Judge Fitzhume remember me and I couldn't have that, could I?"

"He says he didn't mean for it to go so far," Edwards told me. "He says he didn't want to hurt you and he really didn't mean to kill Jeffreys, but the judge brushed him off like he was trash. As if the girl's death meant nothing. He says that if the judge had just said he was sorry, admitted he'd screwed up, that would have been the end of it.

"But Jeffreys told him, 'Shit happens, kid. Get over it.'" Edwards shook his head at the waste of it all. "He kept saying that this wasn't how it was supposed to be, it wasn't what he wanted."

"No Innisfree for him," I murmured.

"Huh?"

"Not important," I told him.

* * *

It was almost midnight before I got back to the SandCastle. Edwards had offered to have someone drive me, but I swore I was okay. And I was, except for an incredibly sore shoulder. All I wanted was a long hot soaking bath and two more aspirin. I put my .38 and its holster back into the locked metal toolbox I keep stowed in my trunk and went up to my room with the candles I'd bought earlier.

When I unlocked the door, I was startled to see that the lights were on.

As was the television.

And a man was asleep on my bed with the remote control in his hand.

Dwight opened his eyes when I closed the door and set the candles on the ledge of the tub. He gave me a drowsy smile and looked over at the clock radio on the nightstand. "Midnight? I thought you were going to be in bed every night by nine o'clock."

As I came closer, he registered my torn and dirty red halter top and saw the scrape on my shoulder and sat upright. His smile turned to concern and all sleepiness disappeared.

"Deb'rah? What the hell happened to you?"

I went straight into his arms for a long slow kiss that made me forget all about my sore shoulder and aching head.

At last we reluctantly drew apart and he said, "How did you get so banged up? What happened?"

"It's a long story," I said, as I slipped off my torn halter top and began to unbutton his shirt. "Let's get in the Jacuzzi and I'll tell you all about it."

At her family farm for the Christmas holiday,
Deborah Knott is shocked by a young girl's
death—and by the murders that follow...

Please turn this page
for a preview of

Christmas Mourning

Available in hardcover.

CHAPTER
1

Marley was dead to begin with.

— *A Christmas Carol,* Charles Dickens

—which means I can usually adjourn around five
'clock. After that, I may have to sign some judgments
r search warrants or other documents, but most days I'm
one by five or five-thirty." I made a show of looking at
ıy watch. Although I had ninety seconds left of the five
ıinutes I'd been allotted, it was chilly here in the gym
nd my toes felt frozen. I smiled at the high school fresh-
ıen, who sat on tiered benches beneath secular swags of
ake evergreens tied with red plastic ribbons, and gestured
o the tables over by the far wall. "So I'll adjourn for now
nd be back there if you have any questions."

There was polite applause as I yielded the microphone
o a nurse practitioner from the new walk-in clinic that
ad recently opened up in a shopping center that sprawled
round one of I-40's exits here in the county.

It was Thursday afternoon, the day before the begin-
ing of their Christmas—oops! *Winter*—break.

(Political correctness has finally, begrudgingly, arrive in Colleton County. Forty percent of our population ca themselves Christian and at least sixty percent of *thos* write alarmist letters to the editor every year claiming tha Christ is being dissed by the ten percent who check o "other" when polled about religious beliefs.)

Today was Career Day at West Colleton High, and was the sixth of seven speakers that the principal, who' also my mother-in-law, hoped would inspire these way too-cool-to-look-interested students. My name card– *District Court Judge Deborah Knott*—was on one of th long tables that lined the end wall, and I sat down besid my husband, whose own name card read *Major Dwigh Bryant, Chief Deputy, Colleton County Sheriff's Depart ment.*

He can't say no to his mother either.

My only props were a brass-bound wooden gavel, thick law book, some gavel-headed personalized pencil left over from my last campaign, a summary of the edu cation needed to become an attorney before running fo the bench, and a list of the more common infractions o the law that a district court judge might rule on.

Dwight's array was much more impressive: a pair o handcuffs, a nightstick, a gold badge, a kevlar vest, an an empty pistol with a locked trigger guard just to be o the safe side. He also had a stack of flyers that outline requirements for joining the sheriff's department.

"The way the county's growing, we keep needing nev recruits," he said when Miss Emily asked us to do thi shortly after Thanksgiving.

That sneaky lady had invited us over for Sunday din ner and then softened us up with fried chicken, tende aky biscuits and a melt-in-your-mouth coconut cream ie. I don't know what she had to do to get the chief of ie West Colleton Volunteer Fire Department to come, ut it's a good thing that my handouts take a minimal mount of space. Between his hazmat suit and fire ax and wight's show-and-tell, there was no room for anything lse.

I felt a hand on my shoulder and looked up to see one f my eleven older brothers. Zach is next to me in age, ie second-born of the "little twins" and four down from ie "big twins" produced in Daddy's first marriage. Zach s also an assistant principal here at West Colleton.

"Good job," he said, handing me a welcome cup of teaming hot coffee. "Thanks for coming."

"No problem," I said.

Dwight had already emptied his own coffee cup, but he ook a swallow of mine when offered. Sometimes I think e should just open a vein and mainline his caffeine. "I ure hope some of these kids will fill out an application orm for us in three or four years," he told Zach.

"I got dibs on the Turner boy," said the fire chief. His ig hand almost hid a clear plastic bottle of water and he rained it in two gulps. "His brother Donny's unit left for raq last week, but little Jeb there's already turning out ith us on weekends."

I remembered Donny Turner from the church burnings ummer before last and said a silent prayer for all the kids vho have gone to the Middle East these past few years.)ne glance at Dwight's face and I knew he was think-ng of the young deputy who'd signed on for a tour with ne of the private security companies there. To lighten the noment, I said, "I guess I'll get nothing but bad jokes if I say that some of them could wind up going to law school."

Zach grinned. "Adam e'd me a good one this morning."

Adam's his twin out in California and I was sure he' emailed me the same joke. I sighed and rolled my eyes but there was no stopping Zach.

"A lawyer telephones the governor's mansion just after midnight and says he's got to talk to the governor right away. So the aide wakes up the governor, who says 'What's so damn urgent it can't wait till morning?'

"'Judge Smith just died,' says the attorney, 'and I' like to take his place.'

"The governor yawns and says—"

"Yeah, yeah," I said, stomping on his punch line. "'I it's okay with the undertaker, it's okay with me.'"

Zach's grin widened; Dwight and the chief tried to keep their laughs down in deference to the last speaker at the front of the gym, but it was a struggle for both of them.

Rednecks, lawyers, and blondes. The only safe butt left. My hair is more light brown than dandelion gold (thank you, Jesus!), so I don't have to wince at all the dumb blonde lawyer jokes. You'd be surprised how many there are.

"Did I tell you, Dwight?" said the fire chief. "That warm spell last week? We got a call from one of them new houses out your way about hazardous fumes."

Hazardous fumes in our neighborhood? My head came up on that one.

"Yeah," said the chief. "We suited up and went rolling out. Thing is, that's the first time the wind had blown from that particular direction since them new folks moved in."

"Jeeter Langdon's hog farm?" Dwight asked.

"You got it," the chief chuckled.

Back at the podium, the nurse practitioner finished her spiel and headed for her spot at the next table. The school's guidance counselor took the mic and instructed the students to use the rest of the period to learn more about our varied professions.

The kids streamed off the bleachers. All were on the right side of the dress code, but just barely. The boys' jeans were loose and baggy; the girls' had not an extra millimeter of denim, although today's icy December chill had put them all in hoodies and fleecy sweatshirts or sweaters.

My brother Andrew's daughter Ruth and her cousin Richard, Seth and Minnie's youngest child, were both in the stands and both had given me a thumbs up when our eyes met earlier in the period, but neither of them would be over to our tables for career suggestions. Last year when the family met to discuss the future of the land we owned, Richard had announced that he for one was going to stay right there and farm, while Ruth planned to open a stable with Richard's sister Jessica. Both girls have been crazy about horses since they were lifted into a saddle as toddlers.

The first to reach us was a white boy with spiked hair and clear plastic retainers where his forbidden eyebrow and nose rings would normally ride. "Were you ever on *Court TV*?"

I shook my head and started to explain the difference between reality shows and reality, but he had already moved on to Dwight.

Picking up the handgun and hefting it with more familiarity than you like to see in a boy that age, he said, "So like how many guys have you shot?"

A tattooed green viper circled his wrist and stretched its triangular head across the back of his hand. Judging by his stubbly chin, he was probably closer to sixteen than the average freshman and had probably been left back a time or two. With a better haircut and no facial piercings, he would have been a good-looking kid—clear green eyes and smooth, acne-free skin most teenage girls would kill for.

"What's your name, son?" Dwight asked mildly as he reached out to reclaim the weapon.

The boy clearly wanted to wise off, but with Zach looking on, he released his hold on the gun and muttered, "Matt Wentworth."

Dwight lifted an eyebrow at that name. "Any kin to Tig Wentworth?"

"My uncle," he admitted, realizing that we must know Tig Wentworth was currently over in Central Prison, serving a life sentence for the first-degree murder of his stepfather-in-law.

By their fruit ye shall know them.

Here in Colleton County, apples still don't roll very far from the tree and among Cotton Grove natives, the Wentworths were well known as a violent family, root and stock, for several generations back. Hux Wentworth, this boy's oldest brother, had been killed in a home invasion and now that I was reminded, I was pretty sure that another brother...Jack? Jay? No, Jason. That was his name.

Our little weekly, the *Cotton Grove Clarion* had used his arrest and conviction as a lead-in to an article on violations of hunting regulations. Jason Wentworth had been brought up before me back around Halloween for jack-lighting deer, i.e., illegally hunting them at night with a powerful spotlight that would temporarily blind them and keep them immobile long enough to get off a shot. I had fined him and, as the law requires, made him forfeit both his rifle and his hunting license. The odds were three to one that I'd be seeing this kid in court before he graduated.

If he graduated.

Just before the bell rang to end the period, Miss Emily came bustling through the gym doors and paused to answer her pager. I'm always amazed that this small wiry woman who barely tops five feet is the mother of Dwight and his sister Nancy Faye, who are both built like their tall, big-boned daddy, a farmer who was killed in a tractor accident when they were children. Dwight's brother Rob and their other sister Beth got Miss Emily's slender build along with her red hair and green eyes. Normally, Miss Emily's a force of nature and there was no hesitation on the part of the school board to make her principal of West Colleton and its two thousand plus students when this shiny new complex replaced rickety old Zachary Taylor High where Dwight and I had gone to school.

But as she clipped the pager back in its case, she looked suddenly tired and drained and, for the first time, almost old. Her eyes were bright with unshed tears by the time she reached our table and looked at Dwight with anguish.

"They just called," she told him. "The Johnson girl died."

If you or someone you know
wants to improve their reading skills,
call the Literacy Help Line.

WORDS ARE YOUR WHEELS
1-800-228-8813

VISIT US ONLINE

@ WWW.HACHETTEBOOKGROUP.COM.

AT THE HACHETTE BOOK GROUP WEB SITE YOU'LL FIND:

CHAPTER EXCERPTS FROM SELECTED NEW RELEASES

•

ORIGINAL AUTHOR AND EDITOR ARTICLES

•

AUDIO EXCERPTS

•

BESTSELLER NEWS

•

ELECTRONIC NEWSLETTERS

•

AUTHOR TOUR INFORMATION

•

CONTESTS, QUIZZES, AND POLLS

•

FUN, QUIRKY RECOMMENDATION CENTER

•

PLUS MUCH MORE!

BOOKMARK HACHETTE BOOK GROUP
@ WWW.HACHETTEBOOKGROUP.COM.